Tales of New America

by

Gunther Roosevelt

Callister Green Publishing
5320 Callister Ave.
Sacramento, CA 95819
johnmark@surewest.net

ISBN-13: 9781491000847
ISBN-10: 1491000848

Contents

Be Careful What You Wish For

The couple looked to be in their mid-thirties, the woman, perhaps, a little younger, with a three year-old boy. It wasn't their nondescript sedan, nor their ordinary clothes that gave them away to Ryan, the border guard. It was the tell tale nervousness of both as he took a little longer than usual scrutinizing their papers.

"Please, pull over there to that parking spot," the young man told the driver, a Mr. Jon Jones. Mr. Jones compressed his lips momentarily, another tell, and did as ordered.

The North Jackpot Highway Inspection Station had a number of large metal warehouses to store winter equipment and highway repair vehicles. There were drive-through buildings for semi trucks, and a small office complex for the inspectors' lounge, the dispatchers' rooms, and management offices. There was a militia barracks close by, and a place for interrogation rooms and holding cells.

All of this was in the flat, nearly barren, sagebrush high desert; although North Jackpot, just above Jackpot on the Nevada side, was growing into an actual town.

The parking spot the Jones' pulled into was in front of the interrogation building. Ryan had himself temporarily relieved so that he could escort the Jones' into interrogation, and hand them over to the militia captain in charge.

Ryan was twenty, and knew there was something frightening about a young man in uniform taking command of older people. People want to negotiate their way out. How can they bargain with a youth who looks like he can only follow orders and nothing else?

He felt sorry for these people. That horrible sense of "Caught!" while trying not to show it in the hope that it's all just a minor bureaucratic glitch and they'll soon be back on the road heaving great sighs of relief.

Not a chance, though. They're dirty and their life is going to change dramatically in a short while.

"Follow me," Ryan told them, and they apprehensively complied. Then he told them to sit in the waiting room: a sterile, harshly lit place with plastic chairs, a dingy yellow linoleum floor, gray walls, acoustic tile ceiling, a tall metal counter with computer stations for officers to process (ahem) customers.

The Jones' were good-looking people. Caucasian, both brown haired, relatively trim, but not athletic. Their toddler, a boy, was well behaved. Maybe he was tired, or maybe they'd given him a little cough syrup to make him somnolent. Everybody hates a fussy child, and they draw unwanted attention.

Capt. Walters (it said so on his uniform) came in through another door. He conferred with Ryan, accepted the papers, looked at the Jones', nodded to Ryan, patted him on the shoulder, and released him back to service at the road station.

"Please come with me," Walters told the couple. He ushered them through the door he'd come in back to a hallway, and led them into an interrogation room. There was a table bolted to the floor, a glass mirror on one wall, a camera in the corner at the ceiling and chairs for them to sit in. There was a computer for Walters at his end of the table.

Walters picked up a phone from the wall and said, "Sherry, would you come into room three. We have a small child for you."

He turned to the couple and spoke to the woman. "One of our staff will accompany you to our nursery. There you will leave your son, and we will proceed to discuss your situation."

They were alarmed with the news of immanent separation from the child. But what could they do? Soon enough, a large woman with sandy hair, wide hipped in khaki pants and shirt entered, escorting Mrs. Jones and the child away.

While they were gone, the captain began typing on the computer while looking over the papers Ryan had given him.

"Could you tell me what the prob . . ."

"Please don't interrupt me. Your wife will be back shortly, and then I'll proceed."

Jon grimly nodded. He studied the captain, a middle aged man, perhaps fifty, looking for signs of compassion, friendliness, anything that signaled comfort and solace. "Well, what's the worst they can do to us?" he silently reasoned. "Send us back? That would be bad, but then they could try again somewhere else."

"Try not to worry. Hope for the best, imagine the worst won't be so terrible. They'd manage. He's white. We're white. That must count for something from what he'd been told. This captain doesn't look very bright. Homely, a bit fat faced, thick at the waist. But it's the dumb ones you have to worry about. Yet, maybe more susceptible to a bribe? Who knows now when the people I'm used to dealing with are such idiots and brutes?"

Mrs. Jones returned, weakly smiled at her husband, sitting next to him again. The captain looked up, and said to her, "I think you'll be happy with the care we'll give your son. You needn't worry."

"No. I mean, yes. Everything looked very nice. He should be fine."

"Now, you're wondering why we've detained you, no doubt."

The Jones' nodded.

"Well, it's pretty simple. You aren't Jon and Karen Jones. You are trying to enter Idaho from Nevada under false pretenses, and we'll have to know why."

"But that's impossible," Jon said, trying to be forceful, but not too loud or adamant.

Walters sighed, then drew out two gadgets from a drawer. One a thumbprint reader, and the other was a retina scanner. He plugged them into the computer, and then used the devices on both of them. When finished, he struck the keyboard's return key, then swiveled the monitor around so that the Jones' could see the screen.

"Now, Mr. Sean Finley and Miss Sandra Adams, how many more lies do you intend to attempt today?"

They were mute.

Walters nodded. "As many as you think can help you. I understand. Now, it says here that you were a professor of Humanities at Berkeley."

"Yes."

"What subject?

"Primarily, World and Comparative Literature."

"And your job, Miss Adams?"

"Secretary in the Chancellor's office."

"Is the child both of yours'?

"Yes."

"You have a birth certificate certifying you are the father?"

He hesitated. "Not with me. It was to come later."

"And how much money are you bringing into the New American region?"

Another hesitation. Was the captain fishing for a bribe? Was he after a percentage or a flat fee?

"Not much. Just enough to get established. More would come later on."

"An exact figure please."

"20K more or less."

"Twenty K . . . I love that language usage. As if I must know what a "K" is, and it makes it seem somehow smaller. What exactly is 20K, Mr. Finley?"

"Twenty thousand dollars."

"American or New American?"

"New American."

"Of course. 20K American dollars is worth what? . . . A thousand or so of the other? Are you transferring any gold or jewels?"

"No."

"The lies they just pile up, don't they?" the captain smiled. He was used to people like Finley and Adams thinking people like him were stupid. Handsome and clever people often assume that homely and less intellectually employed folks are dumb. And a militia captain at a minor highway post is certainly lower than a university professor with a skilled concubine.

The world favors the pretty in every contest of people otherwise equal in skill and energy, but the pretty forget that those equals end up some place; occasionally on top, but generally nearby. Failure to achieve a high status doesn't equate to a complete failure to achieve any status or position.

A punk is brought in on suspicion of a crime. The detective questioning him is forty-five; his suit is cheap, his face is florid, he's been a cop twenty-two years, and must be dumb as a cow to hold on to a job like this for so long without much reward. The punk has no idea that he's already been read. The cop's been doing this so long with liars and their faces — all the tics, the tells, the micro quivers of little muscles, the movement of eyes. He doesn't need to bother with lie detectors that some can fool, MRI or CAT scans of the brain that measure blood flow that give away lying that none can fool, or retina readers that detect dilation of tiny blood vessels when people prevaricate.

It never fails that those who think they're clever judge books by their cover.

On the one hand, the cop thinks it's funny that the criminal believes himself smarter; but on the other hand, it's insulting and payback is due the offender.

Even so, Walters knew he had to wait to spring his revenge.

Well, not his revenge, but that of the State of Idaho and the New American Region.

"Do you know what's being done with your vehicle as we're speaking?"

They shook their heads.

"It's carefully being taken apart. Thus far," he said turning to his computer and tapping a few keys, "we've found seventy thou — that's 70K to you — in New Am dollars, 30 ounces of gold, and an assortment of diamonds and other precious jewels. Will we find more?"

He didn't think so. By the look of their faces, crestfallen and despairing, it revealed they'd found everything! He doubted they would hold out further. But you never know, he told himself. He shouldn't think himself so smart, either, that he underestimated the cunning of criminals even when trapped. Humans never stop hoping to evade consequences, and so they always try to hide a hole card.

Nevertheless, his impulse was to say, "I guess I'll be able to build that swimming pool I always wanted now." Just to rub it in. These smart California refugees trying to sneak into my country, on their terms, with their sick souls and ruinous morality. Like they had a right to wreck a second America with their selfish, vain, sanctimonious self-righteousness.

"What do you think will happen next? What should we do with you?"

"Why not just let us go?" Sandra said hopefully. "We haven't done anything to you. We just tried to get in."

"Where's the harm in trying?" Sean added.

"Why did you want to get in?"

"It's still the United States of America. We have a right to travel where we want to in our own country."

"That's only on paper. You know that. You want in here for another reason."

"We can't live there anymore. It's all broken down. Life is impossible for people like us in California."

"No, it's not. You were doing quite well there from what I see. Isolated. Gated communities, and so forth. Protected."

"But that's no way to live! You fear for your life. You need bodyguards everywhere. Someone's always trying to kidnap you, or your baby. You live inside a garden in a prison. The filth outside the walls, you can't imagine the poverty, the violence, the despair. There are millions. Millions outside your door who don't look like you, think like you, talk like you, or act like you."

"Okay. I see why you want to get out. But why do you think you'd be welcome here? What are you offering us? Why should we accept you? In the first place, you come as liars. These ID's, these letters of sponsorship, these fake resumes, is this how you intend to join us? As thieves and liars, wranglers, bribers and so on? If we have something here that's better than what you left, aren't you bringing us something rotten with you? And with so much money, you think you can buy your way into a new life with people who've paid for it the hard way."

"We had to do something," Sean said.

"Then today's your lucky day," Walters told them. "We need people. We have an agenda. Maybe you've heard?"

"Some say you want to take back all the places we've lost."

"Yes, that's right. The country my forefathers created, and yes, I have ancestors who actually fought with George Washington. Now, I'm guessing that you intended to sneak in and live out your lives as if nothing else mattered much. Your mistake. We have built a martial nation. We intend to conquer and kill our enemies. You will help us do that," Walters said lowering his head at them as he spoke.

"I can't do that," Finley said.

"Would you die to protect or defend your child? Or are you a coward through and through?"

"I, uh, I hope I would fight for my family."

"Then you will."

"Let me explain your future to you. All your funds are confiscated by the State. You both will be going to prison for three years. Don't look so shocked or sad. It's not what you think. It's more of a work place. You will live together. You will have more children. You must have five children. Naturally, or by adoption, it doesn't matter, but that will be accomplished within seven years if all goes well with you."

"You, sir, will never teach again. We will never expose our children to someone who's been as intellectually and morally corrupted as you. You will marry. You may not divorce until all your children are grown. If you become a danger to your children, they will be removed and placed in an orphanage so stay sober and sensible."

"You will both learn a trade in prison. You will become religious, and will be given a choice of religions you may join. Islam is not one of them. You will attend services regularly. Neither of you shall ever be eligible to vote. You will both be trained to serve in our militia, but never exceed the rank of sergeant. Your children will train all through school, and will serve a mandatory period after high school in the armed forces. They will be members of the militia or Reserves until they are fifty."

"If you have or are expecting to inherit further income from outside the Region, you shall not receive it. If you leave the Region, you may never return, and if apprehended during an operation by the Region in former territories, you will be summarily executed."

"You look a bit shattered. Don't worry. It will pass. You'll find that life in New America is worthwhile. There is little crime. People have good manners. Public morals are maintained. Children and women are protected, but we intend to take back what was once ours, and we intend to kill and harm a great many people to do that. And you are going to help because this is the way the world is, and we prefer to lead than follow, own than owe."

"That is all."

The Milk of Human Kindness

Capt. Walters looked up from his desk as Ryan came into his office pulling off his gloves, and blowing into his hands. Snow melted from his boots as he stood in the doorway.

"Whatcha got for me," Walters asked him.

"Couple a lezzies tryin' to sneak in."

"Okay. Put 'em in Room Three. Everything still works in that one. Gimme a few minutes to finish this paperwork. Stay with them until then."

It took Walters five minutes to finish up his weekly report justifying various decisions and dispositions of immigrants legal and illegal.

He then checked the computer for the camera output from Room Three, and was surprised. He saw two middle-aged women, which the black and white camera with its poor resolution was unkind to. He knew immediately what he was going to do with them. He picked up the phone on his desk and buzzed the room.

Ryan answered. "I want you to sit in on this one, Ryan. Okay?"

"Yes sir."

"Don't say anything. Just observe."

"Got it." Ryan wondered what this was about then. Another teaching moment, no doubt, but why? Oh well, the captain could be whimsical but he was never capricious.

A moment later the door opened and Walter's strode in.

It took a moment for his face to register on the women. The light went out of their eyes and their faces fell.

"Hello, Karen and Jane," Walters said to them. "Please don't worry. I'm going to give you what you want."

The women were perplexed, as was Ryan who shot him a look of disbelief.

"It's nice to see you again." He remained standing and offered them his hand. They weakly shook it in turn being dazed with the encounter.

He sat down across from them with a computer on his end of the table. He picked up their various documents, forgeries really, and looked them over.

"You won't need these," he said looking up. He turned to Ryan and added, "I know these women, Ryan. Years ago, I guess twelve or so, they were my neighbors in Sacramento. Just a few houses down."

Looking back to the women, he noticed their aging faces and hair. Both had once been blondes, and for lesbians, they had remained surprisingly trim. Karen was the feminine one, and Jane the butch, but you couldn't automatically tell by looking. Both wore their hair short.

"Things must have gotten pretty bad to force you both out," he told them waiting for a response.

Karen nodded. Jane said, "The neighborhood's just a small pocket now of decent people, and the, the punks and lowlife come over the tracks and levee all the time to rob, steal cars, break in . . . We're not allowed to own guns anymore. I mean, we never did, but when it got to where we were thinking maybe we should, it was too late. The police are entirely corrupt now, just like they were in Mexico I guess."

"That's why I left when I did," Walters said. "I loved that neighborhood, that city. It was a pretty good place to live, but well, you know."

They nodded.

"Anyway, I don't want you to worry. I'll find a place for you here where you should be all right."

They remained confused and wondering. He noticed it.

"If you're wondering why I should help you instead of sending you away since you've been caught doing something illegal, I'll explain." He cleared his throat adding, "You were good neighbors. Everyone knew about your, uh, lifestyle shall we say?

I'm a Christian now as I was a Christian then. I don't approve of such 'lifestyles', but I'm a realist, too. As long as you're not obnoxious about things, live and let live."

"But here in Idaho, New America, you might be thinking, people aren't so tolerant, and most likely we'd try and keep folks like you out. Well, you're right. If I didn't know you it might be a toss up. Depends on your skills, age, and discretion."

"I never knew what either of you did for a living, so how about telling me so I can get started?"

Karen smiled a little, "I was an office manager for an insurance company."

"Good. That's good. And you, Jane?"

"I was a girl's gym teacher at a high school. Don't laugh. Really, I know it seems stereotypical but, well, that because it is, I guess."

"I'm not laughing, but you will permit me a little smile, I hope. However, that is more problematic for the reason you mentioned. That position will be more open to scrutiny here. Especially when you are known to reside with another unmarried woman. There aren't many job openings for it either, and married women will be taken ahead of you every time, I'm sure. That's just how it is. What else can you do?"

She shrugged. "I don't know. It's been so long. I don't know what else I'd like doing or be good at."

"Okay, well, I'm going to put you into the database. I'm sure I can get you, Karen, set up, and Jane, you'll have to manage from there. How much money did you bring?"

They hesitated.

"I won't take it. I need to know where to locate you, what you can afford. The bigger cities are full, and housing is undergoing a boom in building and prices."

"We've got seventy thousand New American."

"I suggest you rent until you have a job." Walters went on to give them a list of small cities and larger towns where they had the best chance of getting a start.

"Now, I want to tell you about Idaho and the Region. You chose to come here. It's your job to fit in, not to ask others to accept you. When you get a place, keep separate bedrooms. Just for show, but keep them. Tell people you're cousins if asked about your friendship. Make up some reason why you never married. Men, that is. You know, a series of bad relationships until you woke up and realized it was too late, and you didn't care much any more. Whatever, but make up something plausible."

"People are going to know at some point, but you need to give them something to tell the children. It's better if the kids believe you suffered tragic love affairs than well, something else."

"Go to church. Catholic might suit you best since that group doesn't much care about personal lives, or pester folks about their devotion. Register with a parish, and show up at Christmas and Easter like most of them do. Give a little something each month. That'll squelch speculation about you, too. I'm not making recommendations here. You have to do these things if you expect to get by."

"People here have come from all over the country, forced out of their homes, places they loved, like you, and they blame certain kinds of people for it happening. People are very decent here, by and large, but they hate homosexuals for what they did to the laws, the schools, the entertainment, along with liberals and secularists. They won't let that happen again. Not here. Leastwise, not for a long, long time. There are a number of sexual acts that are crimes here. No joke. And sedition. You can join a Party, argue politics and policy, but no more bashing the country. If you act like there's something really wrong with the Region, people won't want you around. We deport troublemakers back to where they came from. If home grown, we exile them."

"You're too old to do military duty, now, so you won't be able to vote."

"You must be discreet. I'll give you my number in case you ever need help. You'll need new papers and ID, you have to be registered in a few databases, and then you can be on your way.

Ryan will take care of that, and I will see you before you go. Okay?"

The women nodded and smiled.

A little while later, Ryan told Walters that everything was set, and the women were ready to leave. He walked out to the waiting room to say goodbye. This time they were effusive in thanking him.

"You're welcome. I don't know if you have any personal faith, but I must say that I think it was more than coincidence that brought you here tonight. You might have spent your adult lives thinking that Christians, the ones like me, had it in for people like you, but you might consider the possibility that people might really mean it when they say they hate the sin, but love the sinner. I'm not trying to make a big point here. You were my neighbors. You were good neighbors. That's why I want to help you. I know what it's like where you came from. I know what it's going to be like where you're going. You'll do all right. Just don't rock any boats. At this point in our lives, people our age, we just want to get by anyway. So, good luck and God bless you."

Karen and Jane lengthened their departure. Outside the door was a strange new State, a new life full of strangers.

Ryan came up to Walters and said, "Okay, Captain. I'll bite. What was it you wanted me to observe?"

"The milk of human kindness."

"Huh?"

"You and I, you probably more than me since you're so much younger, well, we're going to do a lot of cruel things by the time we're finished. When the war comes, you'll be called up. You'll do things you won't look back on fondly. It doesn't mean you weren't right, but doing the hard things, things that make others suffer — that doesn't feel good either. So I want you to see that if you get the chance, not stupidly or recklessly, but just a chance, you try to do some good when you can. Something you can look back on and be proud of having done."

"Those women, I know them. They won't subvert the Region with the way they live. We're always going to have such people around. Our own children sometimes. Who knows? There's a certain level of variation from the norm that we'll always have. We can be tolerant. We just can't let people be stupid about it."

Said the Spider to the Fly

Jason Bennington was not a handsome man. Thirty-one years old, round faced with dark hair, a heavy beard and oily skin, he seemed unaware of his homeliness; confident, instead, in his energy and intensity. His clothes were expensive, but unimpressive on the pudgy man.

Right now, Jason was staring down a table in Room Three at Ryan Milligan, sitting with one leg resting across his other knee, his foot wagging rapidly in nervousness, and perhaps, as a way of venting anger.

Ryan, at twenty years old, was an object of wrath for Jason, and he refused to be obsequious to an inferior.

"Your documents appear to be in order. Your identity is valid. Your bio is on the Internet, you own a small, robotics chip company in Sunnyvale, and you're relocating to Boise sponsored by two robotics manufacturers."

"Yes, that's right. It's all there."

"This transfer is just yourself, though. Where is the rest of your company? Your equipment? Employees also wanting to relocate?"

"I liquidated my company."

"I see. But then how do you expect to begin again?"

"I'll manage. I'll gather investors same as before."

"Why didn't you fly into Boise instead of coming to North Jackpot?"

"I like driving. A chance to see the country, and bring my car with me."

"Okay. I'll be back in a few minutes," Ryan told him as he arose to leave the room. Walking out into the corridor, he took a few steps down the hall and into an adjacent room, one from which he could observe Room Three through a one way mirrored glass.

Captain Walters was there in the dark sitting and watching.

"Whaddaya think?" Ryan asked him.

"Hard to say. He's nervous about something. He's also hiding something. Does he strike you as the kind of man who likes to drive long distances through boring landscape for fun or to clear out his mind?"

Ryan shook his head but thought to say, "I'm no expert, though. I mean, he's a wound up guy, that's for sure, but for all I know, fidgety guys might like long drives, too, through the desert."

"That's possible, but let's go over it. He sells his company and probably has a fair amount of money from it. He takes a nice, relaxing drive across the desert for the sake of pleasure; he's got all the papers he needs for immigration status with solid sponsors. Granted, he's uneasy at being questioned at this station, this interruption — but he's nervous while trying to not look too nervous. I'm wondering if he's a spy and an infiltrator. What was he avoiding by not flying into Boise and going through Customs there? Have the men go over that car until they find something."

Ryan exited while Walters continued to study the man in the next room. He also studied his own prejudices. He knew he didn't like Bennington. The man exuded a vicious arrogance, the kind that isn't simply personal conceit, but enjoys being cruel to inferiors. He knew he didn't have a single religious consideration, or venerated anything beyond himself. That alone made Walters certain that he had to find a reason to keep him out of the Region.

Clever, arrogant, vicious, and Godless men were not more of what was needed. We'll always have enough of those. Maybe it's time to do an MRI on this guy.

It was a few hours later when Ryan reported that the impound lab couldn't find anything in Bennington's car. By then, though, Walters thought he had it figured out. Bennington was smuggling something into Idaho through the least aggressive and badly manned corridor.

Numerous articles in the papers, reports from government agencies, and comments on websites noted that North Jackpot received the least amount of funds, had a low inspection rate, and that it needed improvement, but no funds had been allocated yet for that purpose.

It was disinformation.

North Jackpot did not have as much traffic to inspect as other corridors, but it had more to scrutinize carefully since the idea had been to encourage illegals, to funnel them where suspicion would be even greater. The real facts and statistics of apprehensions were concealed.

The captain had Bennington escorted to the MRI lab and seated where the scan could be administered. This device was a smaller version designed to fit over the head. Miniaturization had continued apace. When the technician was ready, Walters began to ask the man a number of simple questions to establish a baseline of truthful responses. When he had done that, he then held up a paper, which portrayed the odd symbols and language of a computer software program.

"Have you ever seen this before?"

"No." But blood suddenly flowed from one part of Jason's brain to another.

"Is this a Chinese software program?"

"I don't know." Again, a similar response.

"Are you a Chinese spy, Mr. Bennington?"

"Of course not."

"You can't beat the machine, Bennington. Take this man back to Room Three."

In a few minutes, Bennington was sitting where he had been, and Ryan was where he had previously been.

"Okay. What's the deal?"

"Deal?" Ryan responded, slightly amused.

"I want a lawyer."

"That's nice, but you aren't entitled to a lawyer. This is a military post governed by Militia Regulations and Law."

Walters came in and sat down.

"Why did you liquidate your company and seek to come here?"

"Uh, well, we were no longer competitive with the technology that was being developed here."

"Where did you meet your Chinese handler?"

"You're mistaken. I never did such a thing."

"Have it your way. I have here in my hand an authorization for a death warrant to be applied when I sign it. I have contacted my superiors, explained the situation, and they agree with my assessment. I have some latitude and flexibility here, but I don't much care for liars, spies, and uncooperative people. Let's see. It's three forty-seven right now. How does a fatal injection at four fifteen sound to you?"

A bad smell arose in the room.

"He crapped himself," Walters said getting up. Have him hosed down in the shower room. When you've got him cleaned up, walk him through the execution chamber, show him the injection equipment."

All those tasks were fulfilled. Bennington cooperated in a long interrogation over the next few weeks. The question became what to do with him. Turn him to deliver disinformation to the Chinese, imprison or execute him?

The Chinese option was discounted since delivering bad information regarding technology would soon be noticed by them. Imprisonment seemed merciful since he had cooperated, but his information was insignificant. He had sold himself for money, and the promise of a great deal more. His company was liquidated because it had failed. It could neither compete nor bear the costs of simple security for itself or its staff in the San Francisco Bay Area. The expense was unbearable.

He had been able to memorize the Chinese code, which allowed him to shuffle information over the Internet without it being traced, but systems were becoming more secure. The Internet had rapidly demonstrated the tragedy of the Commons.

No one could stay ahead of the corrupters, and it made the World Wide Web more trouble than useful after awhile.

Therefore Mr. Bennington was executed as an example for others who might be like-minded. Boise Customs was given credit for his capture and interrogation.

A Man on a Mission

"So, you say that I can't vote, I'm told, if we go New America?" Pastor Mendel's wife, Sally smiled as she poured Jack a cup of coffee in their living room.

Pastor Jack Carson thanked her for the coffee and returned her smile in that wide, toothy way he had learned when he wanted to be particularly unctuous. He knew a potential harridan when he saw one.

"That would be entirely up to your husband, but I'm sure you have every reason to trust his judgment and consideration of you as head of the family," he replied making reference to the epistles of Paul which famously describe the duties of husband and wife in marriage.

"I'm sure," she smiled, but it didn't reach her eyes. She knew she was being played with by the use of Scripture "which even the devil can quote to his purpose."

You can get a bit cynical after a lifetime of people quoting the Bible to get what they want or deny someone else their desire. A pastor's wife is subjected to many lifetimes of verse quoting, silly minded, or agenda driven folks, and God help her if she loses faith while remaining a dutiful spouse. What consolation has she then if the salt should lose its savor?

Her husband, Pastor Henry, a sixty year-old man, kindly appearing and relaxed, pretended a mere wisp of a smile at their exchange. He knew his wife was intractable; in many respects, insufferable; believing herself to be long suffering when she was simply willful and indifferent to God and grace. Sally had a good life, a decent life, but was ungrateful, and did not appreciate him as a man.

He thought of all the couples he'd counseled over the years and how often everything turned on the woman in the marriage. Some men were awful, of course, bullies and, yes, I'll use the word -- bastards; but far more often it was the dissatisfactions of the wife that created so much unhappiness.

He often thought of Milton's line about Adam and Eve in Paradise Lost, "he, for God; she, for God in him." All the feminist scholars screamed how vilely sexist and patriarchal that was of the poet, but any Christian marriage counselor understood it perfectly. Departure from that model could only create misery between the sexes.

And he laughed inwardly to think of Dickens' Micawber, "Annual income twenty pounds, annual expenditure nineteen nineteen six, result happiness. Annual income twenty pounds, annual expenditure twenty pounds ought and six, result misery."

Annual compliance to God, result happiness. Annual rebellion against God, result misery.

It is the human folly that nearly all -- man, woman, or child -- do not want to be subordinate or dependent; which only seems natural, but keeps reliance on mercy and prayer far from the human soul.

That was why he favored the society and Constitution of the New American States. It best grasped man's basic sinful nature, and woman's essential weakness. The former Founding Fathers had been wildly optimistic despite their own wisdom, knowledge, and righteous fear of mortal encroachments that might subvert their project and noble experiment. The Founding Fathers had left too many doors open for diluting, dismissing, perverting, and distorting what they'd written and clearly explained.

Pastor Mendel, as president of the Yakima Council of Christian Ministers, had introduced the younger Jack Carson that afternoon to an assembly of those ministers at their meetinghouse.

"Reverends, pastors, fellows in Christ, you probably know why I'm here, but let me lay it out for you," Pastor Jack Carson, a minister of Holy Spirit Sanctuary of Kalispell, Montana began his appeal.

Jack represented New America, and hoped to persuade his fellow clergymen of the benefits of joining that regional power of the once United States. He briefly filled them in on the genesis of the Region, it's Christian underpinnings mixed with hatred of government into creating constitutions that expressly defined liberty and unalienable rights along with forbidding income taxes, sales taxes, and most of all, property taxes. "If a man can't keep his most essential need, his living place, from being stolen from him by taxation, how can he prevent anything else being stolen from him by crafty politicians and majority rule? *But they shall sit every man under his vine and under his fig tree; and none shall make them afraid: for the mouth of the LORD of hosts has spoken it.*"

He told them how personal responsibility had been thrust back upon every citizen, the voting franchise limited, and the concern for the less fortunate put back into the private hands of those who cared most and were accountable to volunteers and contributors.

Painting the rosiest picture of New America, when he was done with his presentation, questions arose to challenge it.

"What about racism? And intolerance? I hear stories that you don't welcome all Christians or people if they're black or Hispanic or even Jewish. What about that?"

Rather than launch into a long, tedious defense of the culture of New America, he readily admitted guilt before his accuser.

"That's right. I don't deny that we discriminate, and even our constitution respects freedom of association so strongly that anyone or any private business is free to discriminate against anyone however they please. As far as race and religion goes, if you decide to become a Buddhist or Hindu, you won't find any intolerance, per se, but if you want to adhere to a satanic anti-religion like Islam, yes, you'll have a problem. You'll be asked to leave. As for Jews, they are the ones who prefer not to join us for the most part."

"What about race?"

"Nobody objects to the Japanese not welcoming people outside their race or culture as citizens and immigrants."

"But this is America. It's different."

"That was America, and all those differences were a large part of what destroyed it. Identity politics ruined the idea of the melting pot for good. Even for Christians. I love all my brothers and sisters in Christ. In Christ Jesus there is no Jew or gentile, male or female, slave or free. But the sad truth is that black Christians and white ones go to different churches; same for Orientals and Hispanics. Why? We're all saved; washed in the blood of the Lamb, children of the Living God, and kindly disposed to each other when we meet and share our faith . . . but when we leave the church or retreat or fellowship meeting, we find ourselves bound to those closest to us in color, culture, and likeness. That's human nature, and we should overcome it, but as ministers, we know that most of us, most people don't. We have to accept reality if we want our people, our children to thrive. And they are thriving in New America. While there is absolutely nothing, I repeat, absolutely nothing to prevent other people, blacks, Hispanics or Orientals from creating their own thriving communities or States."

Pastor Carson was one slick missionary, Henry Mendel understood. Of course, the few minority ministers at the meeting were nonplused, a few other liberal ones were discouraged, but most of the white ones like himself were . . . persuaded is not the right word. They were choosing to be on the side of what was working and appeared best for their future and that of their congregations.

While Jack sipped his coffee after Mrs. Mendel had left them, Henry asked, "What now?"

"Well, we establish an office, bring in a few more people, engage as many of the governing and business class along with the ministers and their churches, and promote good works, spend money where it will be useful, and prepare the ground for what's to come."

"What's to come? Exactly," Henry probed.

"What do you see?"

"You keep moving west little by little. Spokane was very close to Idaho, easily influenced along with all the small towns in the east. Olympia no longer collects any taxes from there."

"Right. There was a great advantage there: all those huge National Forests to be divvied up among the people who welcomed the new order of things. Here in Yakima and south in Kennewick, there aren't public lands so close and nearby. Incentives will have to be different."

That sounded ominous to Henry, and he shook his head in dismay. Is this what we're coming to? Is this what I'm coming to, he wondered.

"It isn't Christian, is it?" Jack solicited in sympathy toward Henry.

Henry sadly shook his head.

"Can I make the case for the greater good?" he asked in his most sincere manner; sincere because he meant it.

He continued. "For about a hundred years from 1800 to 1900, this country was as close to Godly as I suppose any nation can get. People knew their Scripture and children were raised on its values whether they practiced them or not. Hypocrisy was the respect that vice paid to virtue."

Henry nodded.

"The industrial revolution and the rise of science, which was a direct result of Christendom, came into play, and more people were able to enjoy more goods than ever before not only in the West but around the world. And yes, many, many people suffered in the mills, factories, foundries, mines, and so on but there was progress and even the most exploited eventually gained benefits from their labor. If not for themselves, then for their children."

"Yes, I understand all that," Henry replied. "Civilization, our form of it, was no crueler than others, maybe less, only God can do the measuring, and it created far more happiness for people here and elsewhere; but that's all history to me. What you're asking me, and others, is to take part in crafting new history where we are complicit with doing or supporting very hard, very bad things; things that shock the conscience. All for the greater good, which I agree with in the abstract, but pains the soul in reality."

"That's true," Jack conceded as he had to questions raised at the meeting about racism and intolerance. He knew not to argue against other people's truths. He'd learned to simply point the way to folks. This way or that? This way leads to more good. That way leads to disorder, misery, poverty, and slavery. Paint a picture using the reality of life all around the people, then paint the picture of all the good an imperfect and frequently harsh New America had created. Here is your social and economic salvation. Yea or nay?

Henry was squeamish. A common problem among kindly Americans, but once they'd committed, it all worked out, Jack also knew. It's a new kind of Manifest Destiny: making the best out of a bad situation, and what remained of America was a very bad situation.

Furthermore, in a short while people wouldn't be paying sales taxes, income taxes, or property taxes, and life would be looking up; not to mention that the only people paying for schools would be the student's parents or voluntary supporters since all education would be private. Mandatory that parents provide it, but private.

"I know which way I have to go," Henry admitted, "but I feel compromised."

"Yes, because you care more about all the other people who never cared about you, never considered how their actions harmed so many others, not fat cats, not the rich, just regular folks like you and your congregation. Fighting back seems extreme, somehow, but it's not. We're just a group of people who want to live, be left alone, and look after each other without a gun to our heads or a world of Godless, conscienceless people claiming they're only doing their jobs in making life hell on earth. We can't make this world heaven on earth, we know that, but we don't have to let the worst prevail either."

"I know you're right. I suppose, even for someone at my age, that I'll just have to learn how to 'gird my loins' and accept the battle as it is," Henry concluded.

Jack nodded and knew that Yakima had been won without a shot being fired.

Vinegar for the Flies

The Governor of Washington, along with the Mayors of Seattle, Tacoma, Olympia, Port Angeles, Bremerton, and various small towns and cities had been wondering for some time what they should do about the encroachments of New America.

Nearly everything east of the Cascades and National Forests separating Washington into two great zones was now New American, and what had remained of the State and National Guard, all the armories, airfields, barracks, and forts there were in NAR hands. All without a shot being fired.

Not that the Governor or mayors wanted any shots fired. They were not violent men given to aggressive responses to injury or loss of authority.

The Governor explained, "I have spoken to the President himself and he has assured me that if New America brings an army to the West in Washington State, he will not stand for it. He will order the use of nuclear weapons if he has to."

"How!? Where, for God's sake!?" the mayor of Tacoma, Paul Singer, blurted out.

"Not here," the Governor spat back at him. "Boise, or Salt Lake City; places like that."

"That's unbelievable," the female mayor of Seattle said.

"You better hope it's true if New America marches west on us," the mayor of Olympia told her.

"I don't believe for a second the President will order such an attack on them. If they decide to come here, they will come. The question is, what do we intend to do if they come?" the mayor of Bremerton announced.

The Governor looked around the room. "We have five thousand men remaining in our National Guard. They are poorly armed and short on ammunition. They lack tanks, helicopters, planes, and artillery. What can we do?"

"We can fight!" the Bremerton mayor insisted. "We can organize militias of able bodied people and fight."

"And be slaughtered," the mayor of Seattle replied.

"These people are Nazis!" Bremerton said. "They're ethnic cleansers, they're vicious, sick, religious fanatics. You have to fight them!"

"With what?" The Governor asked.

****

It was in the third week of April when five battalions of NAR forces peeled off from the Fourth Army moving down Interstate 5 and rolled into Bellingham, a city and metro area of 150,000. One battalion rolled up to city hall, while numerous companies split off to take up duty stations at the police department and a few substations in the county and suburbs. Other units took command of water and power facilities along with radio and TV stations and the cable companies. Telecomm cell towers and internet wifi were commandeered, or rather, hijacked into NAR control.

The area wasn't entirely shut down. Ham radios and the occasional satellite messages got through, but in the main, communications were effectively severed and replaced with programming or messages from General Bruster or his central command.

Dolores Harris, an office manager in the City Manager's Office, a heavyset woman in her fifties, watched the tanks, transport vehicles, personnel carriers pour into the parking lot by the creek and onto Library Lawn Park fronting City Hall.

"The bastards. The bastards," she said aloud to the crowd of people from her office beside her as they stared in shock. "I won't have this. I won't." She'd long been part of the longest running peace vigil in the United States begun by her ancestors many generations ago in Bellingham.

Soldiers in camouflage uniforms and their officers erupted from the vehicles and began entering the building. As more and more filtered in through the halls, many would enter offices and announce that anyone not directly connected to the mayor or city manager were free, in fact, advised to go home, and would be escorted from the building if they did not.

People began collecting their things and leaving quietly. It's tempting to say they were dazed, but they seemed more thoughtful than lost; as if saying to themselves, "So this is what it's like to be invaded or conquered. How odd, yet curious, too, since the people giving orders are just like me. Like being told by the police to go somewhere else."

The mayor's office was across the hall from the city manager's. A general, followed by a corps of officers strode into the mayor's office with an escort of armed soldiers. Ascertaining that the mayor was not present, he turned and strode into the city manager's department, which was larger.

Ms. Harris stood a few yards away with co-workers as the general, a man who looked to be in his fifties, severe in attitude, and appearing forceful, stopped and spoke to the group.

"Is the city manager here?" he asked mildly.

"Yes, I am," the city manager replied as he came out of his office from the back of the room. He was in his fifties, also, fleshy without being fat. He stood in his gray suit, having just thrown on the jacket and adjusted his tie.

The general approached him and said, "I'm General Robertson of the New American Fourth Army." He did not offer to shake hands with the city manager. "We're here to liberate Bellingham and the surrounding areas."

"Liberate us from what?" the city manager required of him.

Robertson smiled thinly, "From yourselves. From folly. You're about to grow up very fast. Now, if you'll join me in your office, we can get down to what that entails."

****

Russell Porter had been at his hardware store as usual when NAR soldiers came by, told him the city was under curfew, and that he had until five that evening to close his store and get home.

He was also given a leaflet instructing him as to what radio or TV channel to tune in to receive reports and information, and also what web pages to visit for further explanations and orders.

He learned that the city had been cordoned off into ten sectors. There were about 60,000 residences in the general area, so each sector had around 6000 homes in it.

He was further informed that only 30% of the white population was going to be allowed to remain, and to check a list of names on the web to see if he was one of those free from evacuation.

He didn't know whether to laugh or cry when he found himself on the "good" list. It meant he, his wife, and three children were safe. But what did "safe" mean?

Evacuation, he assumed, meant exactly what it sounded like, and a little more exploring on the NAR web page confirmed his worst fears: *Those selected for evacuation will have three days to put their affairs in order, arrange for their transportation to leave Washington State by way of Highway Five. No travel will be allowed North, East, or West.*

People are advised not to carry large amounts of cash or valuables, but arrange with banks to forward such goods. Money in all bank accounts will be freely accessible for one year by means of credit or debit cards, wire transfers, or checking.

People may keep any firearms and ammunition they have for the sake of personal security, but any use of them against local police or NAR forces will be met with overwhelming return of fire, nor will the brandishing of any weapon be tolerated, but result in either swift arrest or incapacitation through force of arms. All civil liberties are temporarily suspended until further notice.

He noticed that his neighbor across the street, Dolores Harris, had evidently not made it home before the curfew. He wondered if her house was locked since she had three cats that needed food and water, no doubt.

In the absence of patrols, with only the cordoning off of the general area with various checkpoints, he sent his two boys to tell the nearest neighbors that he intended to get into Ms. Harris' house to see about her cats. He let his young daughter go off with his eldest boy.

Crossing the street, he tried the front door -- locked. The back door -- locked. He started searching the porch area for a hidden key when the people his children had spoken to began coming out of their homes, joining him at Dolores'.

He told them he was looking for a spare key and they began searching, too, until one fellow, shouted, "Got it!"

Rather than tender the key to Russell out of deference to his leadership in the matter, he took it on himself to unlock the front door, and as he went in, turned and said, "We don't need a crowd coming in and letting the cats out."

But Russell, noticing the snub or diminution of his role, followed quickly on his heels. "I'm not taking a back seat to anyone, pal," he told himself.

They turned on a few lights, located the cats, their food and water bowls, and litter box. The cat food was in the pantry and they doled it out along with replenishing their water supply. Russell went into a bathroom and lifted the lid and seat of the toilet, left the door open in case the cats had no other source of water.

Russell and the other man went outside and locked the door, while seven people stood by and heard their report.

"Who should keep the key, just in case?" Russell asked the group.

Just as he finished speaking, a military vehicle drove up and stopped in front of the house. Two soldiers, sergeants, got out, each wearing an MP band on their right arm, and walked toward them.

"What's going on, folks?" the one on the right asked.

One woman spun and demanded, "Why don't you tell us, you bastards?"

"Keep a civil tone, ma'am. You don't want trouble, we don't want trouble. Having a crowd outside after curfew violates General Order Number 27. So what's going on here?"

"The lady who lives here didn't get home. She has cats. We're looking after them and organizing some ad hoc way of dealing with it in case she doesn't get back."

"That's fine, but organize it indoors. That's all we ask."

The man who'd upstaged Russell announced, "Let's go to my house then." And there was tacit agreement among them. As they began a retreat from Harris' house, Russell stopped and asked one of the sergeants how they'd known they were out here.

"Maybe an informant," he softly replied.

Russell shook his head, "I don't think so . . . I think," he paused, cocked his head, and looked upwards at the sky, then nodded to himself.

Neither sergeant acknowledged his surmise, although they were obviously aware of their drones.

He then hurried to catch up to the group as they crossed the street to go to . . . what's his name? Isn't it Tom? Ron? Don! That's right. He felt petty about being miffed by the guy, but remembered that he'd never warmed to him after fifteen years on the same block. They'd hardly said two words to each other in that time. He'd walk his dog by when Don was mowing his yard and he'd barely make eye contact and nod at him. He wondered if he'd made the "good" list. He hoped he hadn't, which made him grimace in self-disgust.

Thus far, no one had said anything about the occupation of their city by New America. As soon as they were all inside Don's living room, he brought it up.

All of his neighbors were white, and he asked, "Anybody here on the evacuation list?"

"What's that?" the woman who'd sworn at the soldiers asked.

He explained the situation to them as some interjected -- O my God, how can they do that? How can it be?

Don proffered his tablet to checks the lists and it turned out that six people out of the eleven gathered were "bad" listed. Not Don, though.

There were moments of stunned silence in a few people followed by epithets, outraged disbelief, out right denial.

Russell didn't know what to say. Would they be angry at him for not having to evacuate? Probably. Wouldn't I be pissed and saying why him and not me?

He decided to proclaim, "I guess this is what it's like to be conquered. Something I never thought to see. Ever."

Someone looked up at him from where they were sitting. "Conquered? How can Americans conquer Americans?"

"Because they don't believe you're American anymore. Not like them, anyway. Ask the South in 1861 how Americans would attack and want to conquer them, too. This is just a different kind of civil war, I guess, except we weren't prepared to fight," he finished.

"How am I supposed to pack up everything we have in three days! And go where!?" a woman wailed.

"Why am I on this list? Why?" another man whined. He turned to Russell. "You tell me since you're not on it, are you?"

"Not that I have seen, but who knows what they have in store for those of us who remain?" Russell was quick to suggest. Just a suggestion that maybe staying might be worse or as bad.

"But why me? Why me?" the man continued.

Russell had a guess. He didn't know much about his neighbors' politics, but maybe they had the kind of politics that New America refused to tolerate. He knew that he was a rarity in Bellingham, a Christian and a conservative. Maybe all that the NA did was check the voting registration lists for party affiliation and census records for race.

"Does everybody have guns?" he asked the group.

"Guns? How can guns help us now? You want to get us killed!?"

"No. The General Order says that those evacuated can take their guns and ammo with them. I think this is because people becoming refugees all of a sudden might need personal security. It seems they want you to be able to protect yourselves and your stuff, if need be."

"Dear God, I hadn't thought of that. I don't have any guns," another man volunteered. "I don't suppose I can go buy one, now."

"Yeah, that's doubtful," Don replied. "I tell ya what. I have a .38 revolver I'll sell you and a handful of cartridges."

"Okay. How much?"

"Five thousand. New American dollars."

"Are you kidding? Who's got that kind of money?"

"You do. Your house is worth, what, twenty times that."

"How do I know I even have a house now? Every penny I've got in the bank I'm going to need for whatever's coming."

"I bet you have relatives somewhere. Oregon, California, Arizona. They might help you out."

"My mother and father live in Seattle. My brother's in Port Angeles. My wife's family is back East. Geez, what am I gonna do?"

Russell asked Don for the key to Dolores' house, promising he'd look after the cats until she returned. He'd seen her name on the "bad" list, though.

****

For the next three days, Bellingham was controlled chaos. The curfew was lifted for six hours during the day for people to make what arrangements they could in preparation of leaving.

The provisional government constantly informed the populace that those unready to leave would be dragged out, thrown into transport trucks, and driven south.

Incidents of citizen defiance were roughly met. One small group of peacenik protesters had been shot repeatedly with rubber bullets, tased into submission, and thrown into paddy wagons, not to be heard from again. Individuals wanting to exercise their free speech at a soldier might get a rifle butt in the teeth; someone drawing a knife or gun was shot down.

You might call the people restive but compliant. There was little to do but go along.

Russell grimly watched events unfold and it brought to mind something he'd read of George Washington saying, "Government is not reason, it is not eloquence, it is force; like fire, a troublesome servant and a fearful master." None of his neighbors, none of Bellingham (or few) seemed to have ever realized that. Now, they have a better and bitter idea. He bet they, like the Bourbons, remembered everything, but learned nothing, though.

As the people drove off, stragglers and holdouts were rounded up, MPs and various platoons went house to empty house planting sensors to monitor the premises in case of entry, water leaks, fire alerts, and so forth, in order to maintain the properties in the absence of people, and from hazards or interlopers.

Russell wondered if the owners' land and homes would be compensated for or were they spoils of war?

Bellingham was like a ghost town as the Fourth Army battalions withdrew, leaving a skeleton force to maintain order as they leapfrogged other army groups making their way down the interstate to Seattle/Tacoma with forays east and west to smaller towns in similar process of what they'd done in Russell's city.

Once the curfew had been entirely lifted, Russell took his family to church the next Sunday, observing the worshippers had been reduced by half, unless people had simply failed to come.

The congregants were thankful they had been spared evacuation, forced relocation, refugee status -- these words seemed weak in comparison to the experience of being suddenly driven out of your home because people with guns didn't like your attitude. How criminal. How cruel. And as their pastor sermonized, how Biblical. This is what people did to each other, and it is the Godless who make themselves weak and ripe for conquest. If they will not serve God, and do his will, they will serve as slaves. When the Israelites abandoned God, He abandoned them and left them at the mercy of their enemies. The New Americans were people of God, New Pilgrims, who were fighting to re-establish Christendom and civilization as one nation under God. And as Jesus said, when the woman is in labor she cries in pain, but when the child is born, she rejoices and is glad.

That is what his pastor told them and what they must teach their children. They were New Americans, now. They were to be mighty warriors for truth. To be forbearing, masculine, determined, and hard minded in the face of a sinful world. Jesus was on the march again.

As Slow as Molasses in January

One star General Patrick Robertson sat across from the Bellingham city manager, John Devries, at his desk.

"Where is the mayor?" the general asked.

"Probably at his law office. That's where he usually is most days," Devries replied.

"I'll send for him," the general said as he rose, opened the door, summoned one of his officers and gave him the errand.

Settling back down, the general added, "We'll need to reset the biometrics. Between you and the mayor, that's all we'll need for full access of the city computer system, I'll bet."

"And if I don't co-operate . . . ?" Devries let it hang.

"What do you think will happen?" Robertson asked.

Devries frowned in looking at Robertson's immobile and implacable visage. He pursed his lips at the realization of the answer.

"Something very bad which I will not like at all," Devries allowed.

The general neither confirmed nor denied his speculation.

"Are you a religious man, Mr. Devries? (He'd glanced at the brass nameplate on the desk facing him.)"

"Not especially," he said wondering what Robertson was leading up to, and why he was having this conversation at all. What did he need him for? To co-operate? To inform the public? To act as a liaison of some sort? Or did the general merely want to flex his muscles? Just what the hell was going on? So he added, "Why do you ask?"

Robertson smiled slightly at Devries expression, "not especially" that meant, "not at all."

"A little faith might carry you a long way through your present difficulties and those to come," he informed him.

"Why are you here? What do you want? What did we do to you?"

"Have you ever been the victim of a violent crime or knew a loved one who'd been brutally violated by force?"

"You mean apart from what you and your men seem to be doing now?"

"You're not a victim, yet. You've only been threatened with violence."

"Uh huh, yes, you could put it that way, but no, to answer your question," Devries told him.

"My parents were the victims of horrendous crimes when I was five years old. They were murdered by MS-13 gang members in Virginia. Raped and murdered by illegal aliens. My parents were young and naive Christians who thought they were being Good Samaritans on a country highway where they saw a woman pulled over with car trouble.

It was a setup for the initiation of a gang member that usually entails finding some random, innocent gringo to kill. Here were two, and one an attractive female.

Of course, the illegals had been in the country and state for years. Often stopped by the police for traffic infractions, drunkenness, DUIs, fighting or abusing girlfriends, but neither the federal, state, or local governments cared to remove them; deport them.

When they caught them for the crimes against my parents, they avoided the death penalty because that was barbaric and a waste of time. Lawyers and judges made sure it was never enforced. In fact, those men and their woman eventually got out of jail. Laughing no doubt in the way the famous American terrorist did when a judge let him get out of being prosecuted on a technicality. He said, 'Guilty as Hell. Free as a bird. What a country!'"

Devries said nothing. Why should he feel sorry for this Nazi in front of him? Nor would he taunt him with asking, "What has all that got to do with me? With us?"

"I mention this because you want some idea of why the people of New America are being rude to our neighbors in

Washington State. You're aware of the fact that Bellingham declared itself a sanctuary city decades ago, and that Seattle and Tacoma also did so."

"I'm aware of that."

"Are you also aware of the number of your fellow citizens who've been robbed, molested, raped, murdered, crashed into by the illegal aliens, Mexican and Asian, that you've harbored through the years?"

"I have no recollection of such a number."

"Would you be surprised that even in western Washington that hasn't got an especially large number of illegals, that tens of thousands have been robbed, thousands, including children, molested and raped, hundreds murdered -- often by drunk drivers, and many more crippled as a result. Are you surprised?"

"Not especially."

Robertson smiled a little more grimly. There was that "not especially" again.

"Who do you think should be held responsible for all those crimes against citizens by people who had no business being in the country to begin with? If your neighbor kills your kid, what can you do? He lived here by natural right. But if someone who could have been prevented from ever being here kills your kid, who's to blame?"

"No one."

"No one?"

"Things just happen. Bad things happen. Who's to say that if a drunken Mexican hadn't run someone down that his, his neighbor, as you put it, might have done the same? It's just bad luck everywhere."

"Like now?" Robertson pressed.

Devries stared blankly back at him, and then a shadow descended over his face. The irony wasn't funny at all. God, how he suddenly hated the man in front of him with a fury he'd never quite known. He wanted to scream, "Not like now, you god damned bastard from hell!"

Devries had a revelation, an immediate vision of what was to come for him and his family, one injustice piled upon another, cruelty after cruelty because this bastard was sending them God knows where and into what kind of storm? Or storm after storm. New America was going to come down hard on him and others with both feet. Exiles, refugees, driven across the world until they had nothing, were nothing, were broken and shorn of comfort and humanity. Oh, God help us! He wanted to cry, then bitterly recalled that he was not especially religious.

There was a knock on the door. It opened and the mayor was delivered into the room by the general's adjutant. Robertson stood up.

"Captain, get the Signalman to reprogram access. The mayor and city manager will co-operate. I suppose we might as well set up in the mayor's office and this department. In the meantime, I'm going to check in on the mobile headquarters and catch up on reports. That's all."

"Yes sir."

The general left the office and began crossing the department to leave city hall when Dolores Harris boldly stepped across his path to confront him.

"Yes, ma'am. What is it?"

"You have no right to be here. No right for what you are doing. Who do you think you are? God?"

"Ma'am, did you really want to be the tall poppy?"

"I beg your pardon."

"Sorry, I'm in no mood to pardon anyone. Lieutenant Baxter, General Order Forty-five for this woman. At once," he told a young officer who had been following him out. The general turned his way past Dolores while Lt. Baxter informed her, "You're under arrest, ma'am." He clasped her arm, exposed her wrist and snapped a single, wide, dark bracelet on her while she remained momentarily shocked.

"What are you doing?" she demanded when she gained the sense of being manhandled.

"Come with me, ma'am."

"*I will not!*"

"*Owwww!*" she cried as the bracelet delivered a powerful electric shock. Baxter released the button quickly, and gestured for her to precede him out of the room. She complied with his suggestion. Another woman came quickly forward with Dolores' purse and coat and gave it to her. The soldier did not object.

****

Dolores was passed on to an MP who escorted her out of city hall and into the rear of a military police van. She was driven to a large, empty warehouse near downtown that had been rapidly converted into a prison with two large areas encircled by chain link fences with areas set apart for port-a-potties, an area for changing and showering privately draped, a main area for sleeping on hard cots, and a processing point of entry.

Evidently, Dolores was the first beneficiary of the NAR prison camp since there was no one else in what she assumed was the women's area, and none she could see in the other large area.

Her personal effects were examined, recorded, and stored. She was given an orange jumpsuit and told to change. She could keep her under garments for the time being, but substitutes were being arranged. Her clothes were then stored.

Transferring to the common area of the prison, the toilets and washroom were pointed out to her. She was given no shoes, handed a wool blanket and a small pillow. That was it.

Dolores attempted to get information out of the soldiers, women in her case, but they said nothing about why she was there, for how long, or what about her cats. She tried to be as tough and detached as the women processing her, but once released into the common area, she retreated to the washroom and sobbed.

Never in her life had she been treated so abominably. Like she was nothing, a mere body, an animal; like people might treat a cat if they cared nothing for them.

She looked at the wristband on her arm. It was made of Kevlar, though she didn't know that. Only that it was very tough. Teeth did nothing to it. She also knew that it was a shock device, but had no idea that it did a number of other things such as monitor her heart, pulse, respiration, blood sugar, stress chemicals, a myriad of other conditions, and relayed them all to a computer AI that kept tabs on her.

If the NAR had truly wished to be cruel, they could have done away with any fences and simply painted lines where the prisoners could not cross, otherwise shock would commence. But fences gave the prisoners a sense of security. They were restrained by physical means, not mental ones. They were being held, and not teased with freedom . . . just over there . . . right across that line . . . maybe the system is down . . . should I try it and see? *Ahhhhhh!*

Dolores laid down on a cot with her little pillow and blanket, trying to forget where she was, not worry about her cats while hoping some neighbor would look after them.

She had nothing to do, though. No phone or tablet with their multiple uses and amusements. No book, radio, or music player. Nothing but her own thoughts that were annoying and disturbing. Like many women, she kept herself busy all of the time.

She got up and approached a soldier on the other side of the fencing and asked, "I don't suppose you might have anything I might be able to read while I'm here, do you?"

"Yes, ma'am. There are a couple of books for prisoners if they want them."

"Could I get one?"

"Yes, ma'am. Go ahead and approach the entrance area. I'll tell them what you're wanting."

The young woman tilted her head to the side and pressed a button, telling the soldier at the processing area what was requested.

Another female soldier met Dolores at the pass through area, a place where food or other items could be transferred to prisoners without having to open gates.

"You currently have a choice of two volumes, ma'am. This one is *The Holy Bible*, and this one is entitled, *The Proper Roles of Men and Women in a Modern Christian Society* by Reverend Orem Hayes."

She involuntarily barked, "Ha!"

"I must warn you that the books are to be treated with care or there will be consequences. Do you still wish to read?"

She grimaced. This was not a joke. Did she need to read and take her mind off her situation or didn't she? Thinking the second volume might be good for a laugh, she requested it and it was given. She retreated to her cot, opened the book to its Preface:

In the absence of holiness we muddle our way through the many stages of life. We seek guidance from The Bible, our parents, teachers, and pastors, but what often seems so easy for them to advise, we find impossible to follow in a straight and narrow manner. We pray for understanding, but it does not come until after tough events and sad facts, it seems.

I don't know if I can make the journey any easier, but perhaps I can offer signposts that help the reader better understand what he or she has been going through, and may serve them in good stead for what may come next.

What a load of crap, Dolores snorted to herself, and gave up on the book. *Holiness?* What crap. Who believed this sort of bull anyway?

That was as far as Dolores' thoughts would carry. In her entire life, it had never occurred to her that 1) she might be fundamentally wrong about anything, and 2) that she had never thought deeply about any particular subject. Dolores had no idea that she was all surface and no depth. Her education had consisted of merely relaying information back to a teacher or professor. As a result, she had always been a B minus student, bad at math and science, mediocre in liberal arts and humanities. Her parents had been equally vapid and shallow-minded. The kind of people who found TV episodic dramas, police procedurals, or situation comedies as engrossing and fascinating at seventy-five as they had at fifteen; people who never noticed or tired of the recurring formulae and manipulations no matter how many times they saw the exact same story with different faces.

Dolores lay on her cot trying to avoid thinking about anything, staring up at the ceiling of the warehouse, watching dust motes in various shafts of light. After a period of time passed, a flurry of new noises occurred signaling to her that company might be coming. She sat up and saw a small group of men in lavender jumpsuits enter the men's common area. There was the mayor, the city manager, a few other department heads and managers, a couple of city councilmen.

Just then, too, the gate to her area slid open and a city councilwoman, Mary Ramirez, a well kempt woman in her early forties, entered. She had the now common deer-in-the-headlights look. Why is it that so many people never expect the worst and are shocked when it happens? Lifelong insulation from personal disaster, perhaps.

Dolores was ripe for conversation and tried to get one going with Mary, but it was useless for the time being. Then more people were processed through in both the male and female sides. The noise in the warehouse grew with charged and animated conversations, expletives and outbursts. On the perimeters of the enclosed areas, robots were deployed to patrol or stand guard. Soldiers were no longer seen, making it impossible for the prisoners to abuse them as they desperately desired.

John Devries, the city manager, assessed the situation after studying the two common areas filling with people of Bellingham. All were elected officials, managers and supervisors, union leaders, the chairmen of all the major political parties, heads of city and county departments, administrators and deans from the various universities, principals from schools, numerous professors and people notorious for political activity in radical causes (but hardly controversial for Bellingham).

He thought he understood. "They're decapitating us." No leaders or organizers. No one to lead the sheep, direct or guide them. A chill suddenly passed through his body as the thought that they might all be murdered came to mind. Like rats in trap, he thought, and shuddered. Oddly enough, pictures from the Nazi Holocaust didn't occur to him. Well, it was a historical event that hadn't gotten much play for many decades. People knew the word Nazi well enough, and Fascist, but couldn't take Commie or Marxist as seriously. You could still find posters of Che on college campuses or pictured on T-shirts worn in leftist protests.

Thinking about his wife and children, he wondered how this could be happening. Would he see his family again? He heard some man singing and looked up. It was a union guy he knew, always trying to be the clown, singing, "*Hail, hail, the gang's all here. What the hell do we care; what the hell do we care . . .*" It petered out. No one was in the mood for gallows humor.

Having met General Robertson, a few of his officers and soldiers, he was struck by how American they were, people just like himself, but now it was beginning to seep in that maybe he had no idea who these people were. They were foreign to him. Apart from language, he supposed they might as well be Martians operating out of a different book of rules, codes, and customs.

How do you appeal to their humanity when they're bloodless?

It never occurred to him that Robertson had appealed to his humanity concerning monstrous injustices visited upon his fellow citizens by true aliens. He found nothing bloodless about his own indifference. He didn't even notice he'd always been and remained indifferent. Nor did he notice that after his initial burst of violent anger, how passive he'd become. It seemed to be the default position not only for himself, but most others.

It was something Robertson had noticed, though. It made him think about the way the Arab marauders had found the Levant and North Africa such easy pickings. Decadence, passivity, love of comfort, and lack of faith formed a royal road to slavery.

Devries heard a new sound and looked up as did all the others. Music was coming in over a speaker system. It took a moment to recognize what it might be. A man nearby said, "It's Gregorian Chant, I think."

It was. The piece was called *Puer Natus Est.* Many more would follow.

Brinkmanship

"The President will see you now," he was told by Stormour's Chief of Staff and led into the Oval Office. As much as he had tried to prepare himself for this moment, he was deeply affected by the legendary room, the weight of history that seemed to emanate from the walls, and the impressive persona of the current President of the United States. Those words carried ancestral weight, almost holy as when a devout Catholic has an audience with the Pope. Jergen loved history, especially early American history and the Revolutionary War period.

There was a desk, of course, in the office. It was the famous *Resolute* desk. Built out of timbers from a British Arctic Exploration ship that was abandoned in the ice in 1852, found by an American whaler in 1855 and sent refitted back to England where Queen Victoria had a desk constructed from its wood and given as a gift back to the President as a token of friendship and goodwill.

And there it was with its ornate carved panels.

Jordan Stormour stood near a soft, brown leather sofa, offering his hand as Donald Jergin, chief liaison for the New American Republic in Washington, D.C. quickly closed the distance and shook it. Jergin was forty-five, the President, fifty-three.

Stormour gestured at the couch across from him separated by a coffee table.

"Would you like something to drink? Coffee or tea, perhaps?"

Jergen thought a moment and decided he wanted a cup of coffee very much. Such things, besides being tasty and welcome, could also serve as props in one's deliberations, a means of offering moments of reflection and strategizing while engaged in having something to sip.

"Coffee, please. Black and sweet."

The Chief of Staff pressed a button on the desk and said aloud, "Three coffees, all black, one sweet. Thank you."

Jergen laughed inwardly as he knew from past experience that his coffee would be under-sweetened. Not deliberately, but because others never correctly guessed that he preferred more sugar, so he learned to accept and drink it as given without correction. It made one look weaker for complaining, or autocratic and supercilious if insisting something be done exactly according to specification.

Which was a weird and funny thing. If he asked for a Coke, a soda loaded with sugar, no one would have given it a second thought, but he recalled many times in the office, fixing himself a cup of coffee while someone next to him, doing the same, would observe him pouring four spoonfuls of sugar into his mug and commenting, "Want a little coffee with that sugar, huh?"

Jergen was always ready for that. "Since when did my intake of a substance become your primary concern? I had no idea you were obsessed about the personal tastes of others." That usually shut them up permanently.

That was one of the funnier things about people, about a lot of men. They had no mental censor, no inhibiter for stopping stupid comments before they spoke them; of not minding other people's business out loud like the guy in the office who had to tell the secretary how hot she looked in a sweater, how good her legs were. They couldn't help it. It just automatically spewed out. Cretans everywhere.

He didn't want be annoying and have Stormour ticked off at him. He would soon have a lot to be ticked off about.

Jergen had a tablet with him. It had been cleared and found to be free of explosives or nasty chemistry. Prior to that search, other devices and papers had been given to the White House for examination that were germane to the discussion about to unfold.

The USA did not formally recognize the New America Republic, but it couldn't ignore the reality of it, either; thus both maintained pseudo-embassies. The US in the capitol of the NAR in Laramie, Wyoming.

Jergen knew the NAR was about to invade western Washington State, and that Stormour had promised the governor he would go so far as to use nuclear weapons in retaliation if they did.

Stormour knew the NAR was staging an army in eastern Washington in preparation of invasion. He knew that his promise to the governor of Washington had been rashly given, yet he could not bear the idea of the NAR proceeding in its almost genocidal manner.

Stormour had previously been the governor of Pennsylvania. In that position, his scope and powers remained nearly the same as they had for hundreds of years, and he was an effective leader, administrator, and manager of the state given its current resources and population.

Once elected president, he realized the office he inherited had lost considerable prestige, power, and range. His effective zone of influence and control remained the Northeast, Midwest, and east coast to Northern Virginia. All other States and regions were outside his jurisdiction. The west coast, ostensibly, belonged to the USA, but no taxes came from it. Those States had become poor and bankrupt. The Southwest was overrun with illegal aliens beyond government control, a bizarre frontier, nearly lawless, a highway for illegal drugs, prostitutes, aliens, guns, and warring gangs in many areas.

The Deep South now included Tennessee, Kentucky, and even West Virginia, and formed a Region of its own, not as developed in government and industry, nor with as aggressive a military, nor as federalist as the NAR, but definitely separate.

He knew that Jergen knew exactly how many soldiers, tanks, artillery pieces, airplanes, helicopters, sailors, ships, submarines, drones, nuclear warheads, laser and missile systems he had at his command. The diminution of his forces was humiliating. The budget was draining forever with Entitlements to keep the Welfare Society functioning.

The NAR greatly outnumbered them on the ground and in the air. Being landlocked, they lacked ships and submarines, hence their push to the west coast, and their annexation of northern Minnesota with access to Lake Superior. Soon, no doubt, they'd gain cities on the Mississippi.

The US Navy was reduced to two aircraft carrier groups, one for each coast. There were four mothballed nuclear carriers in California alone. Would they end up in NAR control and refurbished? That was one of the things they war-gamed. Scuttling them was useless. They could be easily raised, regardless of depth. Blowing them up could result in retaliation such as the NAR destroying their last two functional platforms.

Stormour had quickly realized as president that the job was no longer about presenting a vision to the people, and then attempting to implement it through Congress, full of promises about how these measures, this new agency, this subsidy would result in lifelong benefits and goodness.

His job now was plugging dikes springing a thousand leaks, robbing Peter to pay Paul, pleading with States to deliver revenue. His great idea and election message had been a program to re-establish tariffs as they once had during the mercantile period of history. It would protect domestic manufactures and goods while taxing foreigners underselling Americans. It might have worked in a robust economy, but now it only made people that much poorer without increasing wages.

The coffee arrived, and Jergen was both surprised and delighted to discover it was exactly to his taste. Perhaps someone had been studying up on him? He was impressed, and that much more wary.

"Mr. President," Jergen began, "it is both an honor and a privilege to meet with you. I wish I could convey to you just how deep a feeling we of the New American Republic have for the Declaration of Independence and the Constitution, the connection we feel to the United States of America, of *'our bonds of affection. The mystic chords of memory, stretching from every battle-field, and patriot grave',*" he said.

Stormour recognized the quote from Lincoln, but wasn't sure where to place it. It was the first inaugural address.

"I appreciate that Mr. Jergen, but it pains me to mention that just as Lincoln was in conflict with the South, we are in conflict with your Region of the country. You are on a course to do great harm to other Americans. The United States stands firmly against your objective. It must not happen. We will oppose you."

Jergen nodded. "Sir, I won't waste your time explaining our reasons or our Constitution. You are a conscientious leader, well briefed on our politics and culture, no doubt. What I have to tell you pains me, also. It is simply this -- you cannot, must not, oppose our actions in the west (or anywhere else for that matter)."

Stormour drew back slightly at the affront of being told what he could and must not do.

He wanted to clench his teeth, but relaxed his jaw and replied instead, "How do you intend to prevent the defense of our country?"

"It is our understanding that the USA maintains something close to 350 nuclear warheads. We know for a fact that you told the Governor of Washington you would use nuclear weapons against us if our forces invaded them in the west." He paused to study Stormour's face. It was impassive, but clearly a tacit acknowledgement of the fact.

"Mr. President," he continued, "I want you to briefly study a few matters."

He presented his tablet computer to Stormor's view, tapping a few places on the touch screen. "This is a replica of a nuclear weapon we presented your people with a few days ago. This is a prototype of a rejected design; one of many, but instructive in that it's a design that clearly works. We also furnished all the schematics for this. Are you confident that we know how to build functional nuclear weapons?"

The President glanced at his Chief of Staff at the end of the sofa way from him. He nodded.

"Yes. I understand you know how to build nuclear weapons."

Tapping on the screen again, Jergen pulled up a picture of an area of Utah.

"This is an area of Utah well known for its uranium deposits. Through Canada, we've also been able to import quantities of yellowcake from Africa. You can check with Canadian authorities on that. You may not recall, but Arco, Idaho was one of the first processing labs for plutonium in developing nuclear submarine power plants. This satellite picture shows how extensive that laboratory and processing plant has become since it no longer works for your Nuclear Regulatory Commission. Go ahead and bomb this place if you like. We have others."

The President grimaced. He knew he was being set up. Jergen was running a dog and pony show that somehow, inexorably was going to make him impotent. Make his job futile.

"Continue," he said.

"Standing by in a secure location in Wyoming is your liaison to my country, and a team of your nuclear scientists." He again pressed a few glyphs on the tablet. A group of men appeared in a bright-lit room.

The Chief of Staff had moved over to observe the tablet screen, and spoke, "Mr. Washington (he was a black man chosen deliberately for that reason to be liaison there), do you hear me and see me?"

"Yes sir."

"The President is standing by."

"Yes sir."

"Mr. Washington, what is your report?"

"Mr. President, this team of scientists from the NRC has examined the material here in the NAR and they all conclude that they have sufficient fissionable material to construct a great many atomic, hydrogen bombs. There is no doubt, no possibility of deception. Our instruments have not been tampered with, and the material reacts with other elements in ways that can't be faked."

"How much material were you able to test?"

"More than the United States possesses at this time."

"Thank you, Mr. Washington," Stormour said ending the conversation.

"Even so," Jergen added. "Your weapons could utterly destroy us if you launched them. Our having plutonium and devices to explode it are meaningless unless we can either launch missiles or deliver the bombs directly. Here are three co-ordinates in New York, Boston, and Philadelphia you must send police or federal agents to immediately. They will discover three lead lined containers holding a small amount of plutonium in them (to be returned to us when they're done). Undetectable by sensors."

"This demonstrates our ability to both penetrate your security, and destroy your major cities, too, without the need of missiles. But we do have missiles as you can observe here, if your satellites haven't already observed."

Jergen showed on the tablet videos of missile launches by the NAR in the Utah desert.

He then spoke about their missile shield and defense system, far more advanced than anything the US had after cutting the program decades earlier, having lured their most knowledgeable scientists to Wyoming to develop their ideas and engineering.

He didn't mention their EMP drones, pilotless airplanes capable of destroying electronic systems by means of electro-magnetic pulses. Nor did he demonstrate their laser weapons capable of destroying projectiles in size from artillery shells, guided missiles, ICBMs, and Cruise types.

The capabilities of both defensive and offensive weapons easily exceeded that of the USA. Stormour's heart sank as the reality of the situation settled in.

A call came into the office and the Chief of Staff answered it.

"Mr. President, three containers as Mr. Jergen described have been found in the locations given."

"Mr. President, I hesitate to say it, but you should consider the possibility that we have placed other containers in the same cities or elsewhere with active nuclear weapons and are ready to activate them should we be attacked in any way by your country."

"My country?"

"Yes sir. That's how it falls out. The USA is dead as far as we're concerned. Beautiful while it lasted until the 50's or so, but no longer a viable entity for human beings."

"By God, just who do you people think you are!?"

"The descendants of Celts, Saxons, Angles, Germans, Vikings, Pilgrims, Puritans, Scots Irish, and others who refuse to go gently into that good night. Just who the hell are you?"

Stormour didn't answer. He had no answer. He was a man of motley peoples. A conjuror at building coalitions, pulling disparate groups and separate agendas together. He was a man who'd built his house on sand, but was certain he had good will toward everyone, every person in his jurisdiction: the black woman having babies at fourteen, never getting a job, living on welfare; the illegal Mexican having a baby at no cost in the emergency room and suddenly eligible for federal benefits; to the poor Somali in a cab mutilating his daughter's genitals and refusing to transport a blind man and his seeing eye dog.

Stormour pretended to love them all. It was his duty. The Statue of Liberty proclaimed his creed -- the wretched refuse, the tempest tossed -- they were all supposed to find a place in America, to melt into one race and people, the American race that knew no color, religion, sex, culture, ethnicity except baseball, mom, and apple pie. Damnit! People were supposed to get along and not have petty differences like food, music, clothing, beliefs, or tribalism. Everyone was supposed to be transformed into an average white man of northern European sensibility. It stood to reason. To differentiate by ethnicity, by color, by race -- well, that made you a racist; the most evil of the evil; a monster. Everyone was the same with the same needs, same desires, aspirations, abilities, and concerns. Everyone had the same intelligence. To say otherwise was to be a Nazi.

It wasn't that all these thoughts flew through Stormour's mind, just that they'd occurred before and were referenced in passing.

"Mr. Jergen, you're telling me that any act on our part will result in Mutual Armed Destruction."

"Yes sir, but worse than that. You can't destroy us while we can surely destroy you."

"You're willing to bet on that?" he stared him down.

"Absolutely. If we're wrong, most of us believe we're going to a better place anyhow. If you're wrong, everything's finished."

"The United States will stand down so long as you do not use nuclear weapons under any circumstances on this continent. Do I have your word?"

"You have our word. We do not wish to kill anyone and will do all we can to preserve lives. Our main objective is to restore, not destroy."

"I don't believe that's true."

"Here is what I believe. It was written by John Jay in the Federalist Paper number 2. He wrote *'Providence has been pleased to give this one connected country to one united people — a people descended from the same ancestors, speaking the same language, professing the same religion, attached to the same principles of government, very similar in their manners and customs, and who, by their joint counsels, arms, and efforts, fighting side by side throughout a long and bloody war, have nobly established general liberty and independence.'* What a shame so many like you have abandoned those principles. They're good ones."

Jergen was shown the way out and soon relayed the outcome to Laramie and their president.

New America Begins with One

Are some men born to be dynasts? Most dynasts are probably born into the possibility like Alexander the Great or Julius Caesar, but others like a Rockefeller, Ford, or Kennedy find an opportunity, grasp it in both hands and devour it.

Bill Smucker had no inkling of his destiny when he was growing up in Lander, Wyoming. He was a tough kid, but not a mean one. He hated his last name. Boys who taunted, "Smucker is a sucker! Smucker is a f**ker!" didn't do it for long.

"Take it back, or I'll make you pay!" he'd tell them. And he would if they didn't, or pay for the attempt himself. But it settled the matter.

When his gang of pals would play king of the hill, what some call monkey on the mountain, he was usually the last one standing. Lots of bruises, black eyes, and skinned elbows or knees from that, nothing broken, but what fun!

Bill's dad owned a gas station and garage, including a mini-mart and auto parts supply extension. He grew up with his brothers and sisters working after school, on weekends, holidays, and summers in all parts of the business. They learned to clerk, do the books, manage orders, work on vehicles, and deliver supplies to outlying farms and ranches.

He didn't always like the work or the hours, but he enjoyed business, and his dad taught him the ins and outs of dealing with oil companies, vendors, suppliers, customers, and basic economics. He loved the organization of tasks, things put in order, schmoozing with people, the give and take of negotiations, learning how to judge employees and manage people -- getting their cooperation and best effort without abusing their feelings, for men like to pretend they're immune to being hurt, yet nurse grudges forever, and rarely forget a slight.

Learning how to handle complex operations, juggling many problems at once, and keeping one's head was an art, and the reward of doing it well, making it look easy, was the gravy of raking in cash.

Bill had the bug.

One afternoon when it was slow and he was working on the books, his dad came over to the desk.

"Want a coke, son? It's hot and you've been workin' hard."

"Sure," and told him thanks when it was fetched and given.

"Dad?"

"Yeah?"

"I was wonderin'."

"Right."

"How do you make a lot of money?"

"What d'you mean?"

"I mean, how do guys get really, really rich? You know."

His dad laughed, but just a little.

"You tell me. I wish I knew."

"C'mon dad, I mean it."

"Okay. Well, I can't say I've given it a lot of thought. I learned this business from my dad in Laramie, saved up and started here the best I could; grew it a little from a service station, but we are far from rich."

"Well, how do you think some men get really rich and others don't, then?"

"You have to be driven, for one thing. You have to find a need for a lot of people that isn't bein' satisfied, or you invent something everyone will want and you work like the dickens to get it to market, to finding your buyers and being a good enough salesman to sell it to them. People will tell you it takes money to make money, and they're right. It helps to know people who can help you, who you can persuade to help you or invest in your idea. You have to take risks. Sometime big risks that'll cost you everything. You gotta be willin' to fail and get back up. You see what I'm sayin'?"

"I guess."

"See, I'm not rich 'cause I'm not that kind of man. I could sell this business tomorrow take all the money, and say, invest it all on some big idea I suddenly had, but I won't do it. Can't do it. I'd rather not worry about how I'm going to take care of everyone."

Bill nodded.

"But a man alone, taking his stake and trying to make his fortune, he can do that if he's got the will, the fire, and determination. I'm guessing that some get rich because they have to or they'll die. You wanna get rich?"

He nodded.

"Why?"

"I just like making money, doing all the stuff to run a business, but if I'm gonna run it, I wanna get rich from it."

"I wish you luck. I think men always need a little of that, too. It sure doesn't hurt," he laughed.

****

Not long after this the price of gasoline began to rise even though domestic production increased. The problem was that it couldn't be refined. The EPA made it impossible to increase refining capacity or allow new refineries to be built. The oil companies made money selling the oil abroad, but prices rose in the USA, from 4 to 5 to 6 and even 8 dollars in some places. Another factor was foreign expansion of oil and gas use in India and parts of Africa. Despite the continuing alarmist warnings of carbon dioxide, the Third World had caught on that cheap power created more wealth even if it only went into the pockets of kleptocrats. Such people enjoyed the bump in their Swiss bank accounts and promoted greater use of those fuels.

But in the USA, the long recession became a Great Depression.

With higher domestic gas prices, people drove far less, needed fewer auto parts and repairs, and bought fewer snack items when they did tank up.

Bill's dad was going broke as were farmers and ranchers in the county.

Soon enough, a man from the EPA showed up at the gas station. The underground storage tanks that held various fuels were determined to be more hazardous than a recently manufactured type of tank. They mandated all gas stations must install the new ones.

The old fuel tanks were perfectly safe, of course, and had never been a problem, but the opportunity to inflict the most damage possible on independent station operators was too good to pass up. The hostility of the federal government to the carbon fuel energy sector was unabating.

Bill's father came home in despair. Clutching the sheaf of regulations and mandates, his children could hear his anguished rant as he spoke to their mother behind closed doors.

"They do this like it's nothing, no problem, just a minor fix. The man stood there nearly grinning when I asked him where I was supposed to get the money to do this. That smug sonovabitch . . . like . . . putting a man out of business, destroying his livelihood, what little we have left was a minor problem and no skin off his nose. My God, my God, what am I supposed to do? I'd have to get a second mortgage when we can hardly pay the first one now! . . . and he just stands there, I tell you what I wanted to do. I wanted to get my pistol and blow a hole in his God damned head! It's like they say in Texas, the man needed killin'. How is that against the law when someone comes up to you, a man making an honest livin', and puts you out of business with a snap of his fingers because he feels like it? How is that man not worthy of a bullet in his smug arrogant head!? God damn it, God damn it! That's what a man used to do, didn't he? . . . No, I guess he didn't. The EPA, they're the sheriff, and when the sheriff comes and tells you to stop growin' corn, or ranchin' cattle, or selling gasoline, you just tuck your tail and go. But go where? Where are we supposed to go? Where are the jobs? Not in this state, so we're supposed to pack up like nomads or something and go somewhere we've got no roots and no love for. Aw, damnit to hell! God, God! I just want to kill ev'ry one of those sons of bitches!"

He sold their business and home at deflated prices, moving to North Dakota where he got hired to drive a truck to supply oil rigs. It wasn't the worst pay, but competition meant it wasn't the best pay, either. He was lucky to have gotten the job.

North Dakota was prospering, and all of the children did everything they could to make extra money shoveling snow, mowing lawns, cleaning gutters, clerking in retail, delivering pizzas, or working in restaurants.

Bill eventually went to college majoring in petroleum geology, drilling engineering and science, and business management, working oil rigs in the summer.

Hired after graduation by a major company, Bill spent the next decade globe trotting, spending a good deal of time on deep sea platforms starting as a foreman and working his way up the management ladder to a mid level position making a good deal of money.

In his later twenties, he recalled talking to his dad.

"Still wantin' to get rich?"

"I'm tryin'. You bet."

"Savin' your money?"

"Well, I'm tryin' but not as much as I'd like."

"Why is that?"

Bill was embarrassed and didn't want to say.

"Lemme guess. You're wastin' it on wine, women, and song."

Bill paused long enough for his father to chuckle at having guessed right, then added, "What's your problem son?"

"I guess, when I'm off the job, I get to feelin' lonely, and then once I start tryin' to have fun, I find it hard to stop. Havin' fun means . . ."

"Squanderin' your wages. I understand."

"What d'you suggest, then?"

"Nothin'. It's your problem. You work it out. It's all your choosin'. Where you're gonna find the backbone to resist temptation, I don't know."

"Thanks, dad, for the support."

"You're welcome."

"I was being facetious."

"So was I . . . look, if your ambition is important to you, if it truly matters, you'll figure this out and do what you have to. If you don't, it just shows you're another fellow with pipe dreams thinkin' about what coulda, shoulda been if only, if only, if only you'd had more character."

It gave Bill something to mull over. Back on a platform in the Gulf of Mexico after a rotation on land and another binge of big spending and nothing to show for it, Bill lay on his bunk, pondering his shame, his fate, his lack of character as his father had put it. He didn't fall to his knees, clasp his hands, cry out in agony and despair. He simply closed his eyes and begged God for help, promising he'd do his best to do whatever He told him.

But God told him nothing. All he heard was his own small, interior voice saying, *read the book.*

He ignored it. But it stuck with him until he said, "Oh hell," and grabbed a tablet to download a Bible.

Which one, he wondered? There were dozens of translations. He figured the RSV was popular so he started with that, and for some reason found himself reading the story of the Maccabees. Not quite the most usual place where heartbroken and struggling people go for solace and comfort, but it wasn't succor that Bill needed. He needed strength and power and the Maccabees provided that.

Later on, Bill would become familiar with the entire Bible, but he found his footing in Christianity with the Maccabees, and never lost that original sense of defiance of wrong doing by the corrupt, cowardly, and depraved. The Maccabees were just what he and his country needed.

Bill saved his money, invested in the oil business since he had expertise and some inside knowledge of where things stood and where they were likely to go.

He was thirty-three when he decided to start wildcatting on his own. He thought he knew just the place: the Red Desert of Wyoming. Everyone knew there was oil and gas there, among other minerals and coal, but extraction was prohibited on Federal lands and all shale oil extraction was banned. He thought he knew a way around that.

Four years earlier, he'd read an article in an oil and gas journal about a scientist who was working on a new process for shale oil separation that would be cheaper and easier, if it worked.

All the major oil companies had their own competing and heavily invested processes and lacked interest in this new method he learned after contacting the scientist and his small team. After meeting with him and learning as much as he could about the process and necessary development, he persuaded a number of other men like himself to fund continuing research.

A year and a half ago, they perfected the process, tested it in Canada, and began marketing the product worldwide. It was going to be a highly lucrative company. But not a huge moneymaker for him since it had to be divided with a large group. It's like the companies that sell drilling mud do a great business, but not as much as an oil company.

He wanted to drill into shale oil deposits in Wyoming. He could do it on private land, and the footprint would be small. A single rig could drill a dozen slant or horizontal wells. The biggest problem was temporarily storing the oil and transporting it. That meant large tanks and a pipeline to a railhead for shipment to a refinery, or tanker trucks. You couldn't hide that from the government.

But he thought he had an answer. He would visit destruction upon any who tried to thwart him.

Bill needed to get wealthy, filthy rich, but he had a different purpose in mind, now. That money was to fund Maccabees in America.

A Little Brief Authority

"It's breaking the law. It can't be done," Jim Beeks, Bill's friend, told him.

"That's because you still think Washington is powerful everywhere, all the time. It isn't. It's getting weaker by the week. Pun intended."

"They can still crush you like a fly if they want."

"That's the point. They have to want to, and they don't."

"How do you know?"

"In the Hinterlands, all the agencies are vastly understaffed and underpaid. Their budgets are bare bones. They can hardly pay for the toilet paper in the bathrooms, never mind pens, paper, vehicles, or new computers. D.C. has been robbing Peter to pay Paul for decades now. It's not that they won't see it, but they won't stop it. That would take sending people from D.C. -- FBI, US Marshals, EPA cops who do not want to travel to the wilds of Wyoming like Pinedale, arrest some wildcatter and have to keep coming back over a few years for the trial, while in the meantime, we destroy every office and vehicle they own."

"What, like they'll throw up their hands and say, this is too costly, too much bother? That's crazy, Bill. I mean it. It's like Ruby Ridge and Waco, Texas crazy if you have any idea of what the Feds did in those places. Those smug, arrogant pieces of garbage hate having their noses tweaked. They hate it!"

"Except the department heads and managers aren't those guys anymore. They're bean counters, buck passers, incompetent time-serving hacks. A couple of years ago, two brothers went up into the Bridger National Forest and build themselves a cabin and started cutting timber and hauling it to a mill. They had no right to do it. They squatted and took public trees. The forest service noticed after awhile and sent a ranger up to tell them to get out of there. But they came out with rifles while he was driving up the road and put a few rounds in a rear truck panel.

"Right away, he turns tail and heads back home. Now, you'd think the county sheriff would be next in line to deal with the problem, but he tells the Feds it's their land, their problem.

"So what does the ranger do? Nothing. For a year, nothing. He's going to wait and when they come from down the mountain, he'll burn them out. But one of them is always at the cabin. So they cut timber, sell it, and get by. All illegally.

"Now, the ranger is pissed because it's really his land, right. Not yours or mine, but his. It's his fiefdom and these two working class guys are thumbing their noses at him. So why doesn't he call in the FBI, the US Marshals, the Swat team, the Navy Seals, whoever, to rid him of these troublesome clods?

"Well, for one thing, to call for help would be to admit to his superiors that he can't handle minor problems, goodbye ladder climbing; and two, he does call the cavalry. That is, he puts out feelers, discusses the problem with federal law enforcement people, and the word he gets from them is that they have bigger fish to fry. Tough luck, and by the way, no one wants to come out to ass end Wyoming and play Wyatt Earp.

"So, Jimmy, my pal, my bud, that's how we're gonna play it. And if they get too serious, we'll hurt them. We'll be the Earps and they'll be the Clantons. No one gets physically hurt, but we'll destroy everything they depend on to do their job. Do you believe me?" Bill finished.

"Bold talk, but how do you intend to "implement" your policy?"

"How about a couple of former Navy Seals working on a promise of becoming millionaires?"

"Seriously?"

"Seriously."

"I'll invest, but I have no intention of hanging around."

"That's okay, we'll still be friends."

****

Bill welcomed Dave and Pat into his lodging at the Log Cabin Motel in Pinedale. Both men were in their late forties, retired Navy Seals, and bore themselves with unmistakable military bearing. Dave Morelli was the shortest of the three of them by a few inches, clean shaven with graying short hair, while Pat Kinneson sported a full mustache and beard, neck length brown hair that was starting to thin and recede. Neither was particularly handsome, but certainly rugged and virile, which is attractive to many in itself.

The cabin had a kitchen, a sitting room and a separate bedroom. It was spacious, rustic, yet cozy.

Offered beer, Dave and Pat nodded, took seats in comfortable chairs while Bill handed over the cans and sat on a couch facing them. They cracked the tabs, took a pull, and began the meeting.

"Okay, we've got the Ranger Station and BLM office computers hacked. All their emails will go through us," Dave told him.

"How's that?"

"You want to know how we did it?" Dave returned.

"Yeah, I do."

He grimaced a little. He hated being micro-managed, and why give up trade secrets so he gave Bill a cock and bull story.

"It's pretty simple. We email the office secretaries great coupon offers for local restaurants. They know a bargain and want to save money, so they download the attachment to print them out. That sets the malware in the system."

"How clever," Bill smiled. Pat gave Dave a quick look and nodded.

"Right," Dave agreed. "Then we set wiretaps on their landlines. Every conversation that goes in or out is processed through our computer set to identify keywords so anything related to our operation gets tagged and reviewed, so we know what they're up to before they act."

"What about cell phones?"

The two men looked down and shook their heads. It was too expensive to capture all the data even in a relatively uncrowded area like Pinedale.

"We have all their vehicles Lojacked with GPS we can track anywhere, though," Pat was quick to add. "If they head out to the Operation, we'll know long before they get there."

"And there's this," Dave jumped in with. "BLM has only two official vehicles. Both are old. Obviously the fleet hasn't been upgraded in a long time. They sit in the lot every night. I'm going to drain the oil from one of them, disable the dashboard warning light, and let them destroy the engine. We'll see if they have anything in the budget to pay for a new one."

"What about Laramie? The EPA regional office?" Bill asked.

"Same deal with their computers. All their base are belong to us," Pat chuckled.

"Are belong to us?"

"Old joke," Dave grinned.

"We've got their email, too," Pat said.

"What next, then?" Bill asked.

"Well, it's up to you," Dave told him. "What's your schedule for operations?"

"Build the storage tanks first, but while that's being done, we bring in the equipment, the rig, the pipes, the nano-juice for extraction, then there are the trailers for the riggers. The foreman can stay in town. He'll keep his mouth shut."

"You can't keep the men cooped up out there. They're going to want to come to town for dinner, drinks, hook ups. And they won't be quiet about where they work and what for."

"I know, but I can keep them out there for a month, and we can get most of the set up done in that time. After that, I'll have a talk, one on one, with each one of them and emphasize the need for silence and offer a big bonus for the entire crew if the word doesn't get out. I'll give them an alternate story to tell, some BS that could be true, so they can lie with conviction. I'm not worried about them so much. It's the traffic. Once we start extracting oil and filling tanker trucks, the steady flow will attract attention. People can't help but notice."

"How about having them come and go at night. The Feds never work past five if they can help it," Pat offered.

"Yes, we'll try that, but, well, it's only a matter of time. Truckers will stop for coffee, say what they're up to as they try and chat up a waitress, and pretty soon, people are wondering about what they've been hearing."

"Of course," Dave agreed. "That's why we're set up for whatever comes next."

"Which is?"

"Wait and see, Boss. Wait and see," Dave replied smiling.

"I need some idea," Bill returned with a serious stare.

"Look," Pat jumped in. "We know what we're doing. No one gets hurt, but we know how to discourage people who have no desire to be heroic."

Bill nodded, and let it go at that. This is the pucker factor, he realized. The moment things get very serious because so much is on the line. Not for Dave and Pat. He was sure they could stay out of trouble, keep from being caught, and he wouldn't betray them, but there wasn't any way he could avoid capture if it came to that. Clearly he, his company, Zion Oil, was paying for everything. This was his Rubicon.

"Well, as my dear old daddy used to say, 'in for a penny, in for a pound'," Bill grinned.

"I bet he never said that," Dave smiled.

"Maybe not, but he knew what it meant."

Dave and Pat nodded.

****

BLM Pinedale District Manager, Fred Armlinger, a middle aged, pot bellied fellow had called his boss, the regional supervisor in Laramie, Don Goodpasture, an older, wispy haired, pot bellied fellow.

Fred: "Look here, one of the engines of my two trucks seized up, needs replacing, and I haven't got any money in the budget for the thousand it needs. You've got to help me out here."

Don: "Sorry to hear that, Fred but you're just going to have to find a way to cut back on something else. What makes you think we've got any surplus cash to throw your way? I get the same reports all over the region. 'Help, our computers are broken, our building needs a paint job, the roof is leaking.' What can I tell you? There's no money. You'll just have to manage."

Fred: "Well, I'm not going to use my own vehicle. There's no money for mileage, maintenance, per diem, or insurance either."

Don: "I know (sigh). Tell me about it. I've got a skeleton crew here, as it is."

Fred: "Okay, then. I might as well let you go."

Don: "Sorry I can't help you. That's just how it is these days."

Fred: "I know. I know. Talk to you some other time, then."

Don: "All right, then. So long."

Click. Click.

Dave and Pat debated whether it was time to destroy the second Pinedale BLM vehicle. Perhaps, some sand in the transmission fluid? They decided to let it ride (so to speak) to avoid greater alarm.

By that time, it had been a month and the tanks, derrick, and supplies were in place and drilling had commenced.

Two months later, they intercepted an email from Pinedale to Laramie.

Don,

There are rumors of some sort of oil or gas drilling operation occurring in the shale deposits near Pinedale on private land. Do you know of any permits issued by your office or the State Bureau for such an event?

Thanks,

Fred A.

Pat and Dave responded:

Fred,

There's an exploratory operation permitted on private land by the State Bureau of Mining and Mineral Engineering. Nothing to concern yourself with, but thanks for the heads up.

Don G.

Bill got six months of worry free extraction out of that and had opened up two other rigs. His problem now was over-supply. He needed a pipeline to deliver the oil either to a railhead or to a major transcontinental pipeline carrying oil to a major refinery. The latter alternative was cheaper but cut across Federal land. Getting easements for it prior to crossing public land wasn't a cinch either, but since those private lands were also shale rich, it should be easier persuading the ranchers considering the royalties they'd get from the oil and the rent they'd get from the pipeline.

The easements were acquired *sub rosa*, and the pipeline was quickly built. That seriously cut the tanker truck traffic, but ranchers bragging about their newfound sources of revenue spread the word of an oil strike. Eventually other companies wanted in on the action.

Fred had no doubt that laws were being broken now, and called Don in Laramie. Don denied receiving a previous email and denied telling him an exploratory operation had been permitted by the State.

When he tried to drive out to the rogue operation, though, his truck quit on him.

He called Don and demanded back up, that he send out a vehicle to help him. Don agreed, but when the morning came, all of his vehicles were no longer operational. It appeared that some sort of material had burned great holes in the aluminum engine blocks.

Don suggested that Fred get help from the Forest Service in Pinedale. The Ranger was more than happy to oblige a friend, but that was until all his vehicles suffered a similar fate as those in Laramie.

Don informed his superiors in Washington, but the response was slow. Perhaps it was because their computer system was suffering from a complex worm that made getting the system back in order their highest priority. Viral programs invented by the NSA and Mossad to cripple computer systems had evolved and come back to haunt the poorly run, and rather obsolescent systems the government depended on in its less important agencies.

Fred had become angry enough to commit to using his own sedan to drive out to Bill's area that was rapidly expanding in number of rigs, a few crossing onto BLM land.

Don's office was being flooded with requests for drilling permits (since those companies believed everything Bill was doing was legal). They were denied.

The engine of Fred's car was also clandestinely destroyed.

Fred, Don, the District Ranger were incensed and decided to rent a helicopter to fly over the range. The nearest was in Jackson, near the Grand Tetons, but damned if that one didn't come up damaged and unable to fly, too.

Small planes were considered, and when one owner agreed to rent his Piper Cub out, it was disabled within a locked hangar. Word got around that any equipment rented, leased, or charted for use by the government would likely become a useless pile of junk. Prudent owners informed potential government customers that their property was no longer available.

Various law enforcement agencies had been apprised for quite some time -- local police, county sheriffs, state police, and FBI. The FBI remained uninterested, but the local police lost one of their vehicles and decided whatever problem there was, it was outside their jurisdiction. The County Sheriff's Office became militant and pugnacious about the growing abuse of authority. They decided to drive out with Fred in two vehicles and were en route when a couple of armor piercing .50 caliber rounds pierced their engine blocks.

The County maintained a helicopter and a small plane but declined to offer them for use.

Nevertheless, a reporter from the State capitol of Cheyenne made it his business to hire a pilot and fly a small plane over the territory Bill was working. Taking a great many pictures, he was also able to contact the owner of the ranch and spoke to him, but he wasn't able to notice the pipeline that was mostly underground and otherwise camouflaged.

Bill had been in operation for nearly a year and a half, and true to his word, Dave and Pat were millionaires.

With publication of the secret and illegal shale oil operation, a rather large number of federal and state vehicles destroyed, the intimidation of the police and sheriffs, the visual proof of Bill's pirate-like wildcatting, and many people outraged in Cheyenne and elsewhere in the State, nothing seemed to be getting done about the situation.

"You'd be surprised how little money it takes to bribe state senators and congressmen even when they're term limited," Bill explained to Dave and Pat in his trailer on the ranch; having moved out of town to keep from being held and questioned.

"And so despite a little public and political protest, we've got advocates locally, state-wide and nationally. In the meanwhile, other companies can't come in, and we keep expanding. Nobody loves an oil company, but everybody loves an underdog. We've bought as many local newspapers as we can (subscriber websites, really), bought a lot of advertising on talk radio and FM stations, and even TV spots on what a boost to the economy we've been. The net effect has been to stymie an effective response or shut down."

"Now, as for the Feds, they can't be bothered, it seems. This kind of stuff used to bring them down on people full force, you know. I mean, spread some sand on a puddle, and there was the EPA assessing million dollar fines for disturbing a wetland. The country's farther gone than I realized. If we haven't tweaked their noses full sore into calling out the army by now, it can only be for one reason -- they can't spare the resources from other programs and agencies. Every spare dime is poured into entitlements, welfare, food stamps, Head Start, you name it, to keep the Detroits and Atlantas from burning and spreading out from there. Then there's the part where we've been paying taxes on production and they need that revenue."

"I have a question for you," Bill said meaning both Pat and Dave. "Is it me, or was your, our, operation easy to pull off than it should have been; or at least easier than I expected."

The two former SEALs looked at each other and Dave nodded at Pat to explain to Bill.

"There's a number of factors involved," Pat started. "One. We're warriors. We play by a Bushido Code. Everyday I get up, maybe after my second cup of coffee, I decide that if I die today, that's all right. If it comes to that, I'll die today. How many middle managers of a BLM office or even deputy sheriffs get out of bed everyday and say to themselves, 'This is a good day to die. Bring it on.' No, they wake up, go about their routine, and when a real threat comes up all of a sudden, they think of their family, their life, their future retirement and the fact that they don't want to die. Not now, not ever. You follow?"

Bill agreed. That's how he lived -- by routine and assuming he'd be around awhile no matter what.

"Now, factor in a man driving down the road and he gets a bullet in his engine that tears a great big hole in it, or a bullet in a panel or through the windshield where he's not sitting. Later on, he knows it was simply a warning, something meant to intimidate him and keep him from doing his job. So, does he act like John Wayne or Gary Cooper in High Noon insisting he can't be intimidated? Like hell he does. In his head he might be absolutely certain that the next shot won't be to kill him, but to miss again -- to try and scare him off -- but his body can't grasp it! His body is screaming that he can't be sure the guy out there isn't committed, no matter if they catch him or kill him."

"So what does he do? He calls in the cavalry. Let's get a hundred of me and show we can overwhelm the bastard taking pot shots. Let's get SWAT teams, lots of officers, snipers, and so on. And that works every time until Waco when the people you're assaulting have plenty of their own firepower and you're pulling dead and wounded out of the kill zone. Well, screw that, so you burn them out: man, woman, and child. You simply execute them for having the nerve to defend themselves. Drop a bomb if you have to."

"But here, they can't get a hundred guys in armor, helicopters, tanks, APCs, field command modules. They can't afford it anymore, and oh, by the way, they've come to realize they aren't dealing with cranks holed up in a cabin on Ruby Ridge or something. Their resources are being drained with .50 cal armor piercing rounds, their engines have been burned through by molten metal charges that go through aluminum like corn through a goose, and they have no idea if we might have IEDs or Stinger missiles for any helo, plane or drone they send up. Not to mention all their buildings and offices going up in smoke. A SWAT sniper with an AR-15 platform will run far and fast away from a man with a Barrett .50 cal. So, you see, all your local LEO's are scared and when they call DC for the cavalry, the request gets passed from one guy to the next, back and around, meetings are scheduled, and a lot of people have to sign off, which means when it all goes South, they look bad. They don't get shit canned. Heaven forbid! But they're, what's the word?" he said looking at Dave.

"Embarrassed."

"Yeah, they're embarrassed. For some reason, you wouldn't think that would be such a big deal; and it's not as if these are macho guys. They're strictly civilian rear echelon MFs, but any hint that they have something to be afraid of, and they will never sign off on anything. And more to the point, no one's dead, no one's waving the bloody shirt screaming for justice, no Governor demanding the White House do something. So there you have it.

They're afraid to die today or tomorrow. They know they're up against pros, and they have no idea how many and how well armed. And three, the pros they have will not go into any situation that even hints of a fair fight; of them taking casualties. You remember that high school massacre at Columbine? Those bastards sat outside of the library and listened while those punks murdered all those kids because they didn't have the courage or initiative to storm the room, to risk their lives. The two punks were ready to die that day, but not the SWATs."

Bill took it in, thought about it, and asked, "Well, what would you have done against you if you were them this last year and a half?"

"You take this one, Dave," he said grinning.

"After the very first ambush where they, I mean, we, the good guys, fired into the block of a car coming out to inspect the operation, assuming I can't get access to a tank or APC, I would have set up our own recon foray. I'd have sent another car out, but high overhead I'd have a drone with infra-red vision to pick up the sniper or snipers, then track their movements, see where they went, get a fix on their base of operations, collecting as much Intel as I could, and then set up another foray with a vehicle, and see if the sniper returned to his former position. Then I'd do it again, except that I'd have snipers already set up to bag us when we got into position again. We have countermeasures for that, too, but it's a place to start. But from reading their email, listening in on their phone calls, they never had any kind of plan."

"Right," Pat said. "Their plan was to call in the Feds, and that was pretty much it."

"Right," Dave continued, "But if only they'd learned there were two against them, there's a hell of a lot they could have done to neutralize us, drive or helo in, take over the property, and arrest you . . . but we had plans for that contingency, too."

"Really? Like what?"

"Oh, you wouldn't have liked them, Boss, but we think they'd have worked."

Bill almost laughed in relief that they hadn't gone there.

Bill raised his can of beer and said, "Here's to you, to Bushido."

"To Bushido," they toasted.

"And here's to you, Bill. You put it all on the line, too," Pat told him.

With Dave interjecting, "In a civilian way, of course, but balls out just the same."

Soon enough, Zion Oil expanded into the oil shale regions of Utah, Colorado, and further into the Red Desert of Wyoming. By means of bribes, the acceptance of corruption by now widespread throughout all levels of government, Zion Oil captured the lion's share of leases.

The private take over of the public shale oil lands became a fait accompli. Not even the President of the USA, once he learned how enormous the range of the scofflaws had become, was able to stop it. He needed money, too. Enough to scorn the Green lobbies which had kept a tight lid on resource extraction for decades. The money wasn't just for campaigns and his Party, but for the treasury and corporate funded private charities delivering supplemental aid to welfare, social security, and Medicare recipients.

In the less prosperous and Godless society that the humanists and socialists had brought to pass, avarice was loosed from moral restraint. Everyone outside of the ruling elite (their pillaging never ceased) needed more money than they had or earned for what had once been simple amenities or services. Small things, like enough money to buy a washing machine, take a weekend vacation, send the kids to camp, buy new clothes, pay for a new baby, things once within the range of an average income stressed budgets to the breaking point. Any extra income, no matter how it came, was welcome.

In a matter of ten years, Zion Oil had conquered the West, and the efficiency of their extraction techniques let them expand throughout the world. As the major shareholder, Bill became a billionaire many times over.

The Fighting Whities

Kevin Worley was eighteen years old and what folks used to call a 'strapping lad.' He was six feet, three inches, two hundred and thirty pounds, and said by many to be the best high school fullback in the country.

So why weren't any of the major colleges trying to recruit him to play for their programs? He had received letters from UC Davis, a Division II team, a number of junior colleges throughout the country, and a few other Division III teams in the East.

His high school coach had sent out letters of recommendation to every program he'd ever had a connection with, that had previously recruited a few of his best players. He'd sent the stats sheet of Kevin's high school career, the best runner and scorer in the history of Rhode Island, maybe the whole Northeast. Video data was included highlighting his speed, power, aggressiveness, good hands, and agility.

No response. When Kevin asked him why, he said, "There's a dirty little secret that the coaches in the NCAA have bought into -- that all the best athletes are black. Doesn't matter if it's true or not. It's a prejudice that they find hard to break."

"Most teams have whites on them," Kevin protested.

"Yeah. On the offensive or defensive lines, at quarterback, a few linebackers here and there, and even a few running backs and receivers now and then. But whites are who they turn to when all the blacks they want are gone and the Pacific Islanders, too, I guess."

"That doesn't make any sense," he complained. "What am I gonna do? I wanna play ball."

"The Ivys always need good players, black or white."

"Like playing in the minor leagues."

"Some good pros have come out the Ivys. You never know."

"How many, coach?"

"A few. More lineman, perhaps, but a couple of running backs."

"Since when?"

"Well, no players from the skill positions for a long time, that's true enough."

He wondered what he was going to tell his dad. "Dad, it looks like we wasted all that time, all that work. You helped make me one of the best, and I can't buy a position on a good team. Another kid from Pawtucket who isn't going anywhere. When can I start makin' silverware where you're foreman at?"

He was young, impatient, and a little too quick to despair; yet, being told he was too white for a job threw him for a loop. And as for blacks? He'd played against a lot of nearly all black teams and shredded them. They weren't faster, stronger, or tougher. For three years, once he'd demonstrated he was the league's one man wrecking crew, every game a bunch of dumb, loudmouth, trash talking blacks would dance around, beat their chests (why would they do that -- knowing what it makes them look like?) telling him they were "gonna lay out yore cracker ass", and adding a lot more than that even after he'd trampled over them.

Send one linebacker out of the game with a concussion or broken ribs and, sure enough, his black replacement would promise to "knock the honky crap" out of him until he limped off the field, too.

****

Tom Colson, head coach of the Wyoming Christian College Crusaders, liked to gamble when recruiting players. Especially players like Kevin Worley. Kevin was the best fullback in the country, any half-assed scout could see that, but he played in nowhere Pawtucket in a half-assed league and he was white. Even though his high school had won State three years in a row against supposedly better Providence teams.

Let Kevin, Big Man on Campus, star of the State Champions, eat some humble pie for a few weeks once recruiting season opened up in the spring. Let's see how many offers he gets from ranked colleges, if any.

And that's how Kevin got the letter asking for a meeting and an offer to bring him out to their campus in Maccabee, Wyoming, not far from Laramie.

Kevin's coach looked it over and told him about the program.

"They moved out of Division II nine years ago and were invited to join the Mountain West Conference. That's nothing to sneeze at. Boise St., BYU, Utah, UNLV. Some perennial top ten teams."

"Yeah, but the Crusaders? Never heard of 'em."

"Yeah, never been ranked but steadily improving over the last five years since this Tom Colson took over. First year 3 - 9. Next year 4 - 8. Then 6 - 6, 5 - 7, and 7 - 5. Notice the progression? Steady on. Hear what he has to say. Nothing to lose, right?"

He nodded.

Tom flew out with his backfield asst. coach, Jake Swinner, tens years junior to Tom's forty-seven. Jake remained trim and athletic looking, while stress, late night sandwiches, and more beers on occasion made Tom a bit soft in the middle. He tried to work it off in practice, but those carbs held on for dear life, and a great meatball grinder was hard to pass up.

Tom took Kevin and his family out to the best restaurant the Worley's cared to go to, an expensive steak house in Providence. There was Kevin, his dad and mom, his younger brother, Joe who was about to go to high school and looked like he might follow in his brother's footsteps, having the size and look of a ball player; and then there were two younger sisters, Melanie and Sue, ten and eight.

"Order anything you like, anything that strikes your fancy, something you've always wanted to try. Spare no expense, we can handle it, we've got a great alumni donors and booster club. Mr. Worley . . ."

"Call me Jerry."

"Okay, Jerry, call me Tom, coach, whatever you like, but if you're a man who likes a fine whiskey, try the single malt scotch McCallum 50."

Jerry picked up the drink menu and nearly gasped. A shot of it cost $150. He swallowed, looked up and agreed, "Yes, I think I will give that one a try."

Mary, the mom, was partial to wine, and he ordered an exquisite white Pinot Grigio for her. Also expensive.

When their drinks came, Tom offered Jerry the advice of adding a small cube or two of ice, telling him how it seemed to bring out more flavor.

The dad looked at his son Kevin who was watching him intently, perhaps jealously. Jerry sipped carefully, closed his eyes, and sighed. "That is the finest thing I think I've ever put in my mouth. Dear God in Heaven, oh to be a billionaire."

Mary, having sipped her wine, nodded, her eyes sparkling with delight.

The table was too crowded, the restaurant too busy for Tom and Jake to talk football, and they didn't want to at the moment. They'd rather get to know the family better. Were they religious? Yes, church going Catholics. That's why Kevin played for St. Raphael Academy. A school with a small enrollment, but a powerhouse in sports. Both parents worked, but confessed they hardly got by like so many people these days. These days? Heck, for decades now.

In turn, Tom was questioned about Wyoming, its climate, the college. Christian? What kind of Christian?

Jake explained, "Well, ma'am we're non-denominational, but some people characterize us as evangelical; but let me tell you about what we primarily believe and teach. You might have heard of C. S. Lewis and his book *Mere Christianity*, well, we're based on that principle, but go a few steps further. We think the most important thing that any person can have is to know and follow God, and that starts with Jesus Christ. If a man or a woman knows that Jesus rose from the dead, that he's alive today, a person you can meet, well, like you and I can meet here, not exactly like this, but the sense that he's real and present for us to make contact with in his own, but completely convincing, way, then that's were we start on figuring out how we should live . . . where anyone wants to take it from there, that's up to them and the Holy Spirit."

Tom added, "We encourage our students to get to know Jesus and to develop a prayer life that will suit them best, and to seek guidance from those they trust, such as a priest of the Catholic Church."

The rich food and superb beverages had put Kevin's parents in an expansive mood, the young people were satiated on delights so that after returning to their home, they were relaxed and ready to enjoy an introduction to the exotic and far away Wyoming college.

Tom connected his tablet to their flat screen TV and ran a video of WCC and the football program and facilities. First class all the way. The natural wonders of Wyoming produced oohs and ahhs, after all, there was Yellowstone, Devil's Tower, Big Horn Canyon, amazing Badlands, mountain ranges, deserts, and sagebrush prairies. They saw cowboys on horseback, buffalo, wolves, grizzly bears, the Grand Tetons, and many other marvels that thrilled them.

They saw Maccabee and how it was a beautiful small city of about 50,000 people designed in a prairie sandstone style that was peaceful and lovely; and the college with it's gorgeous red and white sandstone buildings, arcades, colonnades, quadrangles, and towers. It was thoroughly idyllic, Western, and entrancing.

After the video show, the dad, Kevin, and the two coaches got down to the business of making a deal.

Tom knew that Kevin hadn't received any major offers. He wondered if he knew why and debated whether to tell him the story he occasionally regaled a potential recruit with. What the hell, let's lay it out there, he decided.

"Jerry. Kevin. If you don't know the reason the biggest football programs haven't been beating down your door, let me tell you how and why that is."

"You have to understand how it all started. Back in the ancient days of 1966, all Southern teams, and they were the powerhouses, maintained all white rosters. Alabama under the legendary Bear Bryant had won back to back national championships, but in '66 the team was cheated out of a third straight championship by the voting sportswriters based on the fact that Alabama was all white and needed to be punished for segregation in the Civil Rights era. That's what Bear Bryant believed, anyway. Damned if he'd lose another championship based on that, so he scheduled an opening game in Alabama with USC in 1970. USC had a great many blacks on their team and stomped Alabama 42 - 21."

"That was Bryant's way of proving to his loyal and fanatical fans that the team needed blacks. They recruited two blacks, and in the following year in Los Angeles, they beat a heavily favored Southern Cal team 17 - 10. By 1973, a third of the team was black and all of the SEC conference had gone in that direction. Except everyone forgot that an essentially all white Alabama team had beaten USC proving that blacks weren't essential for a winning program."

He sensed that the Worleys still wanted to pretend that having a bias for one's own race and culture was mean and inhuman. Still, he thought it best to face it head on, and asked Kevin, "What are your odds of playing if you signed, say with Alabama, Florida, or USC? Hell, even Brigham Young, Boise, and Utah play only blacks at their skill positions except for QB. You're not a QB. You're a fullback with the most yards and touchdowns in your league's history. Tell me, then. Who's come begging for you to start for them?"

The eighteen year-old would looked over at his dad, back to Coach and said, "UC Davis in California says I might start with them."

"Might, huh? Let me tell you something. You're the best fullback in the country, bar none. You come with us, you may not start as a freshman, but you'll get playing time, and most likely, you'll be the man after that barring any misfortune. There's only one reason, Kevin, Mr. Worley, coaches aren't beating down your door to get Kevin to sign with them. You know the reason."

Mr. Worley shrugged. "It's because he's white," he said softly.

"That's right. Best fullback in the country and the best he can do is Division II ball. And that's what's going to make our team successful and get players into the NFL. We go after the best white players in the country, hell, the world if we have to, and showcase them on national TV where everyone can see how stupid this reverse racism that's been going on since the 60's is. And here's another secret. Kevin, what's your SAT score?"

"1280."

"Right. That means you're a smart kid. We're going to win not only because we nurture and develop the best white players there are, but because our teams are smarter. Our players are just as fast, powerful, and aggressive as the best black athletes, but the thing that's going to get us national championships is that we're smarter. Our offenses learn new plays quickly so that when other teams prepare for us, they'll see things they never expected. Plus, we adjust faster to whatever their defense is doing. Same on defense. The linebackers understand their options better, think faster. We make fewer bonehead penalties. We play with more discipline. You won't see Crusaders dancing all over the field every time one of them makes a routine tackle. We focus on winning. Not celebrating before we've won anything. Our advantage is our brains."

Kevin was listening hard while his dad rubbed his chin mulling over what Colson was saying.

"Here's something else. The education you receive will be a fair one. I mean that your professors, your advisors, the administration will be made up of men who are proud of who they are and the achievements of their ancestors. There is no political correctness at WCC. No speech codes, nobody telling you what you can and can't believe. We have a theology and a philosophy, but we train people to think for themselves. You don't like the theology and philosophy, you'll get a debate but you won't get censored, forced to apologize, or punished. You want to offend someone with a wild idea or opinion? Go ahead. It doesn't mean everyone will like it or agree, or won't be offended, but they won't do anything about it except to throw a few choice words back at you, maybe. You'll find freedom in Wyoming in our college."

That concluded Colson's pitch. Kevin and his dad were impressed. Kevin was ready to sign right then, but his dad urged caution, asked for more time to decide.

Everyone shook hands, but Tom and Jake left disappointed. Driving back to their hotel, Jake complained, "What does it take to get these idiots to see where their interests lay. Damn them."

Tom nodded solemnly. "Dumb bastards have been so thoroughly PCed they can't think straight for a second. The dad agrees his son got no serious offers 'cause he's white, yet he wants to hold out for a ranked college. Screw 'em. Bastards. What a waste."

****

Jerry Worley turned out to be right. A week later an offer came from Stanford in Palo Alto, California. A coach came out to meet him, not the head coach, but an offensive coordinator who explained how Stanford recruited a great many whites since its admission standards were much higher than other colleges, and students had to have a good SAT, which Kevin had. Also, Stanford had frequently featured whites in key skilled positions.

Kevin and his dad were impressed. Kevin flew out to see the campus and it was beautiful. The Bay Area, what he saw of it in the exclusive areas, was amazing, the weather perfect. That's where he wanted to go and eagerly signed a letter of intent.

When he showed up in June for the start of practice, he was disconcerted to meet his competition, five other black fullbacks ahead of him on the depth chart. He realized his freshman year was for nothing but training. He'd never see the ball, but who knows, if he worked hard, proved he was better than the others, he'd get to play. After all, could these black guys both be smart enough for Stanford and talented at the position? Probably not, but he'd see. He had some hope, anyway, even though the backfield coach was black, too. Surely color wouldn't matter if it came to winning?

The Spiritual Brain

"I believe in the spiritual brain," Dr. Campbell proposed as he lectured his advanced theology class at Wyoming Christian College. "And I wonder what it is that God is aiming at. Every living thing experiences purpose consciously or unconsciously, so what is God's purpose in creating sentient creatures such as gracile hominids, Neanderthals, Cro-Magnons, and us. Or rather some of us more than others who seem to be continuing in development regarding the human brain."

"God works in process. Long processes, but somewhere along the line, perhaps among the Scholastics, it was determined that Man was the Crown of Creation and completely capable of responding to God's call to follow and know Him if a man chose to. Man was imperfect, but perfectly capable of sanctification. Brain had little to do with it, soul was everything, except for the feeble minded or insane. Those were obvious impediments to holiness and oneness with the Creator."

"Yet today, we are keenly aware that it isn't class that differentiates human beings of a similar group, as it is IQ. Intelligence. Mental ability and agility. But is smarter necessarily better, Mr. Crawford?" he said pointing to a sophomore. WCC had restored formal address between faculty and students.

"No, sir. A great many high IQ people are often arrogant, selfish, and atheistic while someone else with a much lower IQ may be kind, generous, helpful, and faith filled."

"Quite right, but is there a point where we can begin to doubt that faith alone can sustain a man . . . or woman?" he asked nodding to the distaff aspect of his lecture hall. "Miss Hinckly. Could you address that question?"

"Are you suggesting that brain power is needed to advance a person's faith and understanding of God?"

"Am I?"

"Well, I thought so but . . ."

"Go on."

"I mean, well, no."

"In your opinion . . . yes?"

"I mean, it seems to me that if faith is guiding you it will lead you to wherever God wants you to get regardless if you're especially smart or not."

"Then why is it that the process many call evolution, but I prefer to recognize as the process of natural Development appears to show that the brains of some populations have diverged from general humanity. A certain variant of genes that regulate brain size showed up about 5,800 years ago and exists in 30 percent of people. Oddly enough, our brains have dwindled in size over the last 20,000 years. A male brain has lost the equivalent of a tennis ball's size of material: 1500 centimeters, but that's Development probably making our brains more efficient for a smaller body weight and muscle mass. Even so, there's clearly a genetic factor in differences of human intelligence itself, a biodiversity."

"Clearly, we are not all created equal. We can speculate that God wants us to be smarter so that it is easier for us to know and understand Him better in order to fulfill the purpose for which we were created. I say He wants us to be smarter because it appears that the processes He put in place are purposely at work in doing just that. Perhaps His plan is for everyone to have an IQ of 200, which I've read that some say may be the brain's limit in that the system won't function any better than that given the concentration of neurons, synapses, brain size and so on."

"But if humans are meant to eventually be created equal, shall we say, all alike in IQ, then that means some portion of humanity has to become extinct like the Neanderthal. Either that, or we start engineering equal brains for everybody. An Afghan woman with an IQ of 88 gets handed a baby way smarter than Tesla or Shakespeare. Hmm, I wonder how that will work out," he mused scratching his chin for effect. "But then, the kid won't lack company. Every baby in the village is a genius, too, so they'll probably figure out how to deal with their dumb dads and moms."

"But back to Miss Hinckly's assertion that faith is enough. In the Old Testament we are frequently told in the Writings to seek knowledge, seek knowledge, and then keep on seeking knowledge. In the New, we are advised to be as gentle as doves and wise as serpents; the parable of the Dishonest Steward explaining a little of how to be shrewd. If Jesus said that about 'wise as serpents', is it fair to assume that he wants his followers to have something more than common sense. He wants them bright. Bright as he is, and he thinks everyone is capable of seeing things, knowing things, exploring things the same as he. In fact, he's frustrated when they don't, and calls them blockheads."

"Furthermore, when you study the faith of people we might call simple minded, not stupid, but less given to abstract reasoning, we see a faith that's emotional, highly credulous, anti-intellectual, and viscerally opposed to inquiry, challenge, or contradiction."

"So, where do we go from here? Do we try and help Development along with bio-engineering our offspring to be not only healthier, better looking, but also brainier? Are there possible drawbacks to doing that? We don't want to create people who are so smart that they don't see the point in procreating, for instance. Look at the USA and how so many smart people quit reproducing or had only one child."

"It's no good saying we shouldn't do this or that thing because someone will. We've been partners in the acceleration of human evolution ourselves. Smart people invariably want to mate with smart people. We manipulate nature by breeding plants and animals to suit our needs, stepping up to bio-designing them now as genetically modified foods and animals. Why would we stop there and not experiment on ourselves? Since already we do it in a cruder way. I mean not "we', but other humans using sperm banks or selecting ova and removing and inserting genetic material and so on."

"None of this sounds very spiritual so what was I saying about the spiritual brain? On the whole, I'm very doubtful that humanity can destroy itself by trying to improve its health, its looks, and its brains by manipulation. Why? Because there is in all of life a spiritual river at full flow. Life itself is that spiritual river and it is flowing in a direction. That direction is towards God, always and everywhere except that we, or many, that is, reject it."

"Is humanity flowing toward God en masse, so to speak, over time and with gradual improvement? That's hard to say, but when we look back at the previous 200,000 years of human development would we not believe Mankind is better off even though we continually spasm in terrific wars and destruction? We're not going back to being people with stone axes, wooden spears, and lucky to be around a fire if we can find something burning and keep it going."

"How about this idea? Maybe it's all leading up to the end of Man. We reach a certain point, and poof! We don't need to go to work in the morning anymore, or whatever. The Rapture, the Apotheosis of humanity, the Judgment Day," he laughed.

"No, really." he cautioned. "Maybe we are tending toward a situation that concludes life as we know it here and now where all is transformed to another way of existing, of being and becoming. That sounds kind of nice when I put it that way, doesn't it?"

The rest of the period, Campbell moderated a vigorous class discussion about Man's perfectibility vs. sanctification vs. fallen condition and imperfections, and what intelligence, or lack of it, played in considering what the future may bring.

It was delicious speculation and the students got excited and keyed up in trying to think through their ideas, beliefs, and responding to challenges. It was a glorious free for all of big ideas and give and take; just what they'd hoped college was going to be like.

After class, the professor disengaged from the few lingering students who didn't have another class to get to, and made his way to his office in the Humanities building which he occasionally joked ought to be properly called the Divinities since all the courses were centered on the good, the true, and the beautiful.

Unlocking his office door, a small room with hardly enough space for a small desk, a bookshelf, a narrow couch, and a solid but wooden chair (don't want to encourage students to overstay their welcome) facing across from his desk, he put his notes down, sat in his comfortable and flexible chair and took a few moments to decompress. He would have loved to light up a cigar. He felt delighted with the last hour and his students. They weren't always as responsive or engaged with his thoughts and observations. But today was what made teaching fun; a reason to keep at it.

His mood was broken by a couple of quick raps on the door followed by it opening and the appearance of a lanky and disheveled Prof. Anderson.

"Derek, you busy? No, of course not," he said as he came in, taking his customary place on the couch, lying out with his ankles crossed and feet resting on the far armrest as he twined his fingers behind his head.

"I'm basking in the glow of grace and serenity after having enlightened the barbaric horde, candidates of future human being, Neil," Campbell laughed.

"Good, good. How lovely. Wish I could say the same. A regiment of clodhoppers and dullards for me this semester. Anyway, the reason I came by is I have a new petition I want you to sign."

"Not again?"

"Someone's got to stand up against this forever war. Even you, at some point, has to realize we can't dispossess everyone in America who disagrees with us, who's a different race."

Campbell frowned. Although a sympathizer, he wasn't a strict Maccabean as much of the NAR population was, dedicated to reclaiming as much of former America they could and driving out undesirable people. Neil, his friend, professor of World and Comparative literature, was the leader of a group who lobbied, not for peace, but co-existence with all other Americans. That's what they were called: Christians for Co-Existence.

"The army just went through Boulder, Ft. Collins, and are entering Denver. They've cleansed Seattle/Tacoma and are converging on Portland. This is crazy. Think of the suffering, Derek. We are acting like Caesar with his Roman legions," he said in appeal.

Campbell nodded. It was hard to justify it on a personal level. You can read the books of the Maccabees; their defiance of the Seleucids and the traitorous Jews among them; the cleansing of Judah, establishment of the new High Priest and violence towards those who opposed them or sided with the Greeks, and it seemed justifiable according to their times and the savagery of the ancient world, but to do that today, even without the slaughter since they were essentially unopposed by men of arms -- who could feel good about it?

It *was* for a greater good. Campbell believed that, nor did he believe that as a Nazi, a Stalinist, an Obamist would. The good he believed in wasn't utopian, pie in the sky, the-world-is-one kind of lunacy. The people of the NAR believed in liberal democracy, free markets, personal responsibility guided by Natural Law and serious Christian morality.

It wasn't a Puritan America they sought to create for themselves and generations to follow, but a place of severely limited government (with unbreakable restraints put on it) where people could thrive or fail relying on natural bonds to either help them or reject them according to affection or exhaustion.

Yet, the cost! Or holocaust, as some would insist. He answered his friend, "I know, but we're not monsters entirely. We won't let them starve. We'll settle them in Mexico. They can remake that place or create a buffer zone or do whatever they want. We'll make sure Mexico can't do anything about it, and turnabout is fair play, as they say. They sent their millions and millions into our nation, now they'll get theirs back and more in return. We're not killing people. We're moving them. They don't deserve being on this land anymore."

"Hard words, Derek. As Christians, aren't we the ones who are supposed to bear the Cross. And as Socrates asked, is it better to do harm or suffer harm?"

"I can bear the harm done to me, perhaps. That's life. But I can't bear the harm done to my children and their children by people devoted to their corruption, abettors of great evil, and those who deny God and sin. I can't leave that kind of legacy if I can do anything about it."

"Yes, but the people of Seattle and Denver aren't here in the NAR. We already are protecting our culture, our children, our civilization. Let us win by persuasion as we have in eastern Washington, northern Minnesota. We are acting as conquerors, we are plundering other people who only want to be left alone by us." Anderson felt he was making progress with Derek and was about to launch further arguments when a rap on the door brought a halt to their conversation.

"Yes," Campbell called out. "Come in."

The door opened as Colonel Walters peered in, and then fully as he stepped across the threshold. He wore his army uniform of blue and buff, a nod to the Continental Army of the Revolutionary War. A small insignia of IS, the Intelligence Service, was fastened to his lapel. Other than the insignias of his rank, there were no other decorations.

Henry Walters was in his sixties now. His time in the IS as a border captain across from Jackpot, Nevada in Idaho seemed like another century to him. His skills as a forensic psychologist were valued, and he headed up a department at the central headquarters in Boise.

"Hello, my name is Henry Walters. I'm a colonel in the Army and I was looking for Professor Neil Anderson."

Anderson sat up and swiveled around to sit facing Walters standing at the door. Campbell remembered his manners and stood up to greet Walters, shaking his hand.

"I'm Derek Campbell. That's Neil Anderson," he said as Neil stood to shake Walters' hand, although there seemed a slight hesitance or reluctance to do so.

"Please, have a seat. How can we help you?" Campbell asked gesturing to the chair near the desk. He hadn't noticed the IS insignia since military ranks and various service distinctions were unfamiliar to him.

Walters removed his hat, looked for a place to put it, and seeing no coat rack anywhere, placed it on the desk as he sat down. How fastidious, Campbell thought, and chastised himself for not knowing more military men and the way they conducted themselves. The college is a bubble, he realized. Maybe they should create a new branch of the college devoted to military history, engineering science, war gaming, and other things they teach at the military academies, he noted. Something to bring up with the trustees and Provost.

"A small matter of Professor Anderson's background came to my attention and I need to clear it up," Walters told them. He took a small object, most likely a cell phone from his pocket, and tapped on its screen.

Campbell understood that professors, professionals in sensitive businesses, naturalized citizens were screened as to their background. He was native born, but he knew Neil had been naturalized from South Carolina a few decades ago.

"Let me go over some basics with you," Walters told Anderson, who swallowed, nodded his head, and agreed. "All right. If it will help," he said trying to be amiable.

Walters then asked him where he lived, what his job was, how long he'd been at the college, what his National ID was, and his telephone number.

Anderson proceeded to become more nervous with every question. Walters understood why.

"Now, where is it you were born?"

"Charleston. South Carolina, that is."

"The date?"

He gave him the numbers.

"You mother and father were . . ."

"Cecilia and Nathan."

"Brothers and sisters?"

"None. An only child."

"Cousins?"

"None . . . as far as I know. My father had a sister, but I don't recall her ever marrying or adopting, and my mother was an only child."

"Do you know of anyone named Yevgeny Baryshnikov?"

"No."

"What about Peotr and Olga Baryshnikov?"

"No. Why?"

"Well, we have a sample of your DNA and it turns out to be close to that of a Peotr Baryshnikov of St. Petersberg, Russia. And his wife. They had a son named Yevgeny. He'd be about your age."

Dr. Campbell's face drained of blood as he realized what Walters was implying. Anderson tried to maintain an expressionless mien, but the effort at appearing emotionally blank betrayed him, his eyes having darted here and there a few times.

"This device," Walters said holding up what they'd thought was a phone, "has an infra-red image sensing capability. It can record the changes of surface temperature on a person's face. It's a little cruder than what we normally use when interrogating a subject, but it's not as unreliable as polygraph tests proved to be. When a person is lying, the tip of their nose and inner corner of their eyes will get warmer, appearing red on this screen. Unfortunately for you, Professor Anderson, you've done a good bit of lying and there is a police officer waiting outside to arrest you for espionage against the New American Republic."

Walters rose, opened the door and gestured for a young policeman to come in and take Anderson into custody. For a moment it looked like he might bolt, but then he sighed and resigned himself to the ordeal. The policeman led him away as Campbell, who had risen, stood dumbfounded.

"Perhaps you're wondering why I would conduct this matter in your presence rather than simply apprehend Anderson at home or elsewhere?"

Returning his attention to Walters, Campbell could only nod.

"Anderson is a Russian agent of the FSB. He was planted in the NAR to attempt to create political organs to undermine the spirit and resolve of the people, just as the communists had done previously in the USA. China, along with Russia, have no desire to see an ascendant New America, of course. For the Chinese, infiltration is a bit more difficult than the Occidental Russians."

"I decided to let you see first hand what we're up against, how serious things are, and how a country can be demoralized from within by foreign enemies and what Lenin called 'useful idiots.' It's important that you understand how insidious subversion can be as it masquerades with smiles, friendship, seeming good will, and gregariousness."

Campbell remained dazed.

"Oh, by the way. I read your book, *The Spiritual Brain.* It's very good. Worthwhile. Here's my card. If I can ever do anything for you, please let me know."

Campbell took it and nodded as Col. Walters left his office, his footsteps echoing down the hall.

The professor remained in a state of confusion and pain for some weeks afterward. He'd liked Neil. And even later, he worried about what was to become of him. Treason's penalty was death, but perhaps Col. Walters could find a better use for him in the realm of spy vs. spy. He hoped so. He also became a staunch Maccabean. Screw the world. Corruption and depravity was worth fighting against tooth and nail. Damn them!

How to Raise a Daughter in a Patriarchal Society

"Man, I hope this isn't a waste of time," the young man thought. "I could use some help," Johnny Coe admitted to himself as he sat in the back of the small, meeting room on a metal folding chair of Good Shepherd Church of Ranchester, Wyoming. He'd been early for the event, and as the time for the scheduled speaker was nearing, twenty other men, most of them around his age of twenty-five had filtered in and taken seats.

They were a flannel shirt, blue jean bunch of woodcutters and outdoorsmen, landowners in the former Bighorn National Forest when Gov. Smucker annexed it to the State and turned it into homesteads for men of the Region, including a great many Southerners he'd brought into the State to work at all the new businesses he'd either started or had persuaded to move there.

Creating a large and self-reliant yeoman class had been one of Smucker's goals, and giving hundreds of thousands of young men a chance to provide for themselves on their own land was a boon to independence and Smucker's Maccabee Movement.

There was a stir at the door behind him, and Johnny saw that the older pastor was about to come in while an attractive, older woman in a beige skirt and jacket stood by. Glancing at the clock above the door, he was pleased that they were on the dot in getting this show going.

The pastor, in casual slacks, a dark sport jacket, and open collared, blue shirt strode to the front of the room, his carefully coiffed salt and pepper hair and sun tanned face presenting the perfect image of a good sermonizer. The women of his congregation adored him, and might tingle if he deigned to touch them on the arm to make a point in conversation.

"I don't think I know any of you boys from town, so I'm guessing y'all came down from the mountains to be here. Welcome to Good Shepherd. I'm Josh Oakley, pastor here, and I'm pleased to see you. I'm sure this evening's speaker will give you a lot to think about for the future. Let me tell you something about Mrs. Rhonda Martin, besides being a Christian psychologist, she's a mother of five children so she has a good idea of what y'all are facing or going through in raising your boys and girls. She's from Boise and has been making the rounds throughout the Region offering advice and experience on this critical matter for parents, and fathers, especially. Rhonda has written many articles and a few books on tonight's subject, and they're all available if you're interested in having them for later on to remind you of what was discussed; memory being what it is, 'though I'm guessin' all of yours is in prime condition while mine's not what it used to be. Anyway, please give a warm welcome to Rhonda Martin," he concluded, clapping as she walked up the aisle to the front, joined by the men in polite applause.

The pastor moved aside and took a seat against a wall off to the side.

"Howdy, fellas, I'm Rhonda," she said in a pleasant North Texas accent, "and I'm here to talk about how to raise daughters in what the anthropologists call a patriarchal society. Sounds Biblical, doesn't it? Like in the time of the Patriarchs. Thing is, as far as I know, there never has been a matriarchal society although some groups in Africa have been said to be by other folks. The fact is that men run things and if they're not, they can step in and do so any time they feel like it. But just 'cause they run things, it doesn't mean they're happy or the women and children are happy. Life is complicated and we make it worse when we fail to understand the conditions that best suit our nature and how we can thrive."

"Now, women by nature are emotional and will be ruled by their emotions unless they're taught to develop reason and judgment in a way that isn't used simply to support emotion and feeling, but actively challenges emotionalism itself. The fact is, more than likely, that's not going to happen, so you'll get plenty of smart women who can argue a million ways 'til Doomsday over what they want, but never figure out that what they want is just plain wrong."

"Does everyone here have children?" she asked looking over the men's faces. No one denied it, so she went on, "Y'all know what it's like when your child wants something as bad as can be, and that if you don't put a stop to it, that boy or girl will come up with every thing he can think of to talk or tantrum you into letting him have it. Isn't that right?"

Many heads nodded.

"Well, you don't haul off and punch him in the head to make him stop now, do ya . . . ? Heck no. You measure out the right amount of forcefulness -- that could be your tone of voice, a stern look or frown, the promise of some penalty: a time out, loss of dessert, extra chores, and so on -- to get the child to cease and desist in his behavior. You don't even have to be harsh about it. Sometimes a little laughter or letting your child know you recognize his desire, you understand his feelings, but you're in charge and it's settled can be enough. Depends on the child. Depends on you. You know how much little girls love their daddies, and if you're gullible and weak, they'll wrap you right around their little fingers."

"Boys love their daddies, too, but we know how to tame their high spirits and impulsive behavior -- give them lots of responsibility early and often. Make them feel important to the family, give them work to do. They'll become men sooner and more sensible that way."

Johnny was thinking about his three children with his wife, Mandy. Miranda, age six; Kelly, age four; and Stella, age two and a half; three daughters competing for his attention to the point of resenting his wife getting any affection from him. It was a madhouse at times; and there might be more to come since he wanted a son or two and they might turn out to be girls, too, like the last three. He didn't like knowing ahead of time what sex the baby was . . . What was the lady saying?

" . . . so how do we get our little girls to understand why women can't vote, serve on juries, run for elective office? It hurts to be told you're not right for the job; that boys are better at some things and girls are better at other things in general. That will work for some, but most others have access to the world outside of the Region and see where women are more equal than men, have more rights, privileges, opportunities, and even dominance in a number of professions."

"Our women aren't shut up in *purdah*, that's what mooslims call putting their wives and daughters in a separate part of the house and they can't go out or read or see anything they want on TV or Internet. No, our girls hear about all the naughty and willful things other American girls are getting up to or around the world. They know about Spring Break, Mardi Gras in New Orleans, movie stars behaving badly; all of that stuff. We're not Amish folks, either. And only giving your daughters 'women's work' is likely to backfire to some extent, because frankly, girls complain. We complain a lot. We're always needing to vent. Not all, of course, but a typical woman will."

"So how do we transform our willful, catty, status conscious, gossiping, and grasping daughters into women whose price is above rubies? The mooslims beat their women to keep them in line. You don't see a lot of happy marriages and families there. So what is it that will make a woman happy with her husband, her children, and her life? Make her a cheerful helpmate?"

"Well, for one thing, let her be in charge of the home, but not the family. You have to be men and exert your God given authority firmly, but not abusively. You decide on every major expenditure, and on important family matters. You consult with your wife, even your children if they should have some voice, but you make the important decisions and you don't explain them, change them, apologize, or let others complain about them. You assert authority. You are John Wayne, if any of you know who that old movie star was. You let your daughters know that men are in charge and that's just how it is because that's how God wants it, how he made it."

"It doesn't mean they can't aspire to learning or significance outside of marriage or the family, but that the health of marriage and family is the most important thing there is in this world. If a woman or man feels like things aren't perfect, they didn't get what they wanted, or enough of it to make the rest bearable, well, that's what Heaven's for. That's why we're immortal creatures. Good things we wanted for ourselves, hopes and dreams that never came true in this life are more than possible in the next. That's why we have faith. Not because we're fools grinning and dancing around 'cause we know God loves us and everything is hunky dorry from now on. We will never be perfectly happy in this world, on this planet. And you have to teach your children that, and to accept it with all the good grace and humility that you do. If you're a miserable person, that's what your children will learn, and what your wife will despise, making you even more miserable in a vicious cycle."

"Another thing. You men need to rely on each other to buck you up when things aren't great. Maybe your wife or children sense weakness and see an opening to guide you into pleasing them instead of doing what's best overall for the family itself. I mean, buy your children presents, give special treats to let them know you appreciate them and the way they're striving. Same with your wife. Treat her to romantic dinners and getaways. If she's been wanting something special for a long time, go ahead and surprise her with it if you can afford it. But you mustn't let her get away with not appreciating you. If she's moody, sullen, distant, unaffectionate or cold, send her packing if she won't do anything about it. You can't let her poison the family. If she's hostile to you, you have to do something about it."

"Your problem as men is that you're afraid of conflict and confrontation with a woman who can talk rings around you about their feelings and why they need this, that, or t'other; and they will never stop arguing about it every chance they get because they know if you let them nag you, they'll wear you down. You've got to learn to nip things in the bud at the get go. Maybe they'll pout for a day, but then they'll accept it and go on like it doesn't matter that much. You've got to be willing to be tough. That's what it means to be a leader. Leaders make followers unhappy. Followers are always disappointed in their leaders. Always. Heck, most Christians I know are disappointed in God and Jesus because they aren't giving them everything they want. Show me an atheist, and I'll show you a disappointed little girl or boy who didn't get something they wanted more than anything from God."

"Well, you're God's surrogate in the home. So man up! Most of you probably think that it's simply easier to let things slide, let the wife do what she wants, let the kids have their way, don't put up any resistance 'cause it just makes everything worse. Well, that's what cowards do. And how does that work out for your wife and kids? They become more selfish, proud, rebellious, and contentious. And you then watch football, drink beer, become ignored, and eat your heart out."

Rhonda continued, but Johnny wondered, "Like it's that easy. Just start acting like a drill sergeant or something. Women cry and bawl, and then the littlest one is bawling for no reason except mommy is, and then the others ask 'why are you crying, mommy?' and she says it's something I did or didn't do, and then four females are looking at you like you killed their mother, and it was all out of your spitefulness, too."

Johnny wasn't religious, so he didn't like all this Jesus and God crap. He took his family to church every Sunday, but only because his grandfather made him promise he would until the kids were old enough to go their own way.

"It's makes kids better people in the short term and long term," his gramps insisted. "But how would I know?" Johnny asked himself. "It's not like I've got something to compare it to."

" . . . one thing you can explain when your children are older, later elementary school age, perhaps, is that great civilizations last longer when men remain in charge. Rome, a thousand years, China, 3000 years, Greece almost a thousand years, Egypt, 3000 years. But England, America, the European nations started sliding downhill fast when they gave women the vote. Their countries became feminized, even to the point that homosexuals held more and more power, forming self-sustaining and self-promoting in groups in the Media, in Hollywood, in politics, in the arts, humanities, and literature. Just as the Jews exercised power far in excess of their mere two percent of the population, so too did the sodomites. Small groups can do untold damage, effect terrible changes when they're especially aggressive, insular, well funded, and motivated," she explained.

Yeah, like Smucker and his band of firebrand preachers, Coe thought. The way he organized ministers from the South to come, set up churches and schools, importing hand picked Southern evangelicals and Lost Cause Confederate flag wavers to run and work at the factories he started, the media companies he formed, tech, nanotech, robotics, bio-science, pharmaceutical, and military equipment and weapons manufacturers.

In a decade, the transplanted Southerners outnumbered native Wyoming people and were Hell-bent on secession and rebellion.

Of course, Coe would've ended up in Texas like so many from the Ice States looking for work, outnumbered there by Mexicans, but then, the wetbacks couldn't work a lick and hardly read or write so he'd have found a job.

His father was one who qualified for 500 acres of mountain timberland, a sustainable harvest that could keep a family in business forever if it was well managed and the demand for lumber continued from decade to decade.

But then his dad was killed by a widowmaker (large falling branch) when felling a tree, the bastard, so Johnny took over at sixteen.

But then Johnny was an ungrateful bastard. Five hundred acres free and clear, just like that, because Bill Smucker knew how to build a yeoman class of free men who had much at stake to hold on to, and an eagerness to acquire more. It's hard for most men who own a good (or even bad) patch of ground not to wish that he might have more of what neighbored his. Just a little more. That would be enough. Right?

Give that man a chance to do just that by putting on a uniform or sending his sons off to get what they could for themselves, and a new country could be born; and it could all be done for a glorious cause -- Liberty (and Revenge).

Johnny had done his three-year stint in the Militia. Maybe he should join the Army, get away from home, make a lot of money, and not have to deal with all these women at home. He didn't see himself trying to do what this Texas lady was yammering on about. Man up? Did this lady seem like some sort of shrinking violet, I let my hubby run the show type? No, she did not, he insisted emphatically.

Johnny was the kind of man who had enough native intelligence to run an orderly and disciplined life, but not a happy one. If he wasn't working, he was wanting to vegetate. Having children pleased him to some extent, but it didn't inspire or motivate him. He did what was minimal to humor them, make them think he cared. He was hoping having a son would wake him up the way he saw other men his age raise their boys; teaching them sports, taking them camping, fishing, and hunting. He thought he'd like that, too, but he wasn't sure.

"How did I get roped into this?" he inwardly groaned. Oh, yeah. His church pastor had mildly twisted his arm. He wouldn't let him walk away after service until Johnny promised he'd come. Another good reason to join the Army, he told himself.

The Rule of Movies

"How can we create our own movie studios and production companies, Mr. Drinkwater?" Smucker asked the president of Heaven's Gate Productions, a Hollywood company that had had some success producing cable TV movies, a reality show about a family of Christian ministers, a long running TV drama about an itinerant carpenter who helps people solve dilemmas, overcome trauma, and lead misguided children and parents back to the path of hope with an occasional miracle thrown in.

Smucker had invited Peter Drinkwater to Laramie to show him his plans for the town of Maccabee he was building not far from there, and to sound him out about creating an arts community to spread his vision of a reborn America.

The meeting was informal and took place in Smucker's comfortable living room attended by two assistants and a few other Board members of the corporation he headed.

Mr. Drinkwater, a handsome, dark haired man in his fifties, dressed casually but expensively, leaned forward from the wing chair he sat in and began, "Easily. It's nothing at all but a little bit of money to set up a production company. They're nothing more than a few offices. Setting up production studios is more expensive, but not hard either. The big problem is talent. Putting together people who can make a product that entertains millions of other people."

"Obviously, personnel is critical to the success of any business . . ." Smucker replied, but was cut off.

"Competency doesn't help you here. Let's say you want to make movies. Like most Christians you have a compelling message you want to spread to the world and you think a good movie or two will do it, but here's how things really work," he said as he settled into his usual exposition on the movie business to outsiders.

"All right, you're all mostly older middle aged men here," he added glancing about. "How many of you want to see a movie that your teenage son or daughter is excited about?"

No one said they would.

"A five year old child will watch a movie that his ten year old brother is watching, but the ten year old has no interest in what the five year old is entertained by. Same with the ten year old and his sixteen year old brother. Same with the teenager and his parents. Now, each group forms a distinct audience. What they like, their elders don't, and when it comes to movies, the demographic is king. Most movies are being made for the male 15 to 29 age group. Why? Because they go to the movies more than any other group, and they won't go see movies their girlfriends like, but their girlfriends will go to the movies the boyfriends like. That's why they make all those comic book, action, war, and adventure films. That's why they'll spend hundreds of millions on such films while a romantic comedy costs hardly anything in comparison."

"You have a message to spread? It better be filled with conflict, action, thrills, and adventure that teenage boys love or it isn't going anywhere," he finished.

"You're doing well enough with your message, aren't you?" one of Smucker's young protégés asked.

"Yes, if you can target a niche audience of a few million people and keep feeding them the stuff that entertains them. Gentlemen, it's all about entertainment, not messages. That's your problem. Christians keep wanting to send a message and save souls. But the people who write entertaining stories mostly want to make a living, and they sneak in what they want to say if producers and directors let them. Every story needs a convenient villain so they make a preacher a crazed loony, a former soldier is a crazed gun nut, a businessman is greedy to the point of murder, and so on. The most entertaining stories are being written by the most Godless people in the world. How are you going to compete against that? And where are you going to find the talent to produce, direct, act in, and write what you need? A studio has got to manufacture a constant line of product. Not just when it finds something it thinks will sell."

Smucker wasn't exactly stunned, but disconcerted. He tried to come up with a list of Christian novelists, playwrites, composers, artists, architects that he'd heard or knew of. No one came to mind except for a few dead authors like Tolkien, C. S. Lewis, and Chesterton.

"What about the people who write for you?" Bill suggested.

"Most are non-believers. They use their imagination to pretend to think like a Christian, say. It's a genre of a genre like you have romantic fiction, which has pirate romance, vampire romance, warrior romance; even Amish romance. Well, you have spiritual fiction that could be Christian, or New Age, or Jewish. It all depends, and writers who need money figure out how to adapt to what you want them to write about."

"Hold on, now," Thad, Smucker's assistant, demanded. "I've done a little research, and it seems to me that back in what they call the Golden Age of movies, they had a lot of writers who were important novelists, playwrites, literary people who came to Hollywood and did some pretty good work."

"That's true," Drinkwater replied. "It's not like that now. Well, here and there a contemporary author, a literary figure, writes a movie, but it's rare, and they're usually art house niche films of some kind. You get what you pay for. If you offered twenty million for every screenplay, you'd get the best writers in the world to write your big comic book films . . . if they knew how."

Thad went on, "But people like stories. They want stories even if they're not what you might call good. I remember an article I once read about some anthropologist lamenting the fact that even in the remotest parts of Africa or South America, small tribes would give up sitting around the campfire telling tales as soon as they could get some electricity and run a TV. Then they were glued to it all the time no matter what. Why did those groups abandon their own storytelling as soon as a TV showed up? The guy didn't figure it out, but I could. The old tribal stories were darned boring. They couldn't compete with the more elaborate ones from the TV. No matter how badly made or written, they still beat their local ones."

"Your point?" Drinkwater said.

"Well, we just have to tell stories as good as the ones the major studios are doing. They don't have to be great or even good most of the time. Just as good to make money, to get an audience. Right?" he said looking around.

Smucker thought he had a point. Maybe he'd put Thad in charge of the entertainment division.

"And we sneak in our little messages about miserable atheists, Godless movie producers, greedy, lying do-gooders, and hypocritical liberals," Thad continued. "Explosions, car chases, serial killers, adultery, all that stuff. What's more is we bring Christian writers, film students, actors, singers, musicians, and so on to the college in Maccabee, we create a center for the arts with great teachers, tough criticism, and groom a generation to produce what we're talking about. We create the competition 'cause we'll pay really well, and scoop up the best same as they do in Hollywood. Not everybody who goes to Julliard makes it in the arts or music."

"Thad's made a good point," Smucker joined in. "Maybe the problem all along has been that there hasn't been enough money in it to produce our own Leonardos, Bachs, and Dantes. When every church needed decoration, the competition drove up the quality of the art and music. Well, now every house needs entertainment, but Christians haven't been paying for it very well. Christians want to get rich just as much as a Godless Hollywood director. I say we give them the chance."

Drinkwater laughed, not to mock, but amused with the thought that occurred to him. "So, you're saying that you want

Christians to be as driven by wanton greed, lust, power, and luxury like all the people in Hollywood?"

Smucker looked down, pondering for a moment, and then reluctantly nodded his head. "Most Christians already are," he sighed. "There's hardly a dime's worth of difference now except for that passive/aggressive manner so many adopt. Let me tell you a story. Quite a few decades ago there was a professional quarterback who was very successful, widely admired, and cheered for his Christian devotion. He had a lovely wife and three beautiful young children. He became famous, a local hero, and made a lot of money from salary and endorsements. A clean cut, all around, All American fellow named Joe Thelman.

"But Joe soon took up with a gorgeous Hollywood starlet, cheated on his wife, and left her and his kids. It was all very public and shameful, but shame wasn't that big a deal anymore.

"So, he's in divorce court contesting his wife's demands and his wife's lawyer says to him, 'Look here, Mr. Thelman, you betrayed your wife, you abandoned your children, you committed adultery, and yet you contend you're a Christian who believes in God. How could you have done that?'

"Joe looked at him and replied, 'Because God wants Joe Thelman to be happy.'"

The room burst into laughter. Smucker wiped away a tear in helpless mirth at his own telling of the tale.

"God wants Joe Thelman to be happy," he repeated amidst the hilarity, and the ridiculous absurdity of Thelman's first person claim kept him laughing for a time.

When everyone had calmed down, Smucker told Drinkwater, "You see, that's how a great many Christians think. Not that Jesus wants me to carry a cross, but that he wants me to be happy. No worries. Every preacher will tell you that you have to meet the people where they are, and after that, all you can do is try and plant some seeds. So, that's what we'll do."

When Push Comes to Shove

Dolores Harris, office manager for the Bellingham city manager, was released from detention by the NAR army two weeks after her incarceration. She was called to the entrance gate of the prisoner's ward and told, "Go and get whatever personal items you have, then come back. You're going to be released."

She blanched in shock. The advent of sudden freedom frightened her. People get used to everything. Immediate change is terrifying.

Dolores did as she was told, though, and collected her few belongings, clothing, and returned to the gate where it was opened. She came through and walked a long corridor formed by chain link fencing in the old factory building.

A large storage room had been built and she came to a counter by the door accompanied by her escort, a young female guard in army uniform. She handed another young woman behind the counter a slip of paper. That woman disappeared among the many shelves filled with file cartons. They heard her rummaging among the boxes, and then, "Found it."

She returned with a plastic bag full of Dolores' property -- her purse with all the various items it carried along with her street clothes, shoes, socks, and a coat. She was asked to sign for them on a tablet, which she did without comment or expression. Her two weeks in confinement had left her emotionally bloodied and bowed.

"There is a lavatory over there. You may change into your regular clothes inside," he escort pointed out to her.

She entered the cold tiled bathroom with its shining porcelain features and bright mirrors. She stood a moment, dazed and uncertain what to do, how to begin? She caught sight of herself in a mirror and saw a homely, pale faced, gray haired, weak and useless older woman, and wanted to cry as she had when first brought to the detention facility.

She wondered how she had ever considered herself a person of significance.

She made herself undress and put on her regular clothes, which were a bit looser now for having lost a few pounds during the fortnight she'd been in custody.

Combing her hair, she assessed her appearance again, but only saw a defeated stranger in the mirror.

Emerging from the bathroom, her escort retrieved the prison garb she'd discarded, tossed them in a bin, and guided Dolores out of the building.

"Your vehicle remains where you left it in the city parking garage near city hall. It should start, but if not you can call a garage or Triple A for help. Does your phone still have a charge?"

Dolores found it in her purse, turned it on. It worked and had enough charge for the time being.

The army woman handed her an envelope with papers inside. Here are your instructions on evacuation. You have three days to start South on Interstate Five."

Dolores numbly absorbed the information. She tried to remember where she was, where city hall and the nearby garage was. Her confusion led the escort to point out, "You'll be wanting to go that way, ma'am. It's only a few blocks. Good luck." She stood there for the next moment as Miss Harris made up her mind and began walking down the street.

The private shook her head. "God help her," she murmured before returning to the detention building and her duty station.

After walking a long block, she began to regain a sense of rhythm and familiarity in her stride. A sense of freedom began to awaken in her. She noticed the smell of fresh air and a slight breeze. The sunshine with a little spring warmth was welcome. She began to walk with purpose and longer strides.

When she reached the parking garage, she easily recalled that she always parked on the third floor. Finding her car, she opened and entered it, relaxed a moment to adjust to the sensation, then closed the door and started the engine.

****

Russell Porter got a call from his wife as he was going over accounts at his hardware store. The first few days of the occupation had been lucrative as people stocked up on emergency supplies and equipment either because they were being dispossessed, or because they weren't. After that, with 75% of the population gone from the area, sales slumped considerably.

Even so, he owned the building outright and without having to pay property, sales, or income taxes, he supposed they'd manage under reduced circumstances until the city gradually repopulated.

"Hi, honey," Russell answered cheerfully.

"Guess what? Dolores is back," she told him.

"Dolores Harris?"

"Yes, of course. Right across the street. I just saw her drive into her driveway. I was going to go over and tell her about the cats."

"Okay, you do that. I'll be right home. See if we can help her with anything. See you in a few minutes."

"Okay. Bye.

"Bye."

He grabbed his light coat from the rack, left his office for the show room as he put on his jacket and announced, "Billy, I'm going home for the day. You close up for me, okay?"

"You bet," the young man replied.

He didn't have to tell him that his older employee who was on a lunch break was in charge. The only other man he'd employed, Jed Balin, a genial fellow in his forties, had been the only one among his staff ordered to leave. He'd known Jed was irreligious (most men are, he well understood), but he'd never thought he was too radical for the NAR, but then what did he know about most people?

Driving, at least, was a lot more pleasant since there was such little traffic on the roads; and for many, various traffic lights and signs were considered mere suggestions. Why wait at a light when one else was in sight? Perhaps the local police were still reeling from having their chief and subordinates arrested, and so many officers forced to leave town. He hadn't realized until lately just what a relief it was to not have to fear being stopped and fleeced for silly infractions where no one was exposed to harming themselves or others. He wondered if things would remain like that or would new masters arise to annoy and harass people like him over trivialities?

He pulled into his driveway, parked and got out, immediately crossing the street to Dolores' house, assuming his wife, Adele, was already there.

****

Russ knocked on the door and heard his wife call out, "Come in, Russell."

He passed through the small foyer and saw his wife sitting on the couch with Dolores sitting in a chair across from her. The three cats, all tabbies, one orange, the other two gray, wove around her legs, rubbing against her, hopping into her lap to be stroked. People say cats lack affection but Dolores' appeared to have missed her.

"Hi, Dolores. How are you?" he asked.

"Okay. I've never been in jail before so I'm still processing the whole experience."

"Couldn't have been fun," he noted.

"No. It wasn't. It was a little bit interesting, though. You see people like you rarely see them. And now, they tell me I have three days to pack up and leave."

"Anything we can do to help?"

"Tell me where can I go?"

"Do you have any family? Friends in other parts of the country?"

She snorted a laugh. "Country! Ha! What countries now, don't you mean? We're not one country anymore."

Russ was chagrined. She was right.

"Well, I meant people in other states where you could go and stay . . . or live?"

"I have some friends in Seattle with the Peace Movement. I have no close relatives at all. I'm an only child. My parents weren't connected to their families very much. Do you know if I can go to Seattle?"

"As far as I know. The army has surrounded it but they haven't gone in like here and made anyone leave."

"Yet?"

"I suppose it's coming to that. You're going to want a further destination, I guess."

"Oregon? California?"

"No, I wouldn't go there. You might try the Midwest like Kansas, Oklahoma, even northern Texas. They're growing areas. They need people with professional skills," he offered.

She nodded, absorbing the suggestions, considering the best course of action, but based on what? She had no idea.

"What do I do with my things?" she asked gesturing to indicate all her property and goods.

"Well, you could buy a trailer or a truck to haul it all. We could help you put it in storage or sell it, but there's not much of a market for it now. I say you ought to leave any valuable goods with us and we'll send them on when you get settled or sell them if you need the money. What about your cats? It will be very hard to travel with three cats, don't you think?"

She was stricken at the thought of parting from them again.

"I . . . I don't know how I could leave them again," she sputtered, her eyes watering.

He and Adele nodded in sympathy. His wife gently told her, "What if you took one and left the other two with us? We'd send them on when you're able to look after them again. They're all friendly with us now since we've been taking care of them."

Dolores reluctantly agreed that was for the best. They then arranged to have her general household goods put in storage and her most valuable items kept with the Porters.

After they concluded their detailed planning, Dolores asked Russell, "How come they let you stay and not me?"

He looked away for a moment, frowned, turned to her and said, "I think you have some idea, don't you?"

"You mean I don't fit in with them and you do."

"Something like that," he agreed.

She became stern and told him, "Does that bother you? These people invade our city, decide who can stay or go, just because. Just because they feel like it."

"It isn't about their feelings. It's about their idea of self-government . . . and religion, I guess."

"Religion. Hmph. So that gives them the right to come here and throw us out and take everything?"

"No," he agreed. "But from what I've seen, I think they believe that most people sold their birthright of liberty for a mess of pottage and traded it for tyranny, even though the pottage kept decreasing."

"What are you talking about? What does that even mean?"

"A mess of pottage?"

"That, and liberty and tyranny. That's just words. Silly words."

"Didn't you used to use words like 'peace' and 'fairness' or 'diversity' once?"

She was stumped. She couldn't deny it. All silly words, when all she wanted right now was to stay in her home with her cats and be left alone.

She began to cry. "How could they do this to me?" Russ and Adele sat still, waiting for her misery to subside. Dolores looked up, tears streaking her face, "It's so unfair."

The Porters agreed. It was very unfair. Russ wanted to tell her that Jesus could help her with that tragedy -- of life being a very cruel thing at times, but knew she wouldn't receive the hope it would give her to turn to a higher power when all else had failed.

****

Three days later her car was packed, her orange tabby, Popsy, inside a pet crate and ready to go. Russ and Adele leaned over the driver's side open window to say goodbye and wish her the best.

Dolores was tight lipped at the ordeal before her, but thanked them for their help as best she could, although she deeply resented their advantage over her.

Russ reached into his pocket and told her, "Look, there's something I want you to have."

He showed her a small .22 caliber revolver. Dolores recoiled.

"Don't be afraid. You might need this. *I mean it*," he told her forcefully. "You have no idea what might happen. Things are breaking down where you're going. You need to be able to protect yourself."

"I . . . I can't . . . I don't know. I . . . don't know."

"You can throw it away if you want. -- It's simple. It's easy to use. The bullets are so small it probably wouldn't kill anybody. It holds ten bullets. Point it, pull the trigger. That's it. The noise will likely frighten anybody away. Here's a box of bullets. It's easy to reload. You'll figure it out."

She hesitated.

"Take it. You don't know when you might need it. Here."

He shoved the gun and a box of ammunition across her and stuffed them in her large purse.

"Hide it, but keep it near. Now you take care. All right?"

Dolores nodded, then she backed out of her driveway, swallowed hard and drove away trying to imagine this was simply an adventure she was going on. But Christ, she was scared.

****

Dolores was driving off to stay with an old friend from the Peace Vigil Movement (a dozen people in Bellingham, maybe two dozen in Seattle). Her friend's name was Ciel (pronounced Seal), an older woman over seventy with long white hair that she wore loose as a sign of her free spiritedness, a proclamation of glorious age, and advertisement of herself as a magnificent matriarch.

That was Ciel's assessment, anyway. To most other people she looked like an old hippie mama one step removed from being a bag lady. She lived in a small house on a hill not far from the University of Washington. Parking in the area was always difficult, but Ciel had no vehicle and so Dolores was able to park her small hybrid in the tiny driveway.

Ciel greeted her at the door in a peasant skirt and her best tie dye T-shirt bought a decade earlier at a Burning Man festival in Nevada. Dolores, for some reason, found her garb off putting although she received her hug as warmly as she could holding the cat crate with Popsy in it.

Upon entering, Dolores was stung was a slightly acrid and musty odor as she observed a greatly cluttered front room that had an old sofa, a pair of comfortable chairs and a coffee table, but all were covered in piles of newspapers, books, and magazines. Bric a brac filled shelves along the walls and on the mantelpiece above the fireplace. It was dusty, musty, and sour smelling.

Ciel transferred a few piles of stuff to new places to provide Dolores with a place to sit.

"Can I get you something to drink? Some tea, perhaps? I have this most wonderful herbal tea that a friend of mine blends for me."

"I'd love some coffee. I think the thing I missed the most when I was in detention was coffee. Good, hot and sweet coffee."

"I don't drink coffee. It's bad for people. All I have is tea."

"That's fine," Dolores smiled weakly. "Would it be all right if I let Popsy out of the crate? Are all the doors closed so she can't get out?"

"Yes. She won't do her, any business in the house will she?"

"Well, I have a litter box for her. It's a wonderful thing that's self-cleaning. All I have to do is plug it in."

"Oh dear. I don't like the odors of animals," Ciel blanched.

What have I gotten myself into, Dolores cried out inside.

"The box has a masking agent for any odor," she said hoping it would persuade.

"Well, if I must put up with it, then I must," Ciel answered and Dolores echoed the sentiment to herself.

"Okay, tea it is then," she said and turned to disappear in the kitchen.

Dolores called out to her, "I'm going to go get some things from the car?"

"Yes, yes," she heard from down the hall.

Dolores went out, got a travel bag from the trunk, her purse, and then hid the gun and ammunition in the trunk.

After coming back in, she let Popsy out who then wandered around the front room, sniffing and getting the lay of the land. She was a well behaved cat and didn't meow or protest with loud cries of discontent. Popsy was a good traveler. Dolores was proud of her and glad of her company.

While waiting for Ciel, she scanned the room, noticing how old and outdated most of the books and magazines were. Many were what some called radical publications. One cover from 2009 hollered that DDT was still a deadly poison never to be used again.

As she flipped through them, it seemed that every cover was a violent cry of warning about some modern convenience, medicine, appliance, energy source or food.

Ciel returned with steaming mugs and set one before her. Dolores let it cool before tasting. It was unsweetened, tasting a bit of leaves, twigs, grass, and rose hips. She smiled wanly at Ciel after sipping. It was a perfectly vile concoction. Ciel waxed on about the wonder of its anti-oxidants and cancer fighting properties oblivious to her guest, or even of Popsy wandering about occasionally weaving her way nearby and rubbing across Ciel's leg.

She never asked Dolores about her incarceration, her forced evacuation, any plans for the future. She prattled on about herself.

Finally, Dolores interrupted Ciel, "What are you planning to do when the NAR force us to leave?"

"Who?"

"The New American Republic. The army that's surrounding Seattle. They're going to make us leave the city."

"What do you mean? Why?"

"Don't you follow the news? Watch TV? The radio?"

"No. Those things are bad for you."

Dolores briefly wondered what the old woman did to pass the time?

"I told you how they put me in jail and made me leave my home on the phone. That's why I'm here."

"Did you?" she wondered, pondered it and said, "Yes, I guess you mentioned something about why you needed to visit me. Was that it? . . . No, I don't have Alzheimer's. I just forget things like that. Anyway. This is my house. I own it and nobody can make me leave if I don't want to.

"I'm not sure if they will make you leave. I heard that they didn't clear out the hospitals or old folks' homes, but if you're mostly healthy, I don't know what they'll do," Dolores told her.

"Who are they?"

Dolores spent the better part of an hour trying to explain it to her. Ciel had no computer or tablet, either, so she showed her on her own what she could about the NAR, it's army and what was going on.

****

Dolores settled in at Ciel's, sleeping in a guest room on the second floor of an equally cluttered space. She discovered what the sour smell in the house was. It was Ciel. She didn't bathe all that frequently and her diet caused her to pass gas. Well, why should she? She hardly went out and never entertained. She spent a good deal of time sleeping, though, so that accounted for part of how she passed the time.

She only went shopping once a week, paying a friend to transport her on various errands to different stores. For supper, she favored brown rice with soy sauce, mercilessly steamed vegetables, and a tofu hot dog or veggie burger. Lunch was cold leftovers of the same. She skipped breakfast.

Dolores asked if she might buy a few items to cook for herself and Ciel begrudgingly allowed it, although sure it was for things "bad for you."

Surprisingly enough, the Seattle authorities had been able to keep supplies coming into the city in a steady, regular stream. Vendors and sellers continued accepting their USA money without any problem. The NAR did what they could to facilitate order in the city's goods and services. There were panics here and there with buying sprees and hoarding, but in general, the city functioned close to normal.

Ten days following her arrival, the NAR announced the evacuation of the Seattle/Tacoma area. The cities were divided into sections. The first section, about 100,000 people scheduled to leave, was given seven days to put their affairs in order and move out to Oregon.

Ciel didn't believe it. She was in section four. Each section after the first was given five days. General Bruster, the commander, understood a larger city made people's necessary business take longer to complete.

They had about 22 days to get ready.

****

"You have a son in California. Can't we go there?" Dolores asked.

It had taken a week for Ciel to begin to face reality as they watched the news unfold on Dolores' tablet, and she'd found Ciel's name and address on the list for section four. Dolores had begun to hate her and could barely keep her impatience in check.

A day earlier, Dolores had confided in Ciel how she had left Bellingham and how her neighbor had thrust a gun and ammunition upon her.

"You have a gun!?"

"Not on me," Dolores said, taken aback by Ciel's vehemence.

"You can't have a gun in my house."

"It's not in your house. It's in the trunk of my car."

"It's on my property. Guns are bad. No one should have a gun. You can't have a gun on my property. I insist you get rid of it or you'll have to go."

"It's not like I want to own a gun," Dolores declared and then added, "But it can't hurt to have one. Not with all that's happening."

"I won't have it. You have to get rid of it."

Dolores got up and left the house. She stood by her car for a few minutes wondering what to do? As frightened as she'd first been at the thought of having a gun, she was reluctant now to part with it. She realized that it was the only thing she had in the world that could protect her. She was alone; on her own. There were no police, no safe neighborhood to reside in, no gated community or security guardhouse or anything. There was just an army forcing them out of their houses, onto the highway. God knows what they'll be facing.

She made up her mind. She opened her car's trunk, found a sturdy plastic bag, put the gun and ammo in it, and then walked over to the house next door, hiding the package under a thick bush.

"I got rid of it," she told Ciel after returning inside.

"Good. That's enough of that nonsense, then. Can I get you some tea?"

****

Ciel had a son who lived in Arcata, California. They weren't close, but he agreed to take them in. Dolores was able to make arrangements to transfer Ciel's accounts to a bank there, but getting the older woman to understand that she could take only some clothes and jewelry was a hard slog through the dismal swamp of a disbelieving mind.

Nevertheless, their last day came. Dolores had retrieved the gun and hid it in her purse, storing the ammo in the trunk.

It was midmorning when they left Ciel's house and drove to the Interstate to go south. There was a checkpoint at the onramp where they were checked against a list, recognized as forced evacuees, and then a soldier planted a small device with instant epoxy inside the trunk of the car; a tracking device.

They entered the highway and began their trek. Once past Tacoma, traffic became lighter than Dolores expected. All the exits and on ramps they passed had army vehicles stationed at them. When they passed through Olympia and Tumwater later, traffic was sparse.

They had just gone past the small town of Napavine when they saw a car farther up ahead parked on the shoulder, emergency lights flashing, and two men waving for assistance.

As they drove closer, Dolores saw they were black.

"Pull over. They need help," Ciel told her.

"I don't know," Dolores replied.

"You must. They're people who need help. Pull over!"

Dolores obeyed. Maybe they could help them.

She pulled over to the shoulder and eased up a dozen yards behind them.

The two black men, one tall and thin, the other shorter and stockier, dressed in the current fashion of their subculture, approached them on both sides of their car. Ciel lowered her window, calling out, "What's the trouble? Can we help?"

As she finished asking, the taller man reached her door, leaned into the open window and suddenly put a knife to Ciel's throat.

"You move an' I kill her," he said looking at Dolores. "Gibbe ev'ythin' you got!"

Dolores reached into her purse, found her pistol, gripped it, pulled it out and began firing at the man, three, maybe four shots as he recoiled from the car as quickly as possible. Dolores then drove away as fast as she could, which isn't saying much for a small hybrid.

"Are you all right! Are you all right!" she yelled at Ciel who was gasping in a state of shock.

Ciel didn't respond. Dolores tried to look her over as she drove. "You're bleeding! You have a cut on your neck." She rummaged in her purse and found a pack of tissues.

"Here! Use these!"

Ciel was coming to her senses and grasped the package with trembling hands. Dolores pulled down the sun visor that had a small mirror on the inside. "Tell me how bad it is?"

Ciel located herself in the mirror, dabbed at the cut. It was a thin red line about two inches long, not at all deep.

"How bad is it!" she shouted at Ciel.

"I don't know. Not too bad. I don't know."

As she drove, she watched the road behind her to see if she was being chased, and scanning ahead for an exit ramp, wondering if she should inform the soldiers.

When an exit appeared in the distance, she decided to pull up to the army vehicle. As she did so, six men jumped out with their weapons at the ready before she'd gotten close.

A sergeant approached her cautiously. "Yes, ma'am. What is it?"

Dolores lowered her window. "My friend needs help. She was cut. Some men tried to rob us back there."

The sergeant turned, "Get a medical kit. Please step out of the car, ma'am. And you, too, ma'am, if you can," he told Ciel. The tissues she held against her neck were red.

A soldier had retrieved a first aid kit from their vehicle and approached Ciel. He rested the box on the car hood, opened it, and told her, "Here ma'am, let me," as he took hold of the bundle of tissues and drew it away to examine the wound.

The sergeant drew Dolores aside. "What happened, ma'am?"

She related the tale up to the point of where she used the pistol, hesitated, and decided to be entirely honest.

"You still have the weapon with you?"

"Please don't take it from me."

"No, ma'am, I won't. I just want to be sure you won't use it on us."

"I put it back in my purse."

"Very good."

He went over to the car, reached in, and removed her purse, looked in to find the gun, examined it and saw four rounds had been fired. He then opened the trunk, and began to place it inside. Seeing the box of ammo, he stopped, reloaded the weapon, and closed the trunk. He returned to his vehicle, got on the radio and reported what had happened.

"We'll have people looking for the men. I'm very sorry that happened to you, ma'am," he said then, "Private Ellis! How's the lady?"

"She'll be fine, Sarge. Just a superficial cut. I'll stop the bleeding and tape her up, and she should be good to go."

"Very good. You can be on your way, then. I want to commend you, ma'am. You acted courageously. Well done."

Dolores was such a mix of emotions, adrenaline, and relief that she could hardly gather her thoughts.

"I could arrange an escort for you, if you'd like, ma'am. It will take some time before it gets here, though."

She realized the soldier was being considerate and helpful, but she didn't forget that he was the reason they'd had all this trouble.

Collecting herself, she replied, "No. I think it will be fine. I won't ever stop for any reason now until we get where we're going."

"Yes, ma'am. When you're ready to leave, just go ahead and drive a mile, pull over and get your weapon from the trunk. I took the liberty to reload it. All right?"

She nodded. Ciel had been carefully bandaged and was ready to continue.

"Is there someplace with a bathroom?" she asked the sergeant.

"About five miles further on, there's a rest stop. We have personnel stationed there to provide for the safety of travelers. I'll let them know to expect you. You were very brave, ma'am. Good luck to you."

The radio squawked, another soldier responded to it. "Sarge, it's Command. They found the men who did it. One's got three little holes in him, but he ain't dead."

The sergeant turned to Dolores, "You only wounded him, ma'am, so you don't have to worry about being a killer or anything. Okay? Take care now."

Dolores and Ciel climbed into the car and drove away, continuing south. Nothing was said until after Dolores pulled over and retrieved her purse from the trunk. Sinking back into the driver's seat and placing it close by, she said, "This stays with me everywhere from now on."

Ciel simply stared straight ahead.

The Bug is the Feature

Any modern invasion is preceded by considerable spadework. For the NAR army, little shaping of an actual battlefield took place since there was no opposing force to meet in combat. Instead, the mission of intelligence was to decrease any kind of resistance, anticipate any kind of resistance, and easily counter resistance with preferably non-lethal means while protecting soldiers from harm.

Fortunately, the NAR was highly advanced in weaponry, robotics, drone technology, communications control, hardened computer systems, and the pharmacopeia of immobilizing or stupefying agents as gases or injectable fluids.

One meeting between an Intelligence major and his staff weeks before the army surrounded the Seattle/Tacoma region went like this:

Major: How much data have we collected on black, Latino, and Asian gangs up to this point? How many of their, what do you call them, headquarters or gathering places have been pinpointed?

2nd Lt.: Well, having hacked the police data bases of their gang task forces has helped, but analysis of drone recording has allowed us to pinpoint about a dozen black gang residences, seven Latino ones, but nothing Asian thus far. I think it's a waste to bother on them or worry about that population.

Major: Are you prepared to be held liable if an Asian gang we never bothered to look for wounds or kills one of our men, Lieutenant?

2nd Lt.: I'll see it's done, sir.

Major: Now, what about the anarchists?

In the NAR all people with authority or in a government bureaucracy were personally liable for action or lack of action that resulted in injury or loss to a citizen. No longer were officials, judges, police, or prosecutors exempt from civil suits against them rather than their agency.

It was feared, at first, that no one would want a government position if they were going to be held responsible for any bad outcome from having done their duty poorly or having failed to do it at all, but doctors treat patients even under the threat of a malpractice tort, and so people in government bought insurance just the same.

If a 2nd Lieutenant had been negligent in that he'd failed to be diligent in his duty, not only was he open to army discipline and punishment, but the soldier who'd been harmed, or his family, could sue the officer or fellow soldier who failed to be conscientious.

Finally, just as private citizens had always been liable for damages and injuries to others, public servants were also. It tended to make them less arrogant, power driven, and stupid when violating anyone's civil rights or failing to do their jobs in a timely manner. If a bureaucrat responsible for approving your passport and creating the document failed to accomplish the task by the scheduled date costing the applicant time or loss due to plans being interfered with, that bureaucrat could be sued for triple damages.

Threat of serious accountability put a little spring in a public employee's step.

****

The use of spy drones allowed the IS (Intelligence Service) to monitor human traffic patterns in various neighborhoods. The comings and goings of people gave them a good idea of where the bad guys and people who were most likely to offer armed resistance either lived, would group up in a crisis or when challenged.

The army generally found the white populations were exceedingly compliant to their directives, but expected greater indifference, stealth, intransigence, stupidity, and violence from minorities. That is why the evacuations proceeded first of all with sectors of whites, saving greater problems for later when they could more easily isolate them and cut off food, power, and water if need be.

General Robertson had been assigned the task of clearing out the minority neighborhoods like Central District in Seattle. This morning at nine, he led a staff meeting to discuss procedures and final plans.

"Gentlemen . . . and ladies," he said acknowledging the two female officers present. They and their women's corps were necessary in the task of handling females processed through detention or apprehension of female scofflaws.

"Next week we start on Central District. This is the first major minority group we've tried to evacuate. Any idea of what we can expect?"

IS Col. Meechum was the first to speak. "Intel of texts, tweets, social media among that group shows that, one, the gangs don't want to go anywhere, but they have a problem. No black population. No drugs to sell, no welfare checks and food stamps to prey on, no one to rob. They can't figure out what to do except encourage everyone else to stay. My recommendation is to separate the wheat from the chaff. Capture the gang members, imprison them, make 'em work. Maybe, just maybe, it will give other blacks a little breathing room to put their lives in better order . . ."

"You can take the people out of the ghetto, but you can't take the ghetto out of . . ."

"Yes, Major, we get the point," Robertson interrupted the younger field officer. "Nevertheless, I'm implementing the colonel's recommendations. It may help a few people get a better start. It's the least we can try and do considering. Now, colonel, what was the rest you were about to say?"

"There are a number of incentives we're offering the minority population such as supplies being free and available to them before they cross into Oregon. Food, coupons for goods and gasoline, some cash. I hate to say this, it sounds prejudiced, but these people show up in the tens of thousands whenever any voucher program, government job fair, food giveaway occurs. We can lure them out of the city like the Pied Piper. We're getting the message out to phones and tablets of all the goodies awaiting those who are compliant. The response we're getting from people actually signing up, registering for the program in order to receive authorization at the depots in Vancouver across the Columbia from Portland is over 50%."

"That's good news. After that we should neutralize the gangs. Colonel Jenkins? How about it?"

"Our plan is to let the first wave of those who are compliant leave the city, and the next early morning, at zero three thirty, we hit all the gang houses, remove the bodies, bundle them out to the IS Camp. That should catch whoever's left in the neighborhoods off guard. We'll have plenty of insect drones available in case of people wanting to interfere. After that, it's house to house mop up using the warm body, mobile scanners to see who's hiding out."

"Very good. Now, Major Montgomery, what about the anarchists?"

"Our agents persuaded them to leave the city before we got here. The main group is hiding out east of Seattle past Snowqualmie just beyond Ernie's Grove on the north fork of the Snowqualmie River. Their current plan is to wait for us to evacuate the city, and when our major forces leave, attack various squads with IEDs and in ambushes with small arms fire. They think inflicting a few casualties will cause the NAR to abandon the campaign."

"Are they really that stupid?" another officer asked.

"Yes. Of course they are. They read Mao and Che and think they have it figured out. But guerrillas have to be able to hide within a sympathetic population in order to operate successfully. They don't seem to understand that the population, including the rural one, has been purged of anyone who might look the other way or aid them. We have a nice set of ambushes ready for them ourselves."

The rest of the meeting focused on logistics, the number of particular vehicles available, regiments and battalions at the ready, supplies current and in transit, disposition of forces, and so on.

****

On the day of evacuation of Central District commanders set up as many checkpoints as possible on exiting streets in order to funnel as many people as quickly as possible onto the freeway south. Since these checkpoints were often the first and last direct encounter citizens had with the invading NAR forces, they tended to be as abusive as they thought they could get away with. For blacks, that meant unrestrained volleys of epithets and monologues of vituperation usually coming out of every window of their vehicle filled with a few adults, mostly women, and a number of children, each practicing their brand of racial solidarity and disdain for *mo'fo' honkies.*

Despite the soldiers' best efforts to process the black families out of Central District, the people slowed things down to a crawl with incessant demands for further explanations. It didn't help handing them instruction papers, since they could barely read or understand the simplest directions.

"Where's it say I gotta go?"

"Just follow the arrows, ma'am. They'll get you to the freeway. Soldiers will help you there."

"But how'm ah gonna get this stuff? Don' it say ah got some stuff comin?"

"When you get to Vancouver. Just before Oregon, ma'am."

"Where dat? I don' know no Vancouver. Why you makin' us go. Why you be doin' dis to black folk who nebber did a thing ta you? You's raciss is what. You think ahm yore slave. Ah ain't no one's slave, and you cain' make me be yo slave . . ."

"Ma'am, you have to go. Follow those arrows like I said."

"Like you say, hmmph, like I care about what you say. Umm umm umm."

"If you don't leave now, ma'am, I will arrest you and you will go to jail for two years and they will make you work if you want to eat."

"I ain' 'fraid 'a you. You cain' scare me . . ."

"Now! Drive on, right now!"

"Like ahm yore bitch, umm umm umm," continuing her monologue as she finally sped away.

To the soldiers, it was a maddening. Most of them had no direct experience of black people prior to this. They understood and expected to be despised as invaders, occupiers, conquerors, even as whites under these circumstances, but they'd never encountered out and out stupidity in such massive numbers. Some felt ashamed of thoughts that came to mind about these people, and were repelled not by what some called barbarism, but rather the infantilism. These people seemed no more than wild, ignorant, and crazed children.

How was it possible, many would wonder for years to come, that a sophisticated technological society could harbor an interior population of savages who contributed nothing productive or helpful to it? Why would rational people allow it? It made no sense. Suddenly, it made a great deal more sense to the soldiers (and all their friends and families when they related their experiences back home) as to why they were doing what they were doing. It wasn't just about conquest and gaining wealth for themselves. It was about driving weird, destructive alien creatures out of their midst along with the people who had maintained them here, enabling the insanity.

When the last voluntary vehicles had filtered out of Central District (and various other neighborhoods in the City and Tacoma, the soldiers heaved great sighs of relief and actually looked forward to the next phase of clearing the hold outs. Of which there were a great many, for many people walked over to the checkpoints during the day to give the soldiers a piece of their minds, and gangbangers wandered nearby, taking up positions in yards, on porches, studying the soldiers, trying to assess their armor, equipment, and capabilities.

One woman, in her late twenties, perhaps, disheveled and unkempt, marched her five children, the youngest, a toddler, the oldest, merely ten, down to a checkpoint and began hollering at the soldiers.

"Ah wanna know where mah money's at? Where's mah money you mother******** white honkies! . . . Ah have fi' chil'run. Fi' chil'run, d'you unnerstan' 'at? You mother******* honkies. Who gonna pay fo' mah chil'run? Sum'un gotta pay fo' mah chil'run. You hear me! You hear me! Mother******* peckerwoods."

She was given a choice of the black bus or to go back home. She gradually retreated, muttering, swearing, yelling, arguing as she went.

If a crowd grew around a checkpoint, many more soldiers would appear with menacing implements of riot control, mostly non-lethal, but not exclusively so. They also had a large number of attack dogs: German Shepherds, Malinois, Pinschers, and Rottweilers.

One weapon they had resembled a shotgun that fired a soft slug that spread on impact into a wide area that felt like the hardest punch in the chest anyone might receive in their life. It had an enervating and demoralizing effect on the recipient. They were also equipped with tasers, pepper spray gel, rubber and plastic bullets in AR-15 style rifles.

Squads worked quickly at the first sign of a disturbance. Drivers were instructed to shut off their engines when they came to the checkpoint. If the driver or someone else became too belligerent and uncooperative, they would be immediately tased, pulled from the vehicle, placed in restraints, and quickly put into a windowless bus nearby (depending on their weight, but they'd anticipated that problem and had a low cart to roll them on to and spirit the person away and out of sight). Other passengers were given the choice of driving on or joining their companion. Many joined them since they were related.

The effective and rapid response of the soldiers dismayed the gangbangers.

****

Chinatown and various Asian enclaves of Vietnamese, Filipino, Japanese. Korean, Thai, and Laotian were scheduled for a week later. It was complicated with language problems. Many Asians never bothered to learn much English at all, although their children generally did. Although considered to be generally docile and highly conforming as people, Asians often proved stubborn, intransigent, and combative when pushed farther than they felt was acceptable.

The problem this posed was that Asians were clever and smart. The poorer ones would want free goods and might be Pied Pipered into chasing them to Vancouver, but most others could not be incentivized to cooperate in compliant evacuation.

If too many Latinos and Asians refused to relocate, they would shut power, water, and food off in their areas, give it some time as people gave up and gave in, and then clear out the dead enders.

One method used was what the army did after the first day of clearing Central District.

At 3 am, units pulled up outside gang houses. Electricity had been shut down for the surrounding block a half hour earlier. Mobile scanners could see through walls and determined how many people were inside, and where they were located. Quiet, light, and agile spider-like robots were directed to positions around the building using various sensors to locate openings such as broken windows, a cracked facade, attic vents, any small opening. If one was found, a beetle bot was sent through it to explore. If the opening was large enough, mosquito drones (much larger than actual mosquitos, but smaller than hummingbirds) were sent in. They had small batteries to power them, but could be supplied with energy by aiming a safe frequency of microwaves towards them from a unit the commando squads used to transport their various drones and robots.

Beetle drones could also fly and had a camera that could view in ordinary light, infra-red, or night vision.

The mosquito drones were called that since they had a fine needle extending from their bodies containing a drug (in this case a curare-like agent) that could be injected. The commandos could have used a knock out gas, but it was difficult to regulate the amount inhaled and that might result in death, especially if children were involved.

The drones were electronically tagged so they would appear on the scanner and operators could watch them engage warm bodies.

From what they could see, the house contained nine people spread out in various (assumed) bedrooms. No one was up keeping any kind of watch, using a bathroom or any media to pass the time.

Everyone asleep, though, was behind closed doors. The mosquito drones weren't small enough to crawl under doors so the Captain of the commando squad briefly discussed the matter with his lieutenants and sergeants. He decided to send a walker robot to the front door of the house and see if the door was open. If so, the walker would walk in and start opening bedroom doors to let the mosquito drones inside, one by one until everyone was chemically immobilized. If the front door was locked, then the walker would pound on the door and try to wake everyone up. As doors inside were opened, the drones would fly in and contact the bodies. Once everyone inside was down and accounted for, commandos would enter, put the people in restraints, attach an ankle bracelet to each (similar to wrist ones but more multi-faceted), and transfer the bodies to an awaiting detainment and transport vehicle.

The front door was locked in this case, and so the walker used an arm to slam against the door repeatedly. Watching on the scanner, they could see bodies jump up, some reaching for items close by, guns they assumed, while others, women, they guessed, merely awoke and sat up. People rushed to the doors of their rooms and opened them, conferring with others, but the drones stabbed them with fluid and the people reacted as if actual insects swarmed them, their energetic action helping to disperse the drug more quickly into their systems. Within a minute or so, they began slumping to the floor or in their beds.

With the drones having struck their targets, commandos broke into the house and began processing the inert bodies.

If any neighbors had been awakened, none of them appeared on their porches to see what was going on.

All the gang houses in Central District were thus neutralized that night. If their Intelligence had missed any, they followed up in acquiring data and raiding those. If some houses they raided weren't strictly comprised of gang members, well, that didn't matter.

Immediately following the gang purge, though, water and power was shut off. If people ventured from their homes to raid those of their neighbors for food or water that might remain in their pipes or kitchens, spider robots would run them down and shoot them with a dart, causing them to become immobile and safe for pick up and relocation.

If anyone fired on the robots or commandos who were well armored in lightweight advanced materials, and perfectly safe from small arms fire, they would be fired upon for lethal effect if in the open, or their hiding place would be blasted with explosive rounds to open holes that mosquito drones would use to subdue them. Captured alive, the assailants could look forward to very hard time for many years to come.

In this way, Central District and other ethnic neighborhoods were cleared. Most of those who had been taken by force were transported by bus to the bridge over the Columbia River, pointed south and told to start walking. The ankle bracelets were removed (since they were proprietary technology), replaced by simple shock bands, in case anyone felt defiant or refused to move on.

Washington State had a population of around 8 million people prior to the NAR invasion. No more than 25% of that number was allowed to remain, which meant that nearly 6 million people had been funneled south into Portland, Oregon. That state had 5.5 million people. It was an unmitigated calamity.

The End of the USA

The NAR offered to provide food and medical supplies to the state of Oregon, but were initially refused out of pique and anger at the NAR for its aggressive dispossession of American citizens from their rightful homes.

Yet, the acceptance of NAR status in eastern Oregon, just as it had occurred in Washington, attended by loss of revenues and resources, had a profound affect on the government in Salem.

The governor complained to his wife at dinner, "These people seem to have no idea how weak we really are."

His wife, Marie, understood he referred to the state senators and representatives.

"They say raise taxes, but taxes can't be raised anymore than they are now. People can't pay 'em. The economy's been stagnant for over two decades as it is. The eastern state is completely beyond our control. Washington screams at me about sending the taxes we owe them. Everyone cheats on them . . . talk about black markets, gray markets, barter markets, there's no end. Every time they raise taxes we get less revenue. You'd think they'd learn, but they just pass another law against tax avoidance."

"What about the refugees?" she asked. The initial trickle from Bellingham had become a flood.

" 'Destroy the bridges!' many proposed, but how can we? Especially now with traffic flowing south into the state night and day. Blow the bridges? While people, fellow Americans, are on them?"

"Halt the traffic and clear them."

"How?"

"Seal them and send the people back north."

"You don't think the NAR won't seal their end, too, and dare us to blow them up with people on them?"

"Yes. That's what they would do, wouldn't they."

They'd begged the President for army support, but all he'd done was to ask California to mobilize their National Guard and send it north. That governor refused to do it, though. He could neither pay for it nor spare them.

Every relief agency there was had come to Oregon to help deal with the flood of people -- the Red Cross, Salvation Army, various international groups like Doctors Without Borders, CARE, Feed the Children, and so on, but no one had ever seen such a mass of people before.

The United Nations and every first, second, and third world nation publically condemned the New American Republic and created trade sanctions to oppose them, but Canada, while officially condemning the NAR, unofficially maintained economic ties and was a conduit for transporting their goods, resources, and agricultural surplus.

Nor were there any interruptions of their oil and gas exports.

"Six million people. That's what they estimate. But why don't we just ask those bastards. They know the exact number and I'll bet they'd be happy to tell us," the governor grumbled. He was right. General Bruster had an exact figure of the people being expelled and would have given it.

"I have to take their food. There's no way around it. We can't feed so many people even with the world helping out. And you don't think Russia and China aren't laughing up their sleeve at us? By God! What have we come to? And those idiots in the legislature don't think we're next. Not only do we have to absorb these people, we'll be on the road soon enough as it is, too."

"They can't push everyone out . . . can they?" his wife asked.

"They can and they will. Who's to stop them? I can't. The President can't. No one can. I told the Commandant of our National Guard that we should grab a hundred thousand able bodied men, arm them, train them and fight when the time comes. Know what he told me? Christ, he looked like he was about to cry."

"And he said what?" she asked.

"He told me they had no arms to give them. No ammunition to give them, and almost no qualified staff to train them. Nor feed or house them. He said they might be able to buy the rifles and ammo, but that the only manufacturers who could do the job in the amount of time needed were where? You guessed it. The NAR! But we don't have the money to buy it from them or the Russians or the Chinese or anyone. Do you realize what a good rifle costs? Even at wholesale prices, $1000 times a hundred thousand. That's a hundred million dollars we don't have. To field our own militia would take billions . . . and you know what else he told me? The NAR would mow 'em down in a matter of days with no likely casualties to themselves . . . say that we had artillery. We do. A few pieces, and used them. Well they have mobile laser systems that would destroy any shell we fired in a nanosecond. Then they'd kill the weapon with one of their little guided missiles . . . of course, if we had lasers, we could knock out their drones and missiles, too, but we don't, of course . . . then he told me about a whole array of these robots and little drones like insects, and spider things that are simply moving mines that can run or fly across the terrain and blow up wherever they want 'em to. It's unbelievable what they have, he said. We're like Stone Age people throwing rocks or sharpened wooden spears at them . . . even so, even so, you'd think people who are going to be driven out of their homes and their country would put up a fight, wouldn't you? But we've bled them dry. They don't have much more money than it already takes to live on, to just get by, what with unemployment so high. It's a ridiculous crying shame, is what it is. Nobody ever thought such a thing could happen. Nobody. These bastards are just running roughshod over us. And here's the final straw the commandant told me -- the NAR have been persuading our best men to join them. To desert ranks and join them, and they are, the white ones, and that's most of them, in droves. They're driving across the Columbia and signing up. That means their families are protected from evacuation. And they're not the only ones. Young men, hell, middle aged and older men are crossing over and joining up. They'll keep their homes and businesses. Screw their neighbors. What have their neighbors ever done for them except to vote to tax them more? How can we defend ourselves when the people who are going to be driven out can't or won't fight, and the people who can and would fight are joining the enemy?"

"You know, I read or was told something a long while ago about how the citizens of the Roman Empire didn't resist the barbarians who destroyed Rome, but that they welcomed them with open arms because living under Roman emperors was worse than living under barbarian kings. They had more freedom and kept more of their money even if life got a bit more crude. But it isn't more crude in the NAR. It's high off the hog, and people are starting to notice. The people in Pendleton and Wallowa have never made so much money now that they hardly pay any taxes. Same thing in Lakeview and Burns."

"But why should we absorb these, these Washington refugees? Why not send them to California?"

The governor stopped eating and put his fork down. He felt thunderstruck. Why hadn't he thought of that? Then he realized it was because his first reaction had been humanitarian. Yes, yes, give me your tired, your poor, your wretched refuse, let's see what we can do to help you out. Hah!

Send them away? That would be cruel, but it was the right thing to do under the circumstances. Screw California.

"My dear, you're a genius. That's exactly what we'll do. Funnel them down I 5 and let them be California's problem."

It wasn't easy, once relief agencies had set up tent cities and facilities people didn't want to leave their shelters and the sense of being taken care of, rather than on their own, alone in a cruel world. The NAR provided supplies of gasoline to the governor while law enforcement agencies adopted the tactics of sealing the Interstate exits and on ramps and keeping traffic flowing south into Siskiyou County in northern California.

An observant driver, passing through once prosperous towns and regions of the state, would have seen that little had changed in the last forty years except everything was shabbier. Basic maintenance of buildings had declined. Roofs weren't replaced as frequently, repainting was delayed or simply ignored, landscaping went to being wilder, less cared for, more stores were boarded up, cheap looking discount retailers predominated, and there weren't a lot of new cars.

It was worse in California.

It took three months to get the Washingtonians to move on. There were many deaths. Armed refugees who thought their chances were better in the State tried to fight their way out to the cordoned off roads, being killed or killing police; others preyed on fellow travelers -- robbing, raping, murdering. Many died due to medical problems and lack of medications for serious ailments, their bodies left by the road. Small children were abandoned by parents; many teens ran away. Lack of sanitation caused sickness -- streams and rivers were polluted with human waste wherever people camped.

People with enough money had already passed through or joined friends and family in the state. But the poorer often had vehicle breakdowns and nowhere else to go, nor people waiting for them elsewhere. They were rounded up and treated as criminals, forced onto buses and delivered across the state border.

Had there ever been a greater migration of people (forced or otherwise) at one time in the history of the world?

The governor of California sent National Guard units to Siskiyou County to close all the roads leading into the state, which alarmed the governor of Oregon, but the NAR anticipated it and had commando units deployed. The first night the Cal. Nat. Guard was on station was their last night. Mosquito drones immobilized the battalion, commandos then disarmed them, acquired their vehicles, and equipment, and sent them on their way south on foot except for those who decided to change sides.

NAR agents and missionaries had been working in Northern California for a few years, meeting with farmers, ranchers, loggers to extol the benefits of low taxes, and had promised them that they would become a separate state, no longer ruled by bureaucrats in Sacramento who had long destroyed native industries such as timber mills and mining, and had regulations heaped upon them that destroyed capital investment and any hope of economic growth, not to mention that most of the north was owned by the Fed and State govts.

"Imagine if you could develop your land and resources, owned all of it privately. Do you think you might be better off then?"

Thus, with the help and acquiescence of the local towns and county seat, the NAR protected the north state by maintaining the highway cordon and moving people south into the Central Valley below Redding with gas, water, and food provided along the way, including medical aid stations.

The dispossessed people of Washington were California's problem now.

Knowing You're Being Played Doesn't Change the Game Part One

My dad was in detention for about a month. During that time my mother and I and my little sister and brother stayed at home. My mom was allowed to bring fresh underwear to my dad once a week and talk about what was going on.

Me and my sibs didn't have anything better to do, so we went to school, but it was beyond weird since more than half the kids were gone, and most of the teachers. My high school went from about 1500 kids to maybe 500. They closed off a big section of it to keep from heating the whole place.

My brother and sister's schools were combined with others.

Then there was the strange thing about my father being in custody, but I wasn't entirely alone in that. There were around twenty other high school kids whose mother or father was in jail. Other kids didn't say much, but they knew we were the children of people the NAR didn't like.

After a month, though, my mom came back from the jail and told us that dad and the others were being moved to a camp in eastern Washington and we were going to join them. We were told to pack a small bag with clothes, given a location and time to appear in downtown Bellingham. When we got there in mid morning, my mom was given a wristband, but not us kids. We got on a school bus and drove east. It took hours and hours to get to this place called Chief Joseph State Park. The Columbia River ran by it.

It was a dry, flat, dusty place and as we came to a spot near the river, there were a lot of other buses and people. They were milling about amidst piles of wood, various sheds; a little ways away were a number of buildings. There were a bunch of poles standing up with various attachments at the top. A number of NAR soldiers, men and women, were standing by.

Our bus pulled up among the others and we got off. We were directed to a table, got in line to be given our lunch or dinner. It was some sort of mush, oatmeal, maybe. My dad later said it was the basic meal they'd gotten in detention.

We looked for my dad, but didn't see him. My mom went up to other adults, those she knew had been with him in Bellingham, and asked, "Have you seen my husband, John Devries? He was with you in that jail."

"No. Yes, I know him. He was there, but he's on a different bus, I suppose. Just late in getting here."

That was the case. His bus had broken down on the way. It was good to see him!

"Dad!"

"Tom! How are you? Joanie and Mitch!" It was confusing as he tried to hug us and we tried to hug him all at once, but we got it worked out so we all got his full attention while my mom waited for us to sort it out.

"Elaine," he said at last as mom got her turn and they hugged for a long time. "God, how I've missed you. Missed you all."

We didn't get much of a chance to talk, though, because my dad's bus was the last and an officer of the NAR called us to attend to what he had to say.

"I'm Ryan Milligan, the rank of Major, and I'm in charge of this Detention Camp. My office is that building over there." He pointed to a smaller separate building near a larger one. "If you need to see me about anything you may approach that guard station (he pointed again) and request an interview. You will notice that if you walk further, you will see posts around the camp establishing a perimeter. That is the camp boundary. Those with wristbands will find it painful to cross that boundary. Children will not be harmed if they cross, but all movements will be monitored with robots at our disposal, so if a child wanders off, he or she will be followed."

"Now the first business at hand is that you are going to have to build your camp. We have all the lumber and materials you will need, and equipment. Captain Jones will hand out the procedures and instructions. You will start with the Mess Hall. Once you receive the instructions, you will be on your own. The Captain will inspect the buildings and decide if the work was done satisfactorily. If not, you will tear it down and start over. That's all for now."

Captain Jones passed out papers to a dozen or so people and left with a few other officers and the soldiers except two who manned the small guardhouse. They were mobbed by people demanding to see the Major, but were told it was too soon. No one would be seen yet. Just then music began to be heard over the Camp. I don't know what it was, some sort of choral singing and instruments.

"I think that might be Palestrina," somebody nearby said. "We heard a lot of that in detention.

****

People crowded around those who had the Plans and paperwork. There was a lot of noise and confusion. The mayor of Bellingham, Peter Wilson, started yelling, trying to organize things while my dad stood by him telling people to listen up.

"Let's get this thing organized! All right, everyone? Okay, who here has any construction experience?"

"I once built an extension to my house," one guy said. My dad said he was a Parks and Recreation manager. "I can follow plans or blueprints."

A couple of other men volunteered that they had some experience in woodworking or plumbing.

"Fine," the mayor said. "I want you three men to study the Plan, figure out who should be in charge over all, what each role you'll have, figure out how many men you'll need to do the job without tripping over each other, and then come back and we'll organize a work gang for you. How's that?" he asked looking out at the crowd of men, women, and children.

People nodded their heads or murmured approval. The three men went apart from us, sat down on a load of lumber to figure things out.

"Okay, while they're working on that project, I see that this Plan has designs for a bathroom and shower building next, then a recreation hall, a medical building, then houses . . . or something . . . barracks . . . living quarters. Something like that. Maybe some of you might want to look at these plans and see what's involved and if you can learn to do it."

I put my hand up fast as I could. "I want to do it. I can learn how to do it."

My dad shot me a look, and I looked right back at him. I can do it and I wanted to. Building would be fun.

A number of other men volunteered. Most of the people weren't from Bellingham, but from all the small cities and towns around us.

When the other men went away to look over the plans for the next building projects, I went with them. One looked like he was going to tell me to go away, but then shrugged.

We went over to a pallet of plywood boards and sat down on it best we could to look over the bathroom and shower design plan. As they looked at the drawings, I started to read the work list of things in the order they should be done. I came to plumbing and electrical and realized that it was going to get complicated and hard if nobody knew how to do wiring and how to work pipes and copper lines and stuff.

At the end of the list I saw a notice that said we should ask at the guardhouse for any instruction books we might need. That would be a big help to have some "how to" stuff.

When I handed the work list to another man, I told him what I'd learned from it.

"Hmm, that complicated, huh? Well, I guess any building with plumbing and electricity requires the same skill set to put together. The building looks relatively easy to erect, but all this other stuff . . . well, we'll learn as we go, I guess."

So that's what we did. I learned so that they put me in charge of a group of other kids my age and younger. We got to work on the living quarters. Those were simpler, quicker to build, and everyone wanted to quit sleeping on the ground under tarps and using porta-potties.

Not everyone was needed for building, maybe half, which was mostly men, so the women were directed outside the camp on getting a farm going. We were supposed to have wheat and rice fields, pigs and chickens and cows, and vegetable gardens. We were going to have to make various buildings and sheds for all that, too.

It turned out that my dad was lousy at construction. He couldn't drive a nail straight to save his life. They put him to work carrying and toting materials to various sites and mixing cement but he wasn't good at that either. He said his back hurt.

Men who couldn't pull their weight, as others put it, tended to be looked down on. People might not say it out loud, but I could see some thinking, "that guy's useless, who needs him."

And the mayor who helped get things organized that first day, he thought he elected himself in charge, but since he wasn't too swift at work either; in fact, acted like he shouldn't have to, well, it got that no one paid any attention to him. The guys who became the foremen of the crews were the ones people listened to 'cause they knew what they were doing.

And my crew of kids and teens, we were having a great time. I mean, we had five and six year olds helping supply us with tools and nails, smaller boards when we needed them, things like that. We were happy at what we were doing. It was fun to make things.

Food sucked, though. We got gruel, mush, porridge, oatmeal, the same darn thing for breakfast, lunch, and dinner. And no snacks. Even when we finally got the Mess Hall finished to the satisfaction of Captain Jones and we had a decent place to eat with big refrigerators, gleaming, stainless steel work tables, gas ovens and big burners for big pots, and big sinks for washing and cleaning, well, all we still got was mush, mush, and more mush.

The Rec Hall went faster. There was a big LCD TV in it raised up so we could watch movies and shows, or view instruction videos on how to do this or that on a farm or in building a building.

A lot of the adults said they wouldn't watch the movies because they were all NAR ones or TV shows or old ones with John Wayne in them, but the kids and me, we liked those John Wayne Westerns.

During the day, all kinds of Christian music was played over the outdoor speakers from (I learned) Gregorian Chant, Plainsong, Harp Singing, Bach, Handel, Mozart, Beethoven, hymns, pop anthems, carols, and all sorts of stuff. Everything there was.

On Sundays, they played religious movies on the TV. The adults hated them and some forbid their kids from watching them. They said it put bad ideas in their heads like Hell and Satan, but they couldn't stop them because on Sundays the kids and adults could have treats from the NAR like popcorn, ice cream cones, candy, potato chips and soda if they watched a movie or some shows. And then there'd be a Batman or Superman movie, a great big fun action flick. It was great. All week long we'd wait for Sunday. A lot of adults, too.

I asked my dad about it. "Do you believe in Hell?"

"No."

"But what happens when we die?"

"Nothing happens."

"What do you mean?"

"We just die. That's it."

"That's it? But how do you know that's it?"

"No one has ever come back from being dead to say anything different. Forget about that stuff. They just want you to believe so they can use you for their purposes. Don't fall for what they're giving you."

Ever since we'd been at the camp there were a bunch of meetings by the adults trying to figure out some kind of system of who to be in charge, and how to settle disputes or disagreements. My dad wanted to be elected leader, but no one nominated him. They elected the chief foreman, Rusty Hammond, who'd worked at Parks and Rec before. He was known for working out problems with people in the various building crews. He had good sense and an easy manner. Plus, he was big and looked like he could be tough if he had to.

And somebody had to work out a list of chores, and people to do them like cleaning the bath and shower buildings, the Mess and Rec Halls, the washers and dryers for clothes, and policing the lanes of garbage or debris.

One problem was that if someone didn't want to do their chore, even though it only happened once a week or so, no one could make him. Some people said that they should be docked a meal or two, but when they talked to Major Milligan, he said he wouldn't intentionally starve anyone so long as the NAR had to feed them. He told them that if the camp didn't pass inspection, though, they couldn't use any of the buildings or conveniences until it did.

"They treat us like slaves! Like God damned slaves. I'm sick of it!" my dad swore.

A lot of people said that, especially when the camp was mostly finished and everyone had to go out into the fields. The plans called for a dozen acres of wheat, a dozen acres of rice and a dozen acres of vegetables for freezing, canning, and fresh produce.

We had a small tractor for plowing, a small bulldozer for making berms for the rice fields, a threshing harvester, and lots of other tools and machines along with irrigation systems and pumps to bring the water from the river.

But the vegetable gardens were intensive, and planting and weeding had to be done by hand. And all the machines and equipment had to be maintained, of course, but so many people slacked off that Rusty and his council went to the Major again.

"We can't make everyone do their job," Rusty complained.

"Why not?" Major Milligan replied.

"There's nothing to force them to. They eat whether they work or not or do it half assed or not. Those of us who are conscientious end up doing the work of two or three people. You've got to give me a way to manage them."

"Okay. How about this? If they don't work, they don't get a share of the results of the food when it's ready. You keep a list of who's worked and who hasn't or how many hours of decent work they've done. I mean, with the chicken coops being finished, you'll be having eggs and meat soon enough, and in time to come, pork, milk, cheese, butter, and steak."

Rusty later said, "The thought of all those earthly delights gave me pause. My God, yes, I'd be eating eggs and sausage and ham again. Oh man! So I agreed with the Major we'd give that a try."

But in a week, Rusty saw that the new incentives didn't work. People were still slacking off, sleeping late, going through the motions while others busted their butts trying to get the work done on time.

The Council went back to the Major and told him his idea failed.

"Here's what I propose. A new directive has come down that we should let people gain some immediate reward for their labor, so here's what they want implemented. Every man, woman, and child will receive one thousand pennies; twenty rolls each. Every job, and new ones will be auctioned off. For example, a quarter acre of any field will be sold to the highest bidder. Whatever that field grows can be sold by the owner. Also, a catalogue of goods will be provided and things can bought at fixed prices, one penny to many more for different things like clothes, shoes, and other things."

"We'll sell the right to be a restaurant in the Mess Hall. Your Council can collect taxes so that you can pay someone to keep the camp and buildings clean and functioning. That's all up to you. We'll see how that works out."

Rusty came back and relayed the new plan to us. He had a list of all the different jobs available to buy, or you could call them businesses. I wanted to keep building with my crew, but everything was completed by now. My dad didn't want to work in the fields or with animals and thought, maybe they could run a restaurant. They could buy eggs, milk, chicken, and pork from the new farmers, and they could buy other supplies cheaply from the catalogue like flour, salt, corn meal, yeast.

Pretty soon we figured that a penny was worth half a day's labor. Once we figured out what things cost, and what jobs we'd all have, things started to run more smoothly. People who didn't want to work very hard didn't earn much money, and often squandered their pennies on extravagances.

My dad and mom and us three kids became one of nine restaurants that were sold. We were divided up into breakfast, lunch, and dinner businesses. Ours was breakfast. We had to bid a little more for that slot, but it was worth it. Breakfast is a pretty simple menu, and people like having the same thing everyday. But we had to compete with two other restaurants at the same time so we had to try and make our breakfast tastier or cheaper or have more variety. That made it a challenge, but my dad did his best to study up on cooking and ingredients, and we did our best to cook things right.

The spirit of the camp vastly improved. People bought recreational items like games and balls for various sports. People enjoyed mealtimes, they slept better, were more cheerful. I can't say it was great because no one wanted to be stuck in the middle of nowhere living under the NAR in a Camp, but things were looking up.

My dad said, "Look, we know what they're doing. They're playing us, treating us like rats in a maze. First they treat us like slaves to let us see how we like that. Then they make us live and work like communists to see how we like that. Now they turn us into capitalists and businessmen to see how we like that."

"But I like it a whole lot more," I told him.

"Well, that's what they want you to think. What if someone gets sick? How are they going to pay for that?"

"With their money," I said.

"What if they spent it all? Should they just lay there and die?"

"I don't know. His family and friends, they could pay for it, maybe."

"And if they don't have any money?"

"But dad, everybody here has some money now." It didn't occur to me until later that people could do a lot of things. They could save some money for emergencies, or they could join with others and put it in a fund for all of them, or people could donate to help if they wanted. Nobody had to just *lay there and die* because they were broke.

And then I had a mean thought, what if someone was so disliked nobody wanted to help them, and let them lay there and die. It might not be nice, but was it wrong?

Anyway, like I said things had really improved for us, and the little kids were really happy because they didn't think they were in bad place with bad things going on. A couple of people had bought the job of being teachers, so parents paid to have their kids taught. Life was pretty normal for a lot of us.

And then they brought the blacks in.

Knowing You're Being Played Doesn't Change the Game Part Two

I never knew any black people in Bellingham. There weren't any. All I knew of black people was from sports, TV, movies, music, and Black History Month. In sports, blacks were the best athletes. On TV and in movies, blacks were cool and smarter than white guys who were usually dumb, dorky, or jerks. In music, blacks were all about sex. They had a lot of it, and black guys got the hottest girls, white ones, Asians, super models, too; and in history, blacks were a cruelly mistreated people who we owed a lot to because they had done all the work of making America rich, and got nothing but racism and poverty for their trouble.

But when the buses rolled into camp filled with over two hundred blacks, a hundred men and women each and maybe fifty children, the faces of the adults around me fell flat. They all looked stunned.

Someone murmured, "Dear God almighty, what're we gonna do?"

Because the people getting off the buses weren't dressed in suits and ties or wearing nice dresses or blouses and slacks. The men wore dirty white Tee shirts or grey sweatshirts with hoods and dark baggy pants falling down and the fattest sneakers on their feet I ever saw. The women were generally hefty from chubby to jumbo and dressed in an assortment of garish colors impossibly tight with tops that had to be stretched beyond what nylon and elastic was capable of, and short skirts or shorts that looked to be stuffed with a dozen smoked hams.

There were some girls my age in the camp, one of whom I thought quite a lot about when I lay on my bunk in our quarters. She was lithe and small and sweetly bulged in places I longed to put my hands on, but these black women with boobs the size of small watermelons and rear ends the size of a pair of giant watermelons were the greatest anti-sex image I will ever see. They made the idea of sex terrifying; not to mention their ratty hair, broad fat faces, broad noses and big lips from which such ugly noises came from, and dark eyes from which dark, mean looks came from.

I noticed that they didn't have wristbands but ankle bracelets with a thick pack on it.

Their small children were wild and dressed ragged and dirty, while older ones were either loud in speech or sullen in attitude.

Most of the men, though, were not like the women. They looked trim and athletic. Some were fat, but most looked mean and fit.

For the moment, they stood as a group in an open part of the camp among newer piles of lumber and building materials, and stood staring at us as if wondering what planet they'd been dropped onto, but then I could hear one say, "Lookit dem white folks lookin' at us. Whassa mattah? Ain' we good enuff foh ya's?" And she and the people around her laughed.

"Foh sho! Ya white folks gonna show me ta mah new house," another called out having looked around at the buildings behind where we were standing.

Just then Major Milligan, Captain Jones, and a number of soldiers, male and female appeared. The Major stood on a pile of plywood and gave them the same message he'd given us when first arriving. But he was constantly interrupted by calls for better food, warmer clothing, insults and slurs flung out. He ignored them, passed out the Plans and instructions for them to build their own living quarters, and then left.

"Wha' dar we s'posed a do wif dese thin's? Ah don' know nuffin' 'bout buildin' nuffin."

"Ah wanna eat! Where's mah f***kin' food, fools!"

Captain Jones came over to us and asked Rusty and some others to give a tour to a group of blacks and show them the bathhouses, the Mess and Rec Halls, and the washing room. He corralled half a dozen of the black men, in their twenties and early thirties, I guess, and introduced them to Rusty as the Chief of the Camp. He told them they would be shown some of the amenities available to them. Rusty then led them away to tour our facilities.

A number of the black men and women crossed over to us demanding we tell them where their food was at, and weren't we going to build them houses. If not, maybe they'd just help themselves to ours.

A number of our people like my dad and mom tried to explain how they could get started, how'd they even help them, but those they spoke to had no patience for listening. They said they didn't know how to do this or that so what did it matter if you white folks tell us how since we can't do it anyway.

A table had been set up by the soldiers to dole out mush to them, tarps had been set up for them to sleep under with blankets and the same thin mattresses we had. The blacks, I can't say lined up for the food, rather they swarmed the table with a lot of pushing and complaining about being pushed, loudly demanding their rations first.

"It's mah turn! Mah turn!" many would yell, and children couldn't get past the scrum and begun wailing or shrieking and people would scream at them to shut up or they'd hit them into next year.

The group that went with Rusty returned to the mob scene and started to tell others about the kind of food we got to eat.

"Enuf of dis muss. Ah wan' what da whi' peoples be eatin'. Gimme sum of dem whi' peoples foo, fool!" Some began to holler at the soldiers trying to dole out their meals.

"Gimme dat whi' foo'. Whi' foo'!"

Others joined and took up the cry, "Whi' foo'! Whi' foo'! Whi' foo'! Whi' foo'!"

The soldiers took the big pots of mush by the handles and began to leave with them.

"Whar ya go'n' wid our foo'? Das our foo'! Gibbid back! Gibbid back!"

And that became their new joint cry.

A few women went after the soldiers while others followed as the women made a grab at their arms for the big pots, but then they screamed and fell down, grabbing at their ankles where the bracelets were fastened.

Captain Jones immediately appeared. "Shut up! SHUT UP! All of you!"

The crowd of them became quiet except for some children still wailing and crying.

"Are you ready to behave yourselves?" Jones demanded. No response. Which was good. "If so, you will each receive your ration. If not, you can go hungry."

No one said anything so Jones gestured to the soldiers to resume their duty of feeding the people. As they began to swarm the table again, Jones told them, "Get in line!"

"You folks," Jones said turning to us, "best go about your business. Until their quarters are built, they have no kitchen, bathhouse, washing, or recreation privileges."

I could feel a great sigh of relief from around me. That would be from me, too.

I found myself muttering, who are these people? And what are they? I was shocked, and I wasn't alone. Some of the guys from my building crew, and the younger ones came up to me.

****

"Can you believe those people?" Jack, a kid my age, said to all of us. The little kids looked kind of scared or worried. Well, we were all worried, for sure.

I nodded. "We need a plan."

"Like what?" Buster asked. We called him Buster. That wasn't his name.

"Like stick together, right?" I replied. Everybody nodded.

We took it a step further. We organized all the kids on our side, seventy of us, into groups. We had some older teens, and those guys told all us other boys that it was our job to protect the girls no matter what, and to watch each other's backs. They thought we should learn to wrestle and fight, too, and the girls should learn to use whatever was handy, just in case.

Ron, an eighteen year old, and I asked to see Captain Jones and got permission.

"What can I do for you boys?" he said as we sat down across from him at his desk.

"We want to build a gym," Ron told him.

"Uh huh."

"Yeah, and we want equipment for boxing and wrestling, and martial arts."

"Really?"

"Yes."

"That's interesting. It's a good idea to want to be fit and acquainted with manly sport and defensive arts," he said agreeably. "What about instruction, though? Do you have anyone who can train you in these things?"

"I don't know any men in the camp who know these things," I said. "We could ask, I guess, but I'd rather not. Why can't we learn from videos?"

The captain frowned. "It's too easy to get things wrong, and get hurt. You'll get hurt somewhat, anyway, but we want to avoid injuries that should not happen at all. This kind of thing needs hands on close supervision and coaching."

"What do you suggest?" Ron asked.

"I don't think your parents would like it."

"Why not?"

"Because I'd like to have my men and women teach you. They're trained in these things, but your parents don't like us, and no doubt, don't want us training their children like we train our own. You have to admit that they have good reason to feel that way."

Ron and I looked at each other. I frowned at what the captain said.

"Besides," he said. "You don't need to build a gym. We have one of our own to maintain fitness and readiness. Here's what I can do: anyone, that includes adults, is welcome to come to the gym three evenings a week for training. I'll set it all up. Just assemble at the guardhouse Monday, Wednesday, and Friday at eighteen thirty hours. Uh, that's six thirty. Okay?"

We nodded.

"My dad can't stop me," Ron told him as we stood up to leave. "I'm too old for him to order me. Same with the other guys my age. We can learn and teach the kids if we have to."

It didn't go down like that, though. When word came that they were ready the next Wednesday, there was a crowd of fifty kids and a dozen adults at the guardhouse ready to go out.

****

Something we didn't know at the time was that the bigger shock bands on the blacks served a variety of purposes. One was to monitor a cascade of bio-chemicals that were precursors to violence so that they could prevent assaults and murders. They didn't worry about rapes because the men received a cocktail of drugs through their skin that chemically castrated them. An anti-Viagra, you could call it.

The women were made infertile as a precaution, anyway.

The men complained among themselves about their impotence. Even though they understood something caused it, most likely the ankle bands or food, they thought, they still believed they could overcome it by will power or some magic.

Since the effect of mature women in playing with their members did nothing for them, a number decided that little girls would do the trick.

Since they had no enclosed shelter, the NAR caught on to the molestations quickly through video surveillance in the Camp. The men who were caught were removed from Camp, but neither the blacks nor we knew what happened to them. One of the soldiers said, "Hard labor" when I asked him.

While we were organizing ourselves, some of the black men were, too. One thirty year old, DaSean Jenks, very dark with short dreadlocks, was trying to form a gang, but had nothing to offer anyone in return for following him, but he convinced his people that they should take over the whites' living quarters.

The next day, while most of us were at work in the fields or around the Camp, all the blacks moved into our rooms.

Naturally, we thought the NAR would do something about it. Rusty and the Council went to see the Major.

"What do you want me to do about it?" the Major asked.

"Move 'em out. Shock 'em, whatever."

"It's your Camp. You're in charge of your people."

"I'm not in charge of those people," Rusty told him.

"They're your people, too. They're all from your towns and cities; fellow citizens. What did you do about them before?"

"Other people took care of that."

"How?"

"Well, I mean social workers, the police, if need be," one councilman said.

"Okay, so you'll have to form a police department, I guess."

Rusty and the others looked at each in bewilderment, he said later. Become police? They didn't want to become police.

"Here's what I'll do. We'll get you some protective gear, restraining devices, Tasers and stun guns. Form a squad, and those people who won't leave your quarters, you can arrest and remove to the other side of the camp."

It took over a day after finding ten men who agreed to be our cops to get them equipped and ready to evict the squatters.

I don't quite understand how the blacks managed it, but it seems they had enough food cached and water in bottles to last a day, at least, and barricade themselves inside our quarters.

In the meantime, a lot of families had to double up in rooms or sleep in the REC and Mess Halls, but we had no mattresses or blankets or clothes since they were still in our quarters.

Our police divided into two groups of five, and late morning they started at the farthest out of our quarters and began trying to clear each "street", one at a time.

Me, and a whole lot of others who didn't have to tend to immediate chores watched our police enter a room if the latch wasn't jammed and order the people out. Half the time the people would slowly get up and shamble out, but the other half of the time, they refused to move, said awful things, and had to be stunned, cuffed ankles and wrists, and dragged out. And that was hard work considering how heavy so many of the women were and large the men were in size.

And then there were the children who created such a fuss and trouble that they would get tazed, too. And there were over a hundred quarters to rescue this way, room by room.

We worked out a system, though, so that by the end of the afternoon, we had wheelbarrow teams to transport the immobile ones, and men pitched in without any gear and created more teams led at least by one policeman with a shock and stun device.

Rusty set up a line across the camp and told the blacks that any who crossed it to our side would be stunned. I guess you could say we created apartheid all over again on our own.

So the worst was over and our quarters cleared, but while there, they tried to destroy everything of ours. They ripped our clothes, urinated on our beds and blankets, spread feces around. It was unbelievable, and the reason why, I guess, so many who simply got up and left when ordered to had a gleam in their eye and a smirk on their face.

The Major told Rusty that we were in charge of feeding them, now. He suggested a daily rotation of personnel to do the job, including women. They would have stun equipment, but that the situation would be video monitored and if it got unruly, they'd intervene.

We were able to salvage some clothing and blankets, but those who'd had their quarters taken over had to buy a lot of new goods with our pennies from the catalogues; and in some cases, buy from neighbors out of immediate necessity. Fortunately, it wasn't too cold at night since some had no blankets, while others had to sleep on hard benches where the mattresses had been.

"Let's just go and take some of their mattresses and blankets," I told my dad. "Let's make them pay."

"Two wrongs don't make a right," he said shaking his head.

"Two wrongs! There's only one wrong. They did it. I saw the people who wrecked our room and stuff. I know exactly who did it. Taking their stuff in return wouldn't be wrong. It'd be justice. Fair is fair."

"Tom, do you really want to sleep on one of their mattresses and wrapped in one of their blankets?" my mom put in.

I hadn't considered that and shuddered at the thought. "No, I wouldn't, now that you mention it. Still, we should make them pay somehow."

We created a rotation to feed the blacks, a team to dole out the food and a team to stand by and manage their behavior.

That night we had one of our policemen on duty to keep an eye on things, but Mr. DaSean Jenks organized a party of men to sneak across the line and hit our bathhouses and the Mess Hall. The bathhouses are open all day and night for obvious reasons. The Mess Hall is locked at night, but it's not impregnable.

Around two that morning, a huge racket came from those buildings. The people nearest to them got up to investigate, but it was dark, they'd broken the lights to the bathhouses that lit the way, and they'd blocked the doors there and at the Mess Hall giving them many minutes to wreak destruction.

All our tools for building, maintenance, farm and animal work are chipped with RFID tags and have to be taken out and returned everyday into secure, heavy-duty sheds. We don't have the keys.

By the time we got the tools we needed after the soldier at the guardhouse opened a shed for us, and got to the buildings and forced in the doors with all our police standing by, twenty to thirty minutes had passed.

We didn't have to stun or restrain any of the blacks. They happily ran out and back to their side, laughing, whooping, and gleeful; and then we heard greater cheers and applause when they returned to their people as conquering heroes.

In the bathhouses, all the fixtures were ruined, even though the toilets and sinks were stainless steel. They were torn from floors and walls and used to smash and dent each other. The showers and piping were ripped out, bent and broken - a total ruin.

In the Mess Hall, all the food was flung everywhere - oil, flour, corn meal, eggs, meat, vegetables, spices, coffee, tea, salt, and sugar strewn throughout. Chairs and tables were broken, pots and pans pounded with dents, crockery broken, attempts made to break the refrigerators, ovens, stovetops, work tables, sinks and plumbing.

I have to say that they nearly totaled that place, too.

I couldn't help myself and said, "Still think they shouldn't be made to pay, dad?"

It was mean, I know, but they had just put us out of business. I couldn't figure what it would cost to replace everything. That's what the NAR had us doing now. We paid for electricity, gas, water, sewage treatment, and all the goods we used with our store of money. There was even a system to increase the penny supply as we became more productive and banked our earnings.

Now, we were back to Porta-potties and mush. The hatred I felt towards the blacks was fierce; and me and all the kids, plus a number of adults, became shameless about using every common slur word we could think of or invent in referring to them.

The first thing we did, though, was to commandeer all the lumber and sheets of plywood and build a stout and high fence across the Camp, and removed every scrap of building material. There would be no high ladders they could make, but they say that cunning is the intelligence of the stupid. We had to consider how they might avail themselves of their Porta-potties to climb over, or use the sheets of tarps, their poles, and rope cords, or mattresses and blankets; really anything to get under or over.

The Major said we were in charge of the Camp. Their surveillance monitors were unavailable to us.

Why were they such bastards like that? I mean, we went to their gym and were trained to fight, wrestle, and defend ourselves; and I liked the soldiers who taught us. They treated us well, could be funny, and related to us. So why were they putting us through all this crap? It wasn't funny or informative or helpful. They made our lives so much harder just when they were getting better. It made no sense to me. What gave them the right to play God like this with other people's lives?

****

We did what we had to, though. The Council levied a heavy tax on all of us who worked. The farmers who hadn't brought in any kind of crop had to pay out of a futures contract (don't ask me how that works). Little kids like my brother and sister who worked in our restaurant had to pay out of their salaries.

Fortunately, the work of repairing our facilities went faster than expected, and we remained vigilant at keeping the blacks at bay, so to speak. But that cost time and money, too. Winter would come and we'd need better insulation and heat in our living quarters.

After a few weeks, you might say things were close to normal; that is, the normal that was close to being nice just before they brought the blacks in; but having nothing better to do, DaSean Jenks organized his people to be vocally obnoxious. The fence couldn't keep out the songs, chants, clapping sounds they would make in the evening letting us know what evil racists we were and how they'd like to kill us in our sleep and so on.

The fact was that we hadn't done anything to them. We hadn't brought them here. We hadn't arrested and detained them. We hadn't refused to share our skills with them, but we were the ones who should pay for their problems? It was insane.

Every adult in our Camp, though, got to see exactly what they were like up close and personal since we rotated the teams of people in charge of feeding and supervising. People learned to be hard about it.

Rusty, the Council, and other adults met to try and figure out what to do about or with the blacks. They invited Mr. DaSean Jenks and others to discuss matters with them, to work out some sort of living arrangement or way of proceeding with getting the blacks living quarters and facilities.

"Tha's fine; tha's fine, but here's wha' ah wan'. You gives us what you got and builds yoreselfs some new ones. Tha's all ahm aksin'. You dun 'rested us, treat us lak slaves, and say we gots to work on yo planation. We's ain' gots to slave on no planation jes 'cuz you say so. Fu** dat!"

"Be reasonable, Mr. Jenks. You understand that we didn't arrest you or put you here. We were arrested, too, and put here against our will; just like you. All we're trying to do is make things as bearable as possible. You need shelter and bathhouses and a cafeteria and such. We can help you. We want to help you, but you have to make some effort on your own."

"Whys we gots to make an *effit*? You's white same's da ones dat put us here. Fu** dat! We knows are rights. You owe us dat. Gib us are rights. Da's all I gotta say."

Jenks would return to their side with his pals and announce, "Dey's be gibbin' us wha' we wan' soon. Real soon. Dey cain' hol' out 'cuz we's stonger dan dey is. We be a mighty people, black warriors, mah bruddas and sistahs! We be mighty, and dey be weak white nuthin's."

Then, late one night NAR soldiers ran into the Camp, across to the black side and scrambled up the fence in the dark, close to the perimeter of the Camp.

Soon, we saw in the dim light that they were carrying one of the blacks, a girl, I thought, into the medical building. They were working on her there for a while when a vehicle entered the compound, they loaded her in it and took off for Brewster and a real hospital, I guessed.

The girl was called Manzie Dawes, and they just saved her life. What we eventually pieced together was that she about thirteen, had cut a length of rope cord with her teeth from the stays for the tarp poles. She made some sort of a noose, climbed high enough up a fence and got it anchored on a post and hanged herself.

NAR surveillance was alert enough that night to catch it just as she happened to start to hang. They rushed in and saved her. Turns out she was one sad, depressed young girl. She wasn't pretty, but she wasn't ugly, either. She wasn't fat, but mildly chubby. She was smart, sensitive, and often made fun of. Viciously mocked and ridiculed.

Of course, the blacks accused us of lynching her.

Major Milligan explained as much as he knew to Rusty so that we would know how things stood, what was true and what was not.

"We're not bringing her back. She's a nice young girl who's been through a hell of an upbringing. She needs to be with her own people, but we have a place where she'll be looked after by better class of such folks. Who knows if she'll ever overcome things, but with God's grace she may, if she cares to place her faith in Him. I'm not going to absolve myself and my people for what happened. I, we, deeply regret it. But I am sorry before God, and ask His forgiveness."

A few days later a fleet of buses pulled in and they loaded up the black people and drove off with them.

After breathing a great sigh of relief, some of us wondered what was next? A bunch of Mexicans or Chinese to mess with us? But no one else came. We were left as we were. People settled down into routines, we started making jokes, joshing around and laughing again. We listened to the music, watched the videos, and continued training in the gym in boxing, wrestling, and martial arts.

Someone started calling the period when the blacks were here The Dark Time. It left an indelible impression on us, every one of us. Even my dad. The hatred he experienced directed at him and every one of us was like nothing he ever imagined possible.

The younger people, me and all the other kids figured it out pretty quick. Go ahead and be like that 'cause we'll hurt you ten times as hard as you hurt us. No mercy for monsters who can't live and let live.

The Fighting Whities Redux
Part One

"Mr. Bythewood, this is unacceptable. The proposed Constitution is unconstitutional! They can't just exclude women and other people from voting. It's crazy. Who would go for that? It's . . . it's unchristian, too. It doesn't make any sense! You can't treat us, women, like that. It's totally unjust, unfair. It's plain evil!" Janet Gaines said.

"Perhaps, but it is rational. And is it really unfair?" the professor replied.

"How can it not be? You can't treat people differently like this."

"People are different, though. Men and women are very different, but here's your assignment, Miss Gaines. For next Wednesday, I want you to argue in favor of the voting provision using the most rational and thoughtful arguments that have been made. Who would like to argue against the provision in the proposed constitution?" he asked looking around the classroom. A hand shyly arose from Emily Welby.

"Miss Welby it is, then. Best arguments, please. Winner gets extra credit as usual."

The topic moved on to another part of the new proposed constitution regarding taxation.

After class, Janet, a tall, attractive girl with dark hair walked towards the student union with Kevin, her boyfriend. They were both sophomores fulfilling prerequisite courses.

While it was cold in Maccabee, Wyoming, they'd yet to see any snow even though it was late November. There were a number of fireplaces in the student union for students to sit around and relax between classes. It always felt good to come out of the cold and warm up by the burning hearths.

The cold made Kevin miss Palo Alto, California, though. His one year at Stanford had spoiled him regarding weather and climate.

"Can you believe that?" Janet told him as they undid their scarves, unzipped their coats, and sat down on a couch near a fire.

Kevin shrugged. "I've had to do it. Now it's your turn."

Mr. Bythewood often responded to questions or challenges raised by students by then assigning them the job of answering the question or challenge themselves for the benefit of the entire class. That meant a conscientious student would have to spend extra time in the library or online researching the topic as thoroughly as they could, and then having to present carefully reasoned arguments for or against. Students were put on the spot. Janet cringed when a student did a lousy job. It seemed some people didn't care if others thought they were dumb, but not Janet. She was always ready to prove just how smart she was and accept the laurels due her for brains and diligence.

"I'm right, aren't I? What do you think?"

Kevin didn't want to be drawn into an argument or quarrel with her. "I don't know. Let's see what the arguments are and I'll make up my mind. Hope the other girl persuades me, if you like, but you better not throw the debate."

"How can I? I have to take the position of male chauvinist pigs and win. Grrr. I hate it."

"Good thing you're not pre-law, I s'pose," he laughed.

Kevin felt that he lucked out with Janet. She was tall, five ten, for one thing, which he preferred since he was six four; and she was intelligent, probably smarter than himself, he thought, and that beat all the silly, bouncy cheerleader types who usually were attracted to him, the football hero. And right now the

Wyoming Christian College Crusaders were tearing up the Mountain West conference. It was the twelfth week of the college season and they were undefeated (11 - 0), but only ranked seventh in the BCS standings.

Fans and sportswriters gave Kevin a good deal of the credit for the surge of the Crusaders into the top ten and sudden national attention, but he thought their quarterback and offensive coordinator deserved the accolades. Their strategy was relatively simple in game plans. The first two or three series they ran the ball with Kevin as the main back. If they weren't moving down the field or breaking runs into the seven to twelve yard range here and there, they shifted to passing with a variety of crossing patterns and screen plays. Here Kevin got the chance to break into the open field. He had great hands, but when the ball was dropped into him in stride, he punished safeties and cornerbacks.

The threat of passes to him held linebackers in close, which opened up the pass farther in the middle field. Their offense was superbly balanced in threats to score, and for that, Kevin had to thank Brett Allard, the senior quarterback who every major college had thought too small for the position. But he wasn't any smaller than Joe Montana or Fran Tarkenton who had been NFL legends.

Brett had pinpoint accuracy, and like Montana, had the uncanny ability to hit dump off receivers like Kevin Worley in perfect stride. The major drawback was vision of the field in the pocket, and finding the passing lanes where the ball wasn't blocked by the rushing defensemen in timing patterns. That had made him more prone to interceptions in the prior two years, but he'd improved each year. Sixteen interceptions his sophomore year, 12 as a junior, and thus far, 9.

Brett could scramble, though, and once away from the rush, he hadn't thrown a single pick, as they call it.

Kevin had originally signed a letter of intent to play for Stanford, but when he got there in the summer to start training, he was told they wanted to redshirt him. That meant sitting out a year while retaining eligibility for four years, which meant five years at college. And that made no sense.

It was explained that redshirting was to his advantage. He wouldn't have to ride the bench behind their current fullback who was expected to play for two more years. He would be more physically mature by having an extra year to train.

"Well, how do you know I won't be ready in a year to be the starting fullback?" he asked the backfield coach.

"Jackson has earned the position. He's the best we have right now."

"But you haven't seen what I can do; if not this year then the next. What if I'm better? Would that get me the starting position?"

"Look, Kevin, we have a system in place on how we develop players. You have to trust that we know what we're doing. We have a winning program here," the coach told him.

"But what if I'm better sooner rather than later? Shouldn't I get the start?"

"We'd have to see about that. There's a lot to learn before it comes to that," the coach replied.

"Okay, well, how about if we see at the end of summer training. Let's see how I stack up against the others. I mean, I'll know same as you if the other fullbacks are better than me and by how much, right?"

"Aaaah, the problem is that we have to declare our redshirts according to NCAA rules before that. That's why we're talking now. We declare in July."

"Can I think about it, coach?"

"Take a few days," the coach said and patted him on the shoulder, but when he left the locker room, he was seething. Damn kid telling us how to do our job? I don't think so. He headed out to see the head coach, John Lee, and tell him they might have a problem child on their hands.

Over the next few days at practice, he could see that Jackson seemed a bit better than him, but not the other fullbacks, and the difference he saw between himself and Jackson was that he clearly knew the offense better. How could he not? But Kevin had better hands, and so it seemed to him that he should be second on the depth chart behind Jackson, and not warming his fanny for a year.

He talked it over with is dad, but was advised caution: go along to get along. Everything was in the Coach's hands like a Captain of a ship. Piss him off and kiss the NFL goodbye, maybe.

"No, dad, I think they should worry about pissing me off. I don't have to stay here. I can transfer if I have to. I think that Wyoming college might still want me."

"Who knows how pissed off they might be since you went with Stanford?"

"Maybe so, but I'll bet they take me anyway. They said I was the best and they meant it," he said making up his mind what he wanted to do if he had to.

Grimes, the backfield coach, came up to him after a few days later and asked him for a decision.

"Coach, I've been thinking hard about it, but I don't want to be here five years. I'll pass on that redshirt."

Grimes merely nodded his head. No point in saying anything since John Lee would have to do all the talking now.

After practice that afternoon, the head coach approached him and said, "Kevin, I'd like to see you in my office after you shower." He walked off leaving Kevin with that sinking feeling of being in deep trouble.

When he got to Lee's office, a very sumptuous space, Grimes was also there seated on a couch, arms spread out along the top of it. John Lee sat behind his fine, broad desk in a padded, black leather chair that could recline and roll.

"Have a seat, Kevin," he said nodding at a chair similar to his own before the desk. He hadn't stood when Kevin entered the room, and neither had Grimes.

As Kevin sat down and faced him, Lee said, while rocking a bit in his seat, "I'm told you don't want to redshirt this year. Why is that?"

Kevin reiterated the objections he'd made with Grimes, and then added, "Coach, I've been paying careful attention to my competition and the only player I can see calling better than me is Jackson. He's a bit stronger, we're about the same speed and quickness, but I've got better hands."

He held his up as if to illustrate how large and dexterous they were.

"So it seems to me that I ought to be in line behind him and maybe next year challenge for the position. Is that out of line? Am I overstating my ability?"

"I like a boy with confidence, son. That's one of the things we look for in our players, but the fact is you're telling me how to do my job, and that's overstepping things."

The problem he couldn't explain to Kevin was that if he became better than Jackson, by a little or by a lot, and sat Jackson down his senior year to start Worley, the ramifications it would have on the team. For one thing, it would just about destroy Jackson's chance of being drafted by the pro's. Then it would send a message to all the black players on the team that the coach had no loyalty towards them, and that would create tension in the locker room. The black players would grouse, start fights in practice, and ignore the coach's instructions or corrections. God knows it could spill out onto the campus and town where some players might beat up and rob some whites or talk a blonde coed into visiting their rooms, ending up molested or raped. It had happened before with black players. Often, in fact. Stanford was as careful as it could be in evaluating black players but when the blacks numbered more than a few, things got dicey. Almost half of John Lee's team was black. That's why they had Grimes and other black coaches. To handle their own kind. But he couldn't tell Kevin that.

"You brought me here to play coach, and I want to play like you wouldn't believe, and what I'm seeing on the practice field you're seeing, too. I'm good. Maybe almost good enough to start."

"You have a lot of potential, son. There's no doubt of that, but besides your wants and the overall good of the team, it'll help us quite a bit if you redshirt this year. How about it?" he ended, leaning forward on to his desk, eyes fixed on Kevin's.

For a nineteen year old, Kevin experienced pressure like he'd never known before. John Lee's eye bore into him like God, and he could feel Grimes' lasering him from the side. He swallowed hard and said, "I'm sorry, coach, but I'm here to play."

Lee frowned deeply, sat back into his chair. "That's all for now, Kevin. You can get back to the dorm."

"Yes sir," he said rising, leaving, and closing the door behind him. He felt relieved away from John Lee's presence, but he knew he was going to pay for his decision.

The coaches became cool towards him. Nothing overt was said or done especially to wound him, but their coolness communicated a message to his teammates -- he was selfish and wouldn't sacrifice for the team. It made him a pariah among many of his peers, but not all. Athletes are not necessarily dumb, and a few could be quite cynical about the men who run the game. They were there to get what they could out of their ability, and winning was fun, but many coaches are asses and jerks. They'd seen it since grammar school.

Kevin was able to make a few friends on the team, and he had his dad contact the head coach of Wyoming Christian College about transferring there.

****

"Do we still want that fullback from Rhode Island?" Colson asked his backfield coach, Jake Swinner, after he entered the office.

"That, uh, Worley kid? I suppose so. Why?"

"I got a call from his father. Seems that Worley isn't happy at Stanford. They wanted to redshirt him and he objected. Also appears that he noticed he was good enough for second string, at least. He wants to transfer here."

"I'll take him. Get the little bastard on a plane."

Colson shook his head. "Not if he has to sit out for a year. I need him now. Allard's a junior. I want them both for his senior year. That's our best shot at the conference title, I think."

"Well, the rules say he can transfer and play if there's a hardship. A lot of black players have pulled that one and gotten out of one school for another."

"You think Worley's mother might have heart trouble and he needs to be closer to home since he's from a poor family?" the head coach smiled.

"Yeah, well, it's a funny thing about heart trouble in women. Different parameters, not always so obvious."

"You think the Worleys would go for that?"

"They called you. They want in."

"Can we find a doctor? The NCAA may want some proof of hardship," Colson wondered.

"I say we get the parents the most extensive medical exams they've ever had in their lives. Everybody past a certain age has some kind of ailment that might be said to be debilitating, right?"

"Are we going to pray there's something wrong with their health?"

Swinner laughed. "No, but I think they might, God bless 'em. They want their kid to have a better chance."

"Okay. That's what we'll do."

The medical examinations for Kevin's parents turned out to be a two-fer. Both had conditions. The mother had a degenerating hip that would need replacing in the near future, and the father showed signs of heart disease. The staff for the Crusaders were able to emphasize the medical problems and demonstrate the poverty of the family in order to plead with the

NCAA officials that Kevin needed to be closer to home to cut down on the cost of air travel.

Tom Colson spent a few hours on the phone with the NCAA trying to schmooze and cajole. It was a delicate fence he had to straddle. He couldn't complain about the ease in which black players got exceptions for transfers and insist a white kid deserved the same break, but if he mentioned a few black players names and could throw in one white player who'd gotten an exemption, he might persuade with the right amount of coaxing and ass kissing.

The Crusaders lucked out, though. They weren't considered a top tier team and wouldn't be as scrutinized by the media if say, Alabama poached a player from LSU. That would raise a major hue and cry. Stanford might moan, but they'd get a scholarship back to use on someone else, and they had no intention of ever playing Worley or wanting him around polluting the practice field as a team pariah.

That's how Kevin came to WCC and was able to start his second year.

The Fighting Whities Redux
Part Two

"The first matter I have to mention is that excluding the right to vote by sex or property and income status violates the basic American principle of no taxation without representation. It also violates uniformity in the Rule of Law as we conceive it. That argument alone ought to be enough to trump any that the other side proposes," Emily Welby insisted.

She and Janet Gaines sat side by side at a table facing the rest of the class. Prof. Bythewood, was seated with the students and took notes.

Emily, a small blond haired girl who appeared shy and timid in and outside of class, was expressing herself confidently as she addressed the question of exclusive suffrage in the proposed Constitution.

"But to take the sex argument alone, why should women be excluded from the vote? Studies have shown that women tend to make better managers than men; that they work more cooperatively; that female managers listen better. Even in matters of life and death. It has been shown that female airline pilots are more attentive and listen better to traffic controllers and take instructions better. This was exemplified in a famous crash where a cockpit of men in a jetliner were warned numerous times that there was a small plane in their vicinity and they needed to keep an eye out for it. Instead, the men ignored the warnings and the flight recorder showed them so involved in talking about sports and their weekend to come, that they never acknowledged the warnings and that small plane collided with theirs, killing everyone aboard."

"Women serve as auxiliaries in the armed forces. Are they to be denied any say in the running of a country they have risked their lives for and served extremely well? Is this new nation going to be like Saudi Arabia? Are women going to have to ask permission for the right to travel, speak, drive, or go shopping?"

"Even as Christians, how can we allow this discrimination when even Jesus Christ didn't recognize male nor female, gentile or Jew, free or slave as different peoples, but equals in faith?"

"If we're going to discriminate, why this as a basis? Why should a drunken wife beating louse with an inheritance have a vote while a sober, life saving female doctor have none? Why not discriminate based on IQ or musical ability or eye color? Because they are all completely arbitrary and whimsical determinations just as this proposed law on voting is," Emily finished with a flourish, and then looked across at Janet with a nod as if to say, "take that!"

Janet gathered her thoughts and looked over her note cards and began, "St. Paul instructs us that the husband is the head of the family and that wives ought to submit to their husbands in matters of authority, just as husbands should submit themselves to God for guidance and wisdom. As Christians, we don't ask for an entirely egalitarian society because we recognize there are hierarchies in life and in our very being. If God created society as a natural patriarchy, who are we to deny it or attempt to thwart it? We are not to be proud."

"The question, then, is not whether we have a vote or not, but whether we have a voice? The unfranchised can speak freely, form associations, collect money and lobby for their causes and promote their own well being or that of others."

"Furthermore, the history of universal suffrage has proven to be a scheme of plundering and pillaging the wealth of the middle class for redistribution to the rich and the poor. In every State that allowed women the vote, spending on social conditions immediately doubled and increased year after year as emotional irrationality caused women to embrace socialism in the greater society as it was practiced in the home."

"Let me explain. The idea of "from each according to his ability to each according to his need", the Marxist ideal, only works in one place: the family. A man's ability to earn a living and to freely use it for the good of his wife and children is socialism, per se, since the children can do little to satisfy all their own needs."

"A wife's dependence on her husband's income for herself and children creates great anxiety should the man be deeply flawed or impaired. A woman's greatest desire is for security, and for this reason, is emotionally incapable as a sex, in general, from evaluating the necessity of small government. If her children were going hungry, what mother would not beg, borrow, or steal to feed them? But then she applies this logic to the overall society when she hears of men out of work, children going hungry, people not receiving medical care. Whereas previously, she would have formed civic charities to aid the needy, with the vote, politicians persuaded women that government should do the job, and so women and the needy, who also were able to vote, robbed their husbands, brothers, and even their children to feed the government huge sums of money that was almost entirely wasted. Today we see the result."

"As families had less and less money, women went into the workforce. That lowered wages so that more families needed dual incomes to enjoy a life that had previously been provided by the husband alone. Women delayed marriage and had fewer children, which lowered consumption and production since fewer babies meant fewer goods needed to be created. Women who stayed at home . . . well, their husbands had to work longer hours to try and make up for declining income. He spent less time with his wife and family. That created strain. He was exposed to more women in the marketplace leading to a higher rate of divorce, harming society further."

"Just as we recognize Natural Law, that it comes from God, but all people can discover it without having to know God, so too, we need to recognize that men are our natural leaders; and we have to go one step further in recognizing that not all men are equally capable of prudent judgment. The poor are just as greedy as the rich and have no right to grant themselves other people's goods and money simply by outvoting them. Miss Welby made a point about uniformity to the Rule of Law; well, patriarchy is also the Rule of Law, Natural Law. Civilizations thrive so long as they are masculine rather than effete and decadent. We have seen what feminization does to a nation in the USA and elsewhere."

"On the surface, disenfranchisement may not seem fair, but God doesn't seem fair, either, in the way he treats us, but it is right because it is the way things are and were created to be. And our duty is to do what's right, not to have our way in everything. This proposal in the Constitution is wise, just, and fair when looked at in the right light. I recommend it for your approbation," she concluded.

The professor stood up and said, "Well done, both of you. Let's have the class decide the winner. Hands up for Miss Welby."

A dozen hands went up.

"Hands up for Miss Gaines."

The rest of the class, around twenty arose.

"Miss Gaines, you're the winner, but I'm going to give extra credit to you both. Thank you. You may return to your seats."

"Well done," Kevin whispered as Janet took her seat next to him.

"Oh yuck, puke, and blech," she whispered back. "I hate myself."

Kevin felt like shaking his head over the fact that Janet was such a willful and opinionated girl, but she was so much more interesting to talk to than girls who gushed about some YouTube video of cats doing something cute. Janet was kind of a pain, though, but an interesting one like a loose tooth you keep working on with your tongue because it's loose and gives you something to do; and it's kind of fun to fool with it. The day it's yanked out is a bit depressing. It had been entertaining, oddly enough, to have a loose tooth to play with and then it was gone.

Janet would be such a great girl if only she could make a little attitude adjustment. It was fine that she was smart, but she was also damn proud and blind to any opinion apart from her own.

Kevin liked WCC, Wyoming, and the spirit of the people in the State. He was a little bit proud of himself, but for a different reason. He felt like he was learning how to be a man.

He was proud of how he'd stood up to the coaches at Stanford and their bullying tactics. He was grateful to coach Colson and Swinner. They let him prove he could play, and then played him. They had no anger towards him for overlooking them for another college. They seemed like decent Christian men and treated him fairly. (They had been angry, of course, but were forgiving sorts, and were too busy to carry a grudge.)

And frankly, as terrible as it sounded, he was glad to be surrounded by guys like himself: white guys. Sure, there were a number of teammates he wasn't buddies with or felt warmly about, but it's that they understood each other. There were no undercurrents of anxiety or stress where race or prejudice entered into one's thinking. If someone didn't like you, it was because they didn't like you and nothing else.

And what a season so far! To go from the practice squad to starting, and then winning like they had thus far to become challengers for the national championship, well, that's what made sports so great. The excitement, drama, joy, and pure thrill of competing at the highest level, what could beat that? Risking one's body seemed small in comparison to the rewards.

And Stanford? They'd lost two games and were out of contention. That fullback Jackson? Seven not very productive games then a knee injury, and his replacement sucked at blocking, running, and catching. Their halfbacks were hardly better. So they relied on passing, but when you have to pass a lot in college, you throw a lot of interceptions or you get sacked a lot, and the quarterback fumbles a lot, then he gets gun shy of taking brutal hits. They weren't expected to win another game with two more left. They'd probably end up in some third tier bowl and lose that, too.

But there was no time to gloat between football practice and classes. There were no gym majors, basket weaving, or bonehead courses at WCC. Kevin wasn't sure what his major would be, but was leaning toward civil engineering.

But thinking about Janet, what was he going to do with her? Should he tell her how much he liked her, admired her, wanted to sleep with her, but that she was not feminine enough in her behavior? Why did she have to be so rigid, angry, and determined?

He wasn't a Christian goody-two-shoes, but she didn't seem to have any real feeling for submission to the transcendent. Whereas he felt he was growing a deeper feeling about the ineffable nature of being alive.

Maybe being part of a team, of subordinating himself to a greater good, a bigger cause than selfish desire was part of it. Of course, he wanted to succeed, be a star, get drafted by the NFL, make a lot of money and be celebrated if he performed well, but inside, he was beginning to see that life, living, was being a part of something more: family, country, people.

What Janet was, he decided, was catty. Not like dumb sorority girls, but intellectually catty. It wasn't enough that she was smart, but that other people had to be stupid in her eyes, and she was ready to let them know it, insist on it, or complain of it.

As attractive as she was, it made her less so. He wondered if he meant enough to her that she might consider him worth trying to please and amend her behavior? He understood that he was what some people called an alpha male, and was more desirable a partner than the average Joe Shmoe, and thus had a greater pick of attractive girls, but he wasn't a cold, inconsiderate bastard. He just wanted a warm, loving, pleasing, and tender girl who was also smart, laughed at his jokes, and was easy to get along with. Janet stressed that portrait. Not immensely, but enough.

The problem, as he saw it, was how to know when this person was the best you could do in the time you had to choose, or should one hold out for someone closer to the ideal? Did someone close to ideal even exist? Men had been asking themselves that for quite a few millennia.

He liked Janet. She was pretty, had a great figure, was of a size to his liking, but her intellectual cattiness made him realize she was a basically unhappy person. Nothing was ever quite right enough in her estimation. If she knew that, was told that, could she change? Does anyone ever change?

Fish or cut bait? A dilemma. But it could wait until the football season was over. Men are like that: good at delaying confrontations with reality and consequences. Most men have no idea how weak they are nor how proud. Fatal conditions.

****

"So where do you stand, now?" she asked Kevin.

"I liked your arguments."

"I hated them. It was a bunch of bull," she spat out.

"So, you're against Natural Law and patriarchy?"

"Damn right."

"So you're for murder, rape, and theft."

"What? Huh?"

"Natural Law. You know, the idea that some things are inherently wrong and everyone knows it or would if they thought about it."

"Of course I'm not against Natural Law like you mean it."

"Then you hate patriarchy."

"Yes."

"And civilization. You said yourself that patriarchy is basically responsible for civilization."

"No. Women should be free to vote. That's all."

"Even if it means it will destroy a great civilization?"

"Yes. If it comes to that. If people want to destroy their own society, that's their right."

"But people don't want to destroy it. Women do, though, as you said. They can't help themselves according to what you said."

She looked at him peevishly. Was she being hoisted on her own petard? "That's just rhetoric. It isn't true. Not really."

"How not really? Dismissing something isn't the same as disproving it."

"Do you really want women to be like, 'Oh, Kevin dear, I made you your favorite meal, I washed your favorite shirt, I'm wearing your favorite perfume. Oh darling!' " she simpered adding, "Is that what you want?"

"You tell me," he said stopping her and making her face him directly.

She looked away after a moment. "No, I guess not."

"Don't presume it of any man, then, either. Mockery and sarcasm aren't arguments either. At least not civil ones. People do have different roles, you know."

She had been humbled to being less willful or spirited at the moment. "What if some women don't want such roles? Does everybody have to fit in a box of what's expected of them because they're male or female?"

"Yes, to some extent, but obviously, there are a lot of misfits in the world. Are you saying you're one of them or want to be? That doesn't sound like a happy life."

"I don't know. I'm not happy now, so why should I expect to be happy later?"

He considered a number of things to say, but thought better of it. Her admission didn't so much surprise him as it seemed to surprise her. A self-confession blurted out. A sudden realization -- if I can't be happy with Kevin, with knowledge and learning, with having children and raising them, what can I be happy with? Anything? What does make me happy, she wondered? What is it that I truly love about being alive? She liked a lot of things, she thought. Enjoyed most aspects about life, she supposed, but what do I really love apart from proving how smart I am, how much I admire my own thoughts about everything?

It also occurred to her that if she wanted to change anything about herself, she had no idea of how to go about it. She turned away from him.

"I'll talk to you later," she said and began to walk away.

He watched her go, shaking his head a little as he thought, "That is not the kind of girl I want to marry. I want someone who's basically happy who I can please. Someone who appreciates me." His psych professor told the class that people change but little over the course of their lives. Look around at your classmates. What you see now is pretty much what you'll get later.

The Fighting Whities Redux
Part Three

Four other teams in college football remained unbeaten: USC in the Pac-12, LSU and Alabama in the SEC, and Ohio State in the Big Ten (although it actually had more than ten teams, it retained the moniker for some reason).

The Crusaders had gotten to where they were, ostensibly, as sportswriters claimed, because they were in a weak conference. But their first victories came against non-conference teams Cal and Notre Dame. Cal was the favorite, but were easily defeated 35 - 20. Notre Dame which saw WCC as a tune-up game, adjusted their threat assessment accordingly and were ready to play The Crusaders at home in Indiana.

The Crusaders shocked The Fighting Irish with three touchdowns in the first half, but diminished their advantage when Allard, from their twenty-five, threw an interception returned for an ND touchdown at the end of the first half.

Shut out in the second half except for a field goal, The Crusader's defense began to weaken and gave up two touchdowns with the Irish marching down the field in the closing minutes until an interception in the end zone concluded the game, as the Crusaders ran out the clock with their last possession.

The national sports media looked up at the result, but mostly to reassess Notre Dame's program that year rather than buying stock in WCC.

After crushing Fresno and Colorado State, neither ranked teams, they came up against former conference team, now independent, BYU, a western powerhouse.

They began with a nervous start, falling behind by ten points, then rallied late in the second quarter with a breakaway run by Kevin for forty-five yards, and a subsequent touchdown pass. On the ensuing kickoff, BYU fumbled, WCC recovered the ball and kicked a field goal in the waning period to tie the score.

Coming out in the second half, they scored again on their first drive, their third, their fourth, and fifth, holding BYU to two field goals. Final score 27 - 16.

The sports media took notice, but little more than that. WCC then ran the table with the rest of the conference, usually in blow out fashion leaving the last two games with Boise State (10 -1) and UNLV (9 - 2). Boise was ranked in the top ten, UNLV at 18 in the BCS standings.

They played Boise on its odd, blue colored astro-turf field the Saturday before Janet's classroom debate.

The game proved to be a national favorite as it turned into a shootout with The Crusaders winning in the second overtime 51 - 45. Now, the press turned its attention to WCC, and the possibility of a national title rearing its head if they could beat UNLV. It also brought up the unspoken problem of how to talk about an all white team.

"Coach Colson, what do you have to say about why you have no black players on your team?"

"I don't have much of anything to say about it."

"But there has to be a reason you don't recruit blacks to play for you?" he was pressed.

"Look. What would be the point to go out and get a couple of black players to come here to a Christian college in Wyoming where they're likely to not feel at home, having no community of their own to support them in terms of socializing and entertainment. I have no real means of enticing the best black players to come here so why would we waste the resources to try? Particularly since this is the first year we've shown that we can be a great platform in showcasing their talents and abilities," he concluded, hoping that would allay any obvious charges of racism.

"But Brigham Young and Boise State recruit blacks. Are blacks more comfortable there? Is there more community there? And isn't BYU a Mormon school? Wouldn't that make it even more uncomfortable for the players?"

"C'mon, when we started our program as a Division II team, our strategy was to recruit talented players or those we thought had potential to develop that were overlooked by other teams. It worked for us and we're sticking to it. We scour the country for young men who look like no one else wants them. That makes our team highly motivated."

"That kid Worley was recruited by Stanford, though."

"We were surprised they were as interested in him as you were, and you notice that Kevin didn't come to us as an overlooked high school athlete. He came as a hardship transfer."

"Stanford says you poached him."

"They can say what they want, but I doubt they'll tell you the truth about his situation."

"What's that mean, coach?"

"Maybe their side of the story isn't the only one. Isn't it your guys' job to investigate and not just quote people with an axe to grind?"

****

As high pitched in intensity the game with UNLV was expected to be, it turned out to be anti-climactic. Anyone who was rooting for The Rebels to put a stop to WCC's streak was greatly disappointed. Las Vegas was blown out 49 - 13.

It was what was happening elsewhere that was truly exciting to college football fans since no one seriously believed that WCC would be picked for the BCS championship game.

But the week before, LSU lost to Alabama leaving three other undefeated teams for the final week. As WCC was beating UNLV, all eyes were glued on Alabama that was loosing to

Georgia. Then there was the USC - UCLA game, and Ohio versus Michigan.

All three of those unbeaten teams lost. Alabama in overtime, USC by a last second field goal, and Ohio had their heads handed to them by a fired up Wolverine team and five turnovers.

Decades before when Boise State first ascended in the standings nationally and was one of the two unbeaten teams in the country, the BCS committee passed them by. Yet they won their major bowl game and were the only undefeated team that year. Did the BCS officials intend to make the same mistake again?

It took a week to decide, but Alabama and The Crusaders were going to the Rose Bowl for the Championship Game.

****

Sportswriters needing any sort of controversy to exploit to grab eyes or ears couldn't resist making Wyoming the bad guys who were clearly racist and deserved the beating they were going to get from 67% black Alabama. (It would have been over 70% if not for the expulsions and criminal convictions of some of the players.)

Outside of the South, though, walk into any bar where white patrons go, and you'd find everyone rooting for the Crusaders, while heated debates went on as to who had the better team. An old moniker was resurrected that some basketball team of American Indians had come up with to mock whites by calling themselves The Fighting Whities. But whites didn't take it indignantly as a horrible racial slur. They weren't offended, but instead, had cheerfully embraced it, and the name faded for lack of insult. Now T-shirts and sweaters were being produced with the name and happily worn by fans.

The sportswriters and broadcasters were correct, though, about the situation with Wyoming except they needed to swap out the word racist for racial.

Coach Colson didn't want black players on his team. Despite their athleticism, he knew they were more trouble than they were worth. He expected the game to be brutal and wondered if the referees would call it fairly.

In previous games against majority black teams, the words and assaults on field got vicious: lots of racist trash talk directed at his players, lots of late hits, cheap shots, and taunting. He had to prepare the team for what it would face, but they already knew, and had their own strategies.

It was a famous dictum of on-field fights that it was almost always the player who retaliated to a push or a punch who drew the penalty, and so Crusader players learned how to deliver stealthy blows to a loud mouth thug, absorb the retaliation, and get the call to go their way; then laugh at their victim, ask him where his daddy was, call his mother a slut, and get into the guy's head so much the player became overly aggressive and ignored playing the game the way he'd been coached. There was nothing most black players hated more than being shown up by a white guy.

Thus, the Rose Bowl game was keyed up like a fight of the century event.

At first, though, it looked like it was going to be the mismatch of the decade.

The Crusaders received the ball to start the game. On the second run from scrimmage, Kevin broke through the line, split a pair of linebackers, knocked over a safety, and ran for seventeen yards until a cornerback collided with him on a slant and knocked him down. Whereupon the defensive back hopped up, did a dance around Kevin and drew a fifteen-yard penalty for taunting. Then there was a flag for unsportsmanlike conduct a few plays later, and then one for pass interference, and before you knew it, Kevin ran the ball in from the six and WCC led by seven.

The same things happened when Alabama went on offense. A halfback ran for six yards, popped up and put his face into his tackler's and proceeded to run his mouth. Fifteen yards backwards they went.

Wyoming received the punt, returned it thirty yards, and were shortly in the red zone where Kevin caught a screen pass and got his second score.

If things were chippy to start, they got worse. The Fighting Whities used their strategies to slander, insult, and call their opponents n****rs just loud enough for them to hear it while the refs didn't. They found ways to slip a hand in to pinch a guy in the pile, twist their skin hard, which would cause him to erupt and get a penalty.

The Crusaders led 24 - 7 by the end of the half and all the sportscasters could talk about was the lack of discipline on Alabama's part, not that Wyoming was better. In fact, though, Worley had 68 yards in rushing, and Allard had 147 in passing.

"Look," Colson told his team during halftime. "They came out emotional like we thought they would and you made them pay for it, but don't expect that in the second half. They will calm down, their anger will dissipate, they'll focus on what they have to do to get back in the game. We're going to have to grind it out unless we beat their defense badly in the middle, or our offensive line can open up holes for the backs to break out for first down runs or more . . . defense, it may all ride on you guys. Let's help them make mistakes, cause turnovers, get some sacks. If they come out running, we need some stops. We're going to stay aggressive on offense. We're not going to try and run out the clock. We might try and make them think that's what we're doing, though. Three runs into the center of the line until we have to punt, and then we fake it! That kind of thing, so don't get worried if we look conservative at times. That's just to fool them. Not us. So, men take some time to relax, focus on the task, visualize your opponent, go over what's worked against him and what hasn't. When the coaches and I come back in here, we're going to think mean. Calm, intentional, ready, with a quiet conviction of just how mean we are; especially when we've got our opponent down. Killer instinct, boys. Killer instinct."

With that, Colson grouped with his coaches to go over their stats, and adjust their game plan.

In the other locker room, head coach Donner, sent his black assistant coach to ream out the players. "And another thing. The first player I see get another penalty for the kind of crap you've been doin', not only will they be pulled out of the game, they'll be sent off the field. You'll take a walk of shame, and we'll think about whether we need you next year if you're not a senior."

Donner was white, of course. For a 90% white Southern school, that's how it was in the tradition of Bear Bryant, Nick Saban, and now, Tom Donner.

He let the players stew while he went over the game plan and with a few minutes left, came in and spoke to them.

"I hope you got all the stupidity out of your system, because now it's time to play like men and show the world what an Alabama team can do when they play within themselves, in control, and full of focus and purpose. We're going to go out there in the second half and kick their asses up and down the field. And we'll do it the right way. In control. Your pleasure will come from dominating your opponent and not from shouting at him that you're going to kick his ass while it's your ass that's the one getting kicked. Is that clear!?"

"Yes, coach! Tha's righ'!"

"We're going to open up holes, make good tackles, leave the play, huddle up, and then do it again and again until they're crying as they watch their lead disappear. You're going to see their heads drop, watch their eyes look confused, stare at one another because they can't believe what's happening. Isn't that right!"

"Tha's righ'! Tha's righ', coach!"

"You're going to stop caring what they say about your momma or your daddy because you'll be having too much fun beating them up and down the field. Isn't that a fact!"

"Yes suh! Yes suh!"

"All right. Now let's go out there and show the world what we're made of."

****

Alabama received the kickoff to start the second half and had a good return to their forty-two yard line.

Three plays later, their receiver was dancing in the end zone. Donner was right, they were going to prove they were much better than the Whities. Just like they always do. A lot of heads were nodding on their sidelines, smiles breaking out and laughter. Alabama was back. This was going to be fun.

But Wyoming returned the ensuing kickoff back to Alabama's thirty-nine. Five plays later, Worley broke through a hole into the end zone. Score 31 - 14.

Alabama scored a field goal on their next series. The kickoff was a touchback in the end zone as Wyoming took the ball on their twenty-five. Three running plays into the line resulted in a first down, taking time off the clock. Three more running plays resulted in another first down. Then three more running plays into the line left them three yards short at midfield where they set up to punt having run five minutes off the clock.

Just as promised, they tried a fake play and the punter ran for eighteen yards. They pounded the ball again for two series, barely getting first downs, but getting them, indeed, when on the first play of the next series, Allard ran a play action fake, found a receiver on a slant route and it was off to the races and a touchdown. 38 - 17.

Not an impossible number in college ball. That's merely three touchdowns and there were fifteen minutes left, but there were no smiles on Alabama's sideline.

They managed another ten points while holding Wyoming from further scores, but with six minutes to play, the Crusaders were marching down the field. Alabama couldn't overpower the offensive line and Kevin pounded out the yardage. He was coming up on 150 yards thus far. Finally, with two minutes left, Worley broke through once again from the seven and scored. Trotting in, casually dropping the ball, he was speared from behind by a black linebacker low in the small of his back. It was clearly after the play was over. Worley crumbled to the ground. The linebacker jumped up, stood over him and asked him, "How you like that, you sorry ass mother****er!"

Flags were thrown, the Wyoming players tackled the linebacker as punches flew, the benches emptied and a melee ensued, all the while Kevin lay on the ground not moving as far as anyone could see. Trainers and doctors immediately rushed out to him, but it took minutes to restore order to the game. The black player was ejected, flags thrown against both teams. The field was cleared, but Worley was down and being carefully administered to with a neck brace put in place and eventually being turned onto a board, raised into an ambulance and driven out of the Rose Bowl.

TV cameras focusing close up on him could discern only the slightest movement in his hands, but weren't certain if that was him doing it or from being handled and moved.

TV sets in barrooms and living rooms across America were screamed at with every epithet people could think of. In fact, a tide was turned that night. Alabama, The Crimson Tide went from being a respected national icon, an institution, to a despised group in an instant, and it didn't change in time. The coach and staff were fired.

It was as if whites, nationally, understood for the first time just how much blacks hated them, and there was no going back to any delusion about it. They realized that blacks and whites, as groups would never be able to live with each other.

The last two minutes of the game went on, of course, but the end soon came and Wyoming had won. Alabama was booed by the people in the stadium the whole time they had the ball in those last minutes, as the Alabama fans, nearly all whites, were silent, ashamed, grim, and depressed.

The sportscasters who had built the game into a black and white issue where the whites were the evil racists wrung their hands in the aftermath, some even asking whites not to seek revenge, but be forbearing because of the racial overtones, while black color commentators and personalities were stunned. They could only shake their heads ruefully. They understood the implications of what had occurred.

Early reports from the hospital where Kevin had been taken were gloomy. He appeared paralyzed, perhaps from the shoulders down, but they weren't certain how damaged his spine was. He was rushed into surgery after X-rays showed damaged vertabrae. Afterwards, the doctors were "cautiously optimistic" but wouldn't know until Kevin recovered from the operation and they could take more tests.

Even so, medical science had made some amazing progress with spinal cord injuries, particularly if they could treat it quickly enough. Worley had been paralyzed from the hips down, but it looked like he would eventually be able to walk again. It was simply going to take a few years and lots of therapy and further treatment.

It was many months before he could resume classes in a wheelchair, though, and by then, Janet had moved on. She told him that hospitals creeped her out. A lot of people feel that way.

Football was out of the question as far as the future went, but Kevin would never need to worry about a job or money. He was a national hero and a local icon. The alumni of WCC would always be there for him. They had a national championship, a national fan base, and a growing regional identity that was consolidating or coalescing into a political and economic force.

Kevin and his family would be part of that.

Mexifornia

"It's deja vu all over again," General Bruster remarked to his staff soon after the invasion of Oregon had begun. Oregon had more people, but like Washington, was less diverse. The white population being expelled was generally compliant, and minorities were small in number and impotent to impede the NAR's progress. Bruster liked to joke about just how progressive the NAR army was.

Yet, between Washington and Oregon, some eight and a half million whites had been driven south past Redding, California and perhaps two million others who were black, Asian, and Latino.

An expulsion like this had occurred in Europe at the end of World War Two when millions of Germans residing in western Poland, Czechoslovakia, and elsewhere were driven to Germany in chaos and revenge. Few knew about it, and fewer mourned their fate given what the Germans had done in the previous years to anyone opposed to their conquests.

Nearly all other nations of the world condemned the NAR but attempts at embargo and laying economic sanctions against it were as effective as they have always been -- only a little. The NAR was nearly self-sufficient in energy, metals, minerals, manufacturing, and food. With the acquisition of the West Coast, particularly California, they would have perhaps the pre-eminent center of the world in fruit, vegetables, and fiber (cotton), rice, and corn.

But California, despite it's dwindling white population (a population that was to be expelled by 75% of it numbers along with millions of blacks and Asians, along with many many millions of Mexicans) was logistical nightmare.

General Bruster expected fierce resistance from the Mexicans and blacks. Robertson explained the situation. "They've had two years to prepare. They are currently stockpiling food, water, and ammunition, and whatever explosives they can get their hands on. The Federal government has been supplementing them with supplies and ordinance. Usually they would restrict it to the National Guard, but in this case they aren't worried about arming thugs, criminals, and gangsters. They just want to see if they can stop us and make us pay. The Mexicans are a naturally bellicose people. The men enjoy a good fight and look forward to it. They have plenty of courage, but lack discipline and follow through since they tend toward laziness and fatalism. The blacks, well, they lack courage, discipline, and adaptability. Take 'em out of the ghetto and they're lost."

"Yes, but the point is they won't be going out of their ghettos and it might be like Warsaw in 1944. Didn't the Jews hold out for about two months? And without any arms to speak of. Not like what we see being distributed and cached," General Bruster replied.

"Look," Robertson offered. "We have what? Five or six areas to worry about? Some of Sacramento County, Richmond, Oakland, San Jose, parts of Hayward, and then nothing much until Stockton, Modesto, Fresno, places like that until we hit the Southland. There's no way around staging sieges as far as I can see it."

"There's going to be thousands of dead if we go that route," Col. Meechum replied.

"What do you suggest?"

"There's no way around it. Preemptive strikes. We have the drones, we know the traffic patterns around gang houses. We hit them all one night. We let the smoke clear, study the traffic patterns as they regroup, hit them again and again like that. When the neighborhoods are mostly clear, we send in the Scan teams to mop up."

"A lot of innocents will die," Robertson responded.

"Better them than us," Meechum said.

Gen. Bruster agreed.

Robertson had to admit there was no way around the fact that they were pushing millions up against a wall, and a lot of those would fight back. This was where a General admitted he was going to be a part of mass murder, killings certainly, and to suck it up, accept it, and condemn himself to hell for the greater good of his people and their future generations. But eating that meal of conviction and purpose was wormwood and gall.

The general strategy of removal had been significantly altered, too, given the massive numbers of people and an attempt to use them in colonizing northern Mexico in stages, all while holding the Mexican army at bay (who were sure to be reinforced by sympathetic Central and South American governments with arms and men) was dicey.

Whereas before, people had been given the freedom to load up their vehicles, carry arms, and drive south -- that could no longer work. People had to be separated from weapons and all their goods except for a suitcase. Then they would be transported either by bus, train, or plane. A thousand buses carrying 50 people a day means that 300,000 a week (Sundays off) were transferred. Thus, the operation, conquest of northern Mexico and relocation of the people of California (and those driven into Arizona) had to be simultaneous.

But how were they going to stop all the millions of people who would be loading up their vehicles and taking off ahead of any organization?

"The roads will be madness," Robertson said. "We can close them, shut them down, but we're still talking about tens of thousands, maybe hundreds of thousands of vehicles trying to drive away, stuck in traffic. It'll be chaos like we've never seen it. There won't be a controlled evacuation in stages like before."

"If we can get our men in position before a general panic starts, close the bridges, the Interstates, major highways and arteries, we might be able to staunch the bleeding."

"Think of the manpower, and the fact that they'll be outnumbered by law enforcement, if they decide to fight, and gangsters or guys with guns. How do we relieve them, keep them supplied, when they're scattered throughout the whole region? It's a logistical nightmare," Robertson added rubbing his hand through his short hair. "Gen. Bruster, it's all about logistics now. We have ten divisions and we're about to split those forces. Gen. Anthony in Arizona has seven. There's no question we can drive these people south, but not in any orderly way. We don't have the men."

Gen. Bruster tapped the table with his fingers and he considered the situation.

"I can get four more divisions," he said, and held up his hand to forestall the complaint sure to arise. "That's not enough. I know. But what if we organize a civilian militia from Washington, Oregon, and northern Cal? Maybe it's time for those folks we spared from tyranny, who've been enjoying lower taxes and the acquisition of property cheaply, maybe they need to contribute something to the cause. A few bodies. How many do we need?"

"How about a hundred thousand?" Robertson said.

"General, there's no time to train them," Col. Ewells complained. He was in the Quartermaster Corps and Planning and Logistics for Bruster.

"We split units and stick them in with them. I mean, how much training does it take to carry a rifle and direct traffic? They'll learn on the job," Bruster decided.

Meechum shook his head at the vision of all the headaches that would cause.

That was the plan. To pounce on northern California from Redding to Sacramento and San Jose, clamp down immediate all the vehicle traffic in the region, and lay siege in the areas that were resistant to friendly persuasion.

They also had to contend with the Governor and his National Guard that blocked the roads south of Redding, along the coast, and east of the Cascades.

Once they destroyed the National Guard's will to fight, they would have a two front war going (at least. Who knew what other countries or States might do if motivated? Where did Texas stand, a majority Hispanic State, for example? Would they muster arms and come to the aid of other Latinos? It seemed likely.)

Then half their army had to leapfrog to the border with Mexico and wage war there while the rest funneled the masses for resettlement working their way down the State while Gen. Anthony coordinated the same basic plan in Arizona.

****

It was late winter as the column halted on Interstate Five along Lake Shasta. General Bruster and his staff got out of their vehicles. A sergeant ran up and handed him a white flag on a short pole. He gave it to his adjutant. General Robertson was similarly standing by on Highway One, while General Erwin was waiting near the Donner Pass on Interstate Eighty.

Directly ahead, further up the highway stood the second in command of the California National Guard. Between the two forces stood the bridge over the lake. It was heavily mined to destroy the roadbed if need be.

Bruster, his adjutant and three of his staff, began to walk towards the Californians, their white flag clear to see. As they approached the bridge, they were ordered to halt from a distance. They stopped and saw that the Californian general and a few of his men began the long walk towards them. The bridge was about 1000 meters long, which took about twenty minutes to cross.

As the Guard commander approached Bruster and his group, neither side offered their hands for shaking.

"I'm General Dillon of the California National Guard, these are my staff officers, Col. Grimes and Maj. Andrews. I'm here to inform you that you have illegally invaded this State and nation and are hereby ordered to leave. If you attempt to come any further, I will do everything in my power to prevent you from doing so."

Gen. Bruster nodded. "I understand, General, but if you would, I ask for a moment's indulgence. If I am correct, I believe that air forces and men of the NAR are currently occupying every major airport and military airfield along with small aircraft fields in northern California. Your Air Guard jets in the air currently have no place to land, and our laser drones are capable of shooting them down."

While they had been speaking, a large number of Stealth drones had landed in every airport and taken up position on runways. The control towers were informed that the drones were filled with high explosives and would detonate if approached. They effectively closed all the northern region's air traffic. Planes approaching for landing were rerouted south or east.

"I am aware that we do not have your capabilities," Gen. Dillon responded.

"What about your chain of command starting with the governor? I believe that he, the lieutenant governor, and other State officials are either currently captured or being captured. I also believe your own commanding general's headquarters has been captured. And if not, is under siege and soon will be."

Large numbers of Special Forces of the NAR had infiltrated Sacramento and taken control of the Capitol building, visiting various homes in the area of elected officials and taken them into custody.

"If you would like to confirm that with your people, please do so."

Dillon walking away from Bruster back towards the bridge, took out a small radio and began his inquiries. He became animated over the next few minutes as news was received of the kind of things Bruster had claimed to be happening. Concluding his conversation, agitated and angry as he returned to Bruster, he barked, "You sir, will find that I am not so easily overpowered. We will fight you. Tooth and nail if need be, but we will fight!"

Bruster again nodded. "Yes, General. I know you can put up a very brave fight. But we both know you will lose, and what would be the point? Let us sit down and reason together, shall we?"

General Dillon's face betrayed his anguish. He looked away, his mouth grimacing as he tried to process his impotence. His was a lost cause, and he wasn't even likely to get a shot off at the enemy just to make himself feel better because he knew it was senseless to lead his men into slaughter.

Nor was it funny that he, from a family native to California for six generations, hated what had happened to his State, hated the politicians and what they'd done, should have to surrender his State to these people he mostly agreed with.

He finally turned back to Bruster. "May we keep our arms?"

"Only if any of you care to join us."

He grimaced again. "I can't do that."

"But some of your men might. There are benefits to being on our side."

"I can't stop you from speaking to them. We'll arrange the surrender as soon as we can. Right now, I shall notify my officers on the Coast and in the Sierras to stand down and comply with your officers."

"Thank you, but I have to tell you that any sudden retreat will result in attack and destruction of your forces. Even if your men leave the roads for the woods and fields, the drones will track them. Also, we will allow your fighter jets and bombers to land, but the crews must surrender their aircraft and themselves once down."

This time Dillon nodded, turned and began the long walk back to his side.

Bruster turned to his adjutant and told him, "I want all those soldiers and officers put on the non-evacuation list. Let them know it, and give them authorization papers and codes to present if challenged by anyone. I don't want any of them accidently forced out of their homes."

"Yes sir."

****

Corporal Johnny Coe sat with his squad listening to his captain inform Company C what the plan was for evacuating most of the people from northern California south of Redding to the Bay Area. It wasn't at all the same as they'd used in Oregon and Washington.

"Any questions?" the captain concluded.

"Yes, sir!" Cpl. Coe was first to blurt out.

"Yes, corporal, what is it?"

"Well, sir, I'm trying to wrap my brain around these changes. It seems like you're saying that we're going to surround large areas and just let the people inside go hog wild or something. I don't get it. Why not do what we've been doing? Seemed to work fine. Most people have gone along."

"Were you a part of the teams that cleared out Central District in Seattle?"

"No, sir."

"What about in St. John's in Portland?"

"No, sir."

"Talk to those who were there. We're coming into serious resistance, men. We're going to bomb them and starve them out. No food. No water. No power. But we know they're armed, and so until they're ready to crawl out on their own in surrender, they're living on an island. They can burn it down for all we care."

Someone near by snorted, "That'll improve Oakland." Another laughed.

Johnny had no idea what Oakland was like. Was it like Detroit? He'd heard about that place.

Since he'd joined the army, mostly to get away from his wife and three small daughters where he lived near Ranchester, Wyoming, he'd been pleasantly surprised to find going to war not so fierce an undertaking after all. And his share of all the property they'd liberated was going to be quite a nice chunk of money. Now it was starting to look scary, but at least his unit wasn't going immediately south to engage the Mexican army. Company C with it's various platoons would be camping on a highway somewhere and impeding traffic until that was sorted out, and then they'd be laying siege to uncooperative parties; the natives being restless, and all.

The thought of it made him mentally recite: *Now I lay me down to sleep, I pray the Lord my soul to keep*. Knock on wood.

****

After the surrender of the California National Guard, the NAR Fourth Army rapidly deployed south, bypassing minor cities such as Petaluma, Santa Rosa and others in order to deploy rifle platoons along the Interstates and other highways. Beginning at San Raphael, Vallejo, and past Sacramento, units were stationed every five to ten miles on the roadbeds themselves with barriers set up as time and logistics permitted.

Ideally, half a platoon (about twenty men) would barricade each side of the freeway (if divided), usually before an overpass. They didn't have to barricade the strip of land dividing the freeway, then, if it wasn't elevated.

Using the safety water barrels that were placed in front of concrete abutments, they filled them with sand and created a zigzag to allow emergency vehicles through or various tractor trailers hauling food and supplies or buses headed south with reluctant passengers.

People awoke in the morning to find travel, except on surface streets, curtailed. The business then of granting travel permits (and tracking modules) to doctors, nurses, nursing home facilities, first responders, along with utility workers began.

Early morning, around 4:00 am, while the platoons deployed on the roads, the drones unleashed their missiles at hundreds of targets spread throughout the region at known and supposed gang houses. Each missile killed at least two people, usually more. Perhaps a thousand people died in the first fusillade against resisters.

If there were any secondary explosions as a result, stored ammunition and other ordinance blowing up due to ensuing fires or volatile response to the warheads, that was counted as a great success, but didn't occur as often as hoped.

All the TV and radio mass media outlets were taken over (or shut down as redundant) with various General Order instructions given to the public. Most people were under curfew except those mentioned above and people whose jobs involved acquisition and distribution of food and medicine (sometimes energy supplies but with restricted vehicle traffic, gas stations remained stocked).

In the third day of the occupation, 3rd Platoon Company C, was stationed in the middle of I 880 in San Jose on an elevated roadbed. Halves of the platoon were positioned across from each other on the divided highway. The gap was too far to bridge so any traffic between the two units could only be accomplished by exiting and then entering the other side through the cloverleaf underneath them.

On the southbound side, Cpl. Johnny Coe sat in a lawn chair (appropriated for army use by verbal requisition - "thanks, we'll be taking these, bill the army") not far from the Porta-Potty (also conveniently requisitioned) eating an MRE, and complaining as usual about it.

"Hamburger. God, I hate this crap," he said to know one in particular.

"Actually, they taste pretty good to me. I'm surprised," Pvt. Russell Porter contradicted.

"Yeah? How long you been eating them? What, a week? Yeah, they don't seem so bad at first but try loving them after two years. Sheesh."

A number of other heads nodded.

"Rookies!" someone else snorted.

Four new men had been assigned to the squads. One of them was forty-year old Russell Porter from Bellingham, Washington. Two months ago he was selling hardware in his store when the NAR swooped down and inducted him into the army, claiming that all able bodied men from 18 - 55 were members of the state militia and eligible for conscription.

He'd spent a month in basic training and then assigned a unit.

"Well, I saw through the binoculars that there's a McDonald's about have a mile down that road," another soldier stood up and pointed. "I say we make a run."

"Yeah, like Bluey (2nd. Lt. Blooner) would go for that," Coe responded.

"What he don't know . . ."

"Booker, you are an idiot. He's not gonna see our leftover MREs or the garbage?"

"Just chuck 'em all off the highway."

"Litterbug."

He shrugged.

"Say you need to go see the other squads for something, make a quick run and then come back. What could be simpler?"

"Your ass being court martialed."

"Hmm," Porter considered. "What if they delivered?"

"McDees doesn't do delivery you dumb web footed bohunk."

"Well, let's see. Saying they have supplies for food, and people at work, and needing to make some money now that people aren't driving around so much, what are the odds that someone won't take the initiative and make deliveries," Porter concluded.

"He has a point," Coe said.

"One other thing, though," Porter added.

"What's that?"

"You want to take a chance of someone messing with your food? You think the people in the store love you for what you're doing here?"

"What do you mean "you"? It's we, Rook. It's we," Booker told him.

"Yeah, you're right. I'm just not yet used to being, well, being one of you guys," Porter said.

"You make that sound like there's something wrong with being one of us guys."

"No, no, no. I didn't mean it like that. I just never thought I'd be in the army. That's all."

"You found a new home in the army, son. Welcome. One big happy family, you know. One for all and all for one," Coe laughed.

Another soldier called Mimic due to his use of various accents threw in an Indian response, "Oh me oh my, jolly good fun. Gin and tonics all around."

"Okay, I say we call McDonald's give them our order and tell them we'll blow them up to smithereens if they tamper with the food. How about that?"

"Do the phones work?"

"The internet is still running, annnnnd . . . I'm looking up local McDees, annnnnd . . . I have a number," Booker told them as he played with his personal phone. "It's ringing now. 'Yes, hello? Yes, hi, this might sound odd, but can you make a delivery? No, wait. Look. It's a big order . . . have you got food? Yeah? That's great. Well, look we're the men of Company C about half a mile from your store . . . on the freeway . . . yeah, soldiers . . . yeah, NAR.' He just clammed up, guys. He's thinking it over. 'What's that? You'll sell us some food and deliver it? Okay, but here's the deal . . . no, we aren't gonna steal it, fer Christ's sake, just listen. Maybe you or somebody there don't love us so much and wanna mess with our food or something right? You understand? You do. That's great, well, we'll be checking the food real careful and if anything doesn't look right, well, let's just say the result might be a bit unpleasant . . . no, I'm not questioning your integrity (whatever that is). I'm just sayin', if it isn't right you might get a more serious response than a bad review on Yelp or something . . . I'm glad we understand each other.' "

Booker started collecting and relaying the orders of everyone and totaling the cost from the store manager.

Forty-five minutes later, a small blue hybrid pulled up to their checkpoint (the exits and on ramps weren't blocked since a vehicle couldn't go very far anyhow). A Latino looking man, the manager, they guessed, got out with some five or six bags of their order. Cpl. Coe took them and divvied them out. All of the men examined their food for contamination, while Booker simply opened a box and started eating.

"Hey, I trust 'em," he said. "Like they don't know what will happen if they mess with us," he laughed.

"Fookin' 'eathens," Mimic added in his best Cockney.

The radio buzzed. It was Sgt. Teller from the other side of the freeway. They'd been watching through binocs at the activity on this side and wanted to know what was going on. Coe explained it to them, and they decided to emulate the fine initiative demonstrated by the squads of southbound I 880.

When Lt. Blooner reported back to his men after having met his superiors twenty miles up the road for the daily briefing, it didn't take him long to smell out a change of attitude and morale, and coming across a scrap of a wrapper which hadn't made it over the side, he put it together.

"Did you save anything for me, Coe?"

"Sorry, sir. Booker, that pig, ate your portion."

"I did not!" he protested.

Bluey, as they called him, asked for more info, considered what to do about it if anything, and decided that, perhaps, discretion was the better part of valor. As long as the men were careful, maintained guard and readiness, what could it hurt? He wasn't going to be a hard core, iron ass killjoy on this. Maybe, he'd let them do it once every other day. After all, they expected to be here at least a month. By then, maybe McDonald's and the other restaurants would be out of food or business.

Every three days or so in the early morning hours, the men could see drone strikes taking place, houses going up in flames. Porter couldn't bring himself to cheer like most of the others, "take that ya fookin' 'eathens!" they'd laugh, having adopted Mimic's term of endearment towards the enemy.

****

Over the next few weeks, the squads kept ordering food from McDonalds, usually every other day, and different vehicles and people would deliver it to them.

Bluey was concerned about his raw recruits and so devised further training exercises. Targets, mobile and stationary were set up for them to practice firing live rounds. They had to field strip, clean, and reassemble their weapons. Tactics in advance and cover, then retreat and cover were practiced as best as possible in various scenarios on the freeway, using whatever materials they could find to set up pretend machine gun nests or enemy forces in cover. They had to walk through or go half speed through some of the drills since they were working on concrete roadbeds, and Bluey had the Sgt.s and Cpl.s make them recite procedures and instructions until they understood how they operated in various conditions.

Bluey figured it was better for the rookies to have at least a mental picture of what they needed to know and do even if they couldn't instill muscle memory through field exercises at real training centers.

Porter, being the oldest, was naturally tagged as Gramps.

In that same period, the drone strikes at night decreased, and a steady number of the relocation buses featured blacks and browns, whereas at first they'd been exclusively whites. It appeared they were making a dent on the millions in the region.

****

It was now mid-March, and the traffic of the day had slowed with the nearing of curfew. Company C had called in their order over an hour before, but the manager complained about getting shorthanded because of you know what.

It was dusk when the big, dark SUV rolled up to the checkpoint, and the young men who'd just settled down into their lawn chairs began to rouse themselves out of them when the doors of the SUV swung open and Mexicans poured out firing automatic machine guns at the NAR squads while a pair from the rear hopped out with an RPG each.

NAR men dove onto the hard roadbed, scrambling for their weapons that weren't far from them. Bluey had been standing when the SUV arrived and was stippled with a number of rounds and went down hard.

On the northbound side, the squads reacted, but the Mexicans were shielded by their big, long vehicle. Cpl. Coe had his weapon, and crouching low, began to run up the zigzag, protected by the sand filled barrels. Porter, seeing him taking off to engage the enemy automatically went after him for no reason he could think of except that he thought Coe needed some help.

Bending low and trying to move along, one of the Mexicans saw the movement while his companions continued their spray and pray tactics. He lowered the barrel of the RPG and fired. Sand barrels exploded at the side of him, while the other Mexican lowered his and fired closer to where Coe had gone.

Another explosion of sand, and the blast sent Coe sprawling. A Mexican appeared in the gap and entrance of the zigzag and fired on the fallen Coe and then lifted his gun and aimed at Porter. Bullets struck the two soldiers, but the Mexican had exposed himself to fire from the platoon across the way and was cut down in a hail of fire.

Another RPG was fired ineffectively, as all the soldiers who could take cover behind the sand barriers had done so, while a few had gotten behind the APC stationed close by. Grenades were thrown, screams were heard, wild firing continued a brief while until it appeared all the Mexicans were down or dead. A few soldiers tentatively crept out to the enemy to secure the area, assess the situation, and examine their own casualties.

After kicking away his weapon, Booker called out, "Hey Sarge, this one's still alive. Want I should ice him?"

"Save him for IS," he heard back.

Booker peered inside the SUV. "Christ, they didn't even bring us our order. C'mon, Sarge, let me ice the motherf*****r."

Their medical corpsman had been pinned down by the APC, but was now at work examining the wounded. Soldiers from the other half of the platoon, including their corpsman had driven over as soon as they could, arriving half a minute after the firing had ceased.

All told, the raid had lasted about a minute and a half.

Lt. Blooner was groaning at the pain from his chest having absorbed three hammer blows, but his armor had stood the test, an incredible thin fabric that seemingly turned to steel and spread the impact energy of bullets at the same time. It still felt like hammer blows and left serious bruises. A hit at the right spot, could stop a heart, but Blooner was alive and relatively uninjured.

Coe and Porter were not so fortunate. Coe had caught two in the body, one through his left hand, and another in the helmet for a concussion while Porter was nearly deaf from the close blast, a small piece of shrapnel had hit his left eye, perhaps destroying it, and he'd been peppered three times in the body, two in the chest, one in the shoulder which had penetrated his light armor.

In a short while, army ambulances showed up and Coe and Porter were loaded on gurneys to share a trip to the field hospital.

"How you doin', Coho?" Booker asked him.

"Looks like I'll live."

"And you, Gramps?"

"Fookin' 'eathens," he grimaced.

"You tell 'em, Gramps. See you soon."

The rest of the platoon took hours trying to decompress from the brief, but adrenaline pumping, attack. They went over every detail again and again. Mostly trying to figure out what the fookin' 'eathens hoped to accomplish. The raid was suicidal. They wouldn't learn until much later how hopped up on drugs the brownies had been.

No wonder they hadn't thought things through. They just wanted a chance to revenge themselves on the soldiers that had bombed their friends in their houses, killing men, women, and children over and over.

Once they heard that the soldiers were getting orders delivered from McDees, the plan suggested itself. Perhaps, they figured they would drive up, kill them all, and quickly drive away. So, load up on oxycontin, tequila, maybe some meth, and *andale*, amigos, lets kill some gringos.

Gen. Robertson sent out an order curtailing the delivery of non-army food, but promised he'd see to it that hot Commissary meals made it to the men in the field at least three times a week. He also arranged for rotation of duty so that men could have days off and relax at a camp they'd set up at some amusement parks with hotels close by like Great America, and a few others in the region.

Marin, San Francisco, San Mateo, and parts of Santa Clara counties had been cleared. Large portions of the East Bay remained and San Jose, meanwhile forces had gone north to evacuate Petaluma, Santa Rosa and all the small towns and cities.

The other divisions under Gen Bruster had invaded Mexico proper and were dealing with the Mexican army in combat. Robertson wished he was there doing a real soldier's duty than this dirty work of herding people.

God help them when they came to LA and San Diego.

Endgame

Southern California was not as chaotic as Gen. Bruster had expected. The millions of whites driven out of Washington and Oregon had mostly scattered away from California, heading east to the Midwest and elsewhere, although there were a number of UN and NGO tent cities having been set up for many refugees, people too poor or broken down to make their way. Kind of like modern Okies.

Mexicans either returned to Mexico or went to Texas, Florida, or other States where they thought they had a chance of getting by.

Asians also went to Texas, Louisiana, and Gulf States where there were large numbers of people like themselves.

Blacks had long been under assault by Mexican gangs in LA and other cities, attacked on the fringes of their neighborhoods, forcing them to leave and head to the Southern States.

Having rolled south with 130,000 men, Bruster ignored the LA and Orange County region and poured into San Diego, instituting martial law.

Addressing his assembled staff and various liaison officers such as the Intelligence Service, Quartermaster Corps, and Congressional oversight teams, he asked for a complete update on the Mexican Army capabilities, "Can these people fight, and with what?"

"Well, they advertise an army of 180,000 men and half a million in Reserve, but they're lucky if they can field 120,000 equipped, and ready to move. As to their Reserves, smoke and mist. There's no unit loyalty or cohesion after a man leaves the ranks. There's no follow up training, field exercises, or monthly assemblies. They don't get paid so the former soldiers don't bother with maintaining any readiness, fitness, or bother to report to any duty," the IS colonel told them.

"But that may change once their national pride is wounded," a major put in.

"No doubt, but where do they get the arms to do anything about it?"

"From their Latin neighbors, from China and Russia. Who knows?"

"Perhaps," the colonel admitted, "but too late I think. We know that the Chinese and Russians have been advising their government to prepare to oppose us, but as far as our sources can tell us, the Mexicans have ignored their warnings and advice. They simply don't believe they're going to be invaded."

"Well, that's good news," Gen Bruster brightened. "Now, what are we facing?"

"They have no heavy armor. No tanks, a hundred or so light APCs, a dozen light armor urban patrol vehicles with small cannons, a dozen mounted artillery guns, twenty mobile howitzers, and a couple hundred humvees or the equivalent."

"Geez, you'd think they had no interest in self-defense at all," another officer said in amazement.

"Yup, and their air force is no better. They have a dozen airfields, a hundred fighter jets that are essentially obsolete. They have a few drones, but no anti- or counter-drone technology. It will be almost nothing to destroy their radar, ground their planes and their few helicopters. They will be blind in no time at all, along with their command and control centers."

"Why so toothless?" another man asked.

The IS colonel explained, "You have to understand that these Latin countries don't maintain armies to deal with external threats, but use them to suppress interior rebellions and riots. I mean, when has Brazil ever feared invasion? And Mexico? The last time was in 1846 when America attacked Mexico City and defeated them. The chase after Pancho Villa by Pershing was a joke. Complete folly."

"Is the Refugee Force ready to assume their duties?" Bruster asked.

"Yes, sir. They're in position now."

"Good. Well, in seven days then, our coordinated invasion will begin through Nogales, Mexicali, and Tijuana with a split to Ensenada."

****

They brought us down in these big black buses to a place called La Jolla, except that they pronounce it differently than the way it reads. At first when someone kept saying La Hoya, I didn't know what they were talking about.

Anyway, we're staying in the dorms of the University of Cal, San Diego. I guess classes have been suspended for the time being, and the NAR have put us up here.

There's over a thousand of us in the RF (Refugee Force). We've been trained by the NAR to do their dirty work. Oh sure, they tell us it's our job to secure our new homeland, that if we want to survive we'll have to fight, but it's just to salve their consciences -- this idea that we can somehow hold out against over a hundred million Mexicans who might want a large portion of their country back.

And us? How many of us are there going to be? They say seven - twelve million.

"Boo hoo hoo." That's what the NAR Major said when we complained about the odds. "You never heard of Israel? If those Jew bastards could hold off a couple hundred million A-rabs and Muslims, don't you think ten million white people can do the same to a bunch of dumb, corrupt, miserable, and poor Mestizos? You never heard of Cortez?"

"We're doin' all the heavy lifting here. All you gotta do is organize yourselves, maintain law and order, and set up your perimeters and defenses. Piece of cake you whining bunch of pussy faced crybabies."

But my captain in the RF explained it this way: "Look here, boys, this is the plan. They clear out Mexico including the Baja which is nice of them because they know we'll want a lot of oceanfront property to relax on, and then from Tijuana south to

Hermosillo and then across to Chihuahua and then up to Juarez. That's our new home sweet home."

"In the meantime, we have to take over what farms there are, what factories there are, what mines there are, and ranches, and figure out how to feed ourselves and make things we can sell to other people. And then we have to repel every attack the Mexicans make. Yeah, a real piece of cake. Easy as pie."

So, now we invade, secure power, water, sewage, law enforcement, government, and settle everyone.

Right now we wait. As soon as Tijuana and Mexicali are mostly cleared we follow up on their heels and all the white people from Nor Cal start coming in.

All the people like my dad and mom from the detention camps will be there right away, helping to organize. Well, it looks like life is going to get even more interesting for the, oh say, next fifty years or so.

****

In Northern California, the NAR had moved in and shut down airports and freeways so quickly that a large majority of the wealthy had been caught off guard and unable to flee. Also, the NAR had seized mortgage and savings banks along with investment banks and shut down financial trading.

Having considered Californians among the most egregious of the America-killing elite, the NAR confiscated their wealth, which would be put to use in establishing the Mexican Colony of refugees.

Of course, many of the rich were able to escape by boat or a few private planes here and there, but most of them were stuck and would be ferried south as future colonists. They might be capable of making their way to Mexico (if they weren't robbed and killed in revenge) or somehow get to Texas, but it wasn't going to be easy.

In Southern Cal, though, a great many more were able to get out of the State, quite a few with their fortunes intact and transferred elsewhere. A great number of movie stars, directors, and producers were caught flatfooted, though, and people throughout the world wrung their hands in trepidation that a great many celebrated people were *trapped* in the horrors of war, and who knew what might happen to those beautiful people?

Even in the midst of the Endless Recession, the wealth residing along the coast of California staggered the imagination. Hundreds and hundreds of thousands of people seemed to be unaffected by a half century of hard times, dwindled opportunities, and hopeless situations.

There were still trillions of dollars in money and property in the hands of the rich, and that would go a long way in paying for the Colony to get a firm footing. The NAR intended to dole out a bare bones budget to the provisional government for many years to come to keep corruption at a minimum.

Eventually, all the personal property, land, and houses seized by the NAR would be assessed (at their now lower contemporary value and a portion of their sale placed in an endowment for future reparations. Yes, the property was taken, but they intended to pay the owners something for it or use the money in resettlement). Still, they didn't want to make life easy for the refugees. Let the school of hard knocks teach a few lessons.

****

"There is a Division of the Mex army in Tijuana now. Apparently someone took some initiative in wondering what we might be doing massed at their border. We've located their bivouacs, barracks, camps and so on. Along with the police stations, they'll be disabled in an hour," Bruster's general of operations told him.

"It's oh four hundred now. Everything moves in at oh five thirty."

Before five am, hundreds of carrier bots snuck or were dropped into Tijuana loaded with thousands of mosquito drones. The "biting" injector drones were filled with a subtle neurotoxin. When injected into a human body, it acted locally in the muscles of a particular area where it damaged (but not destroyed) the nerves, rendering those muscles useless. It took three to five years for the nerves to repair themselves (faster with the right proprietary medicines the NAR possessed).

The "stings" were not generally fatal unless located in critical areas such as the diaphragm, the throat and windpipe, or into the heart. But stuck in the arm, leg, shoulder or back destroyed a soldier's ability to function in combat.

The NAR would be charged in the court of world opinion with war crimes for the use of a neurotoxin, but it seemed more humane to disable a soldier for a period of time than blow him up where he stood or lay.

It was demoralizing for the enemy, also, to immediately suffer a high number of casualties, and then there was the further pressure put on the government's budget and welfare system with having so many disabled men to care and pay for.

Other nations could develop similar tactics and weapons and use them against the NAR, of course, but first they would have to have them, and the NAR's specialization in miniature drones and bots of all kinds was still leading edge tech, and their great (temporary) advantage. But that's all they needed, a brief window to realize their strategic goals.

Carrier bots were directed to the Mexican Army's staging bases and resting places where the bots opened their bins and released mosquito drones. Operators, watching through the carrier bot cameras and sensors could direct small swarms to soldiers standing guard and initiate "stings". The effect led to loud outcries and alarms. That brought men from their sleep, into the open, or they unwittingly opened doors for the drones to enter.

Perhaps, thirty-five percent of the soldiers were quickly disabled, while another 15 - 20% were eventually "stung" until enough men understood the nature of the attack and hid themselves accordingly or fled far enough away to avoid getting "bit".

Overhead drones tracked soldiers who fled, and saw when they grouped up, in which case the carrier bots, having recalled the mosquitoes, took off after them. Numerous miniature drones were not recovered, though, due to damage or being trapped in buildings. Each carried a small but powerful charge and was detonated to keep it from being captured and copied. What neurotoxin it contained rapidly degenerated when exposed to air, masking its original properties, identifiable as a nerve agent, but not exactly what kind of chemistry it consisted of.

The NAR, having determined that no significant anti-tank weapons were present, rolled into Tijuana, Nogales, and Mexicali taking up positions, along with escorts of APCs and lighter armored fighting vehicles, at government buildings, media buildings, radio antennas, police and fire stations, communication buildings, sewer, water, and power utilities.

As sunlight dawned in Tijuana, so did a terrible revelation among its citizens. Soldiers and police forces were quickly overwhelmed. The able bodied were detained while disabled soldiers were loaded for transport and carried a hundred miles south and deposited with some water to wait for their own forces to get them.

****

Many of the people that had been in our detention camp and others were immediately installed to run our new home, the stolen city. The General of the RF was given full command by the NAR, but all the people like me and my dad were either involved in organizing order or maintaining it.

Millions were coming to join us, and millions more were going to be funneled through to lower or east Mexico keeping the roads full and a problem for any Mexican army trying to travel towards us.

Even then, though, the roads were bracketed by mobile lasers that could cut through tires like a sharp knife through a watermelon. If the beaners had any track vehicles, bomb bots would easily disable them.

My job and that of my small unit was to come in after the NAR had cleared neighborhoods, that is driven out Mexicans, and see what was missed and secure the areas for settlement.

The NAR would go into an area, announce (in Spanish) that the people had half an hour to pack up and get out. They could take their vehicles. When a half hour had passed, usually the Mecks hadn't done much to leave, so the soldiers began rousting them out. Not many Mecks had weapons, but a lot tried using kitchen knives as the soldiers came in to get them out.

They got tired of that pretty quick and started sending bots in with cattle prods to encourage people to move out. Shocking, eh?

It took awhile to get the show on the road as my sergeant said, but once enough people were disabled and forced to comply, others began resigning themselves to it.

So, my squad would then come in and go house to house to see who or what was left. We came across a number of old and sick people. We loaded them into special buses where some nurses would look after them while they were carried off to some kind of medical camp.

It's weird enough just walking into some stranger's house, bold as you please, seeing all the details of their lives on the walls, on shelves, and in cupboards, all the furniture they chose to live with, closets full of their clothes and goods, and then you come into a small room with some little old brown guy lying in the bed, looking like they're about to die. It's just plain weird.

I mean, there I am standing by with my assault rifle, geared up, in uniform, supposedly ready to fight an army, but there's just this wizened little guy lying there, big brown eyes wide and frightened clutching a sheet pulled up to his neck.

"De nada, Paco. De nada," someone might say since that's about all the Mexican anyone knew outside of taco and carne asada, por favor, but it was something, I guess.

The worst part was days later when we were clearing out the barrios west of Tijuana where these shacks and huts littered all the hillsides and small canyons around the city. You couldn't believe how anyone could live like that, in all that filth and squalor. It was all ramshackle and crazy. I couldn't help think how great it will be when we tear all this garbage down and clear it out and make it look like nature again. But better, because maybe we can get some water on these hills and make them look a bit more green.

OK. I get it. This is a desert. It's dry, but so is southern Cal so maybe with a little effort, it doesn't have to look so dusty, used, and rundown, although I have to say a lot of Tijuana is totally modern with malls, nice streets and houses, well kept parks and lawns, but that's just in a few areas.

Those areas are the ones we're filling first, of course, with people like us from the camps and the RF. Spoils of war, and we get to assign former LA movie stars and millionaires four-room tin roofed, concrete block, cement floor bungalows.

Yeah, like that's going to happen, Sarge says. "You think those bee-yoo-tee-ful people and millionaires are going to rough it very long? If you think that, you've got another think coming."

"The cream always rises to the top," he'd also say. "They find a way to trade on their looks, charm, or smarts. I mean aren't they all just a bunch of whores really?"

"So, where're we going to end up, Sarge?"

"On top, if we play our cards right. Look. Before, soldiers were just average and low pay guys getting sent around the world, getting killed or maimed, given some medals and told thanks, now get lost. But the NAR guys said, let's share the wealth. Whatever we take and steal, we share with all the grunts. Give people an incentive, and make them full fledged mini-capitalists, right?"

"So here's what we do. We get to live in the best homes now because we took 'em. We get paid better than cops, fireman, sewer engineers or road repair crews because we're the ones on the border keeping everyone else safe; and if someone says 'screw 'em, those dumb bohunk grunts want too damn much', then we pay them a visit and send them packing, 'cause we're the goddamn army and we're not under civilian control anymore. We don't take orders from a**holes sitting at desks. We give orders to a**holes sitting at desks now. We elect our captains, and the captains elect our generals. We fight so we get to stay fat and happy, too; and not like some nothings and nobodies. The worm has turned my friends, indeed it has. No more Mr. Nice Guy for us. Democracy? Screw that. When did that ever do the little guy any good? Truth is, men can't govern themselves any better than one man can govern himself. Let the Spartans call the shots for a while, anyway. We can't do any worse than what all those a**holes did to the country for the last hundred years."

At first, I felt sorry for the Mecks we were throwing out of their homes, like I said. It was weird seeing all those places filled with all their stuff, and feeling like it was filled with indignant and disapproving ghosts, accusing me of being mean to them, but you get used to anything, I suppose, like when we were in the camps. It really is us versus them. That's how things work in this world. So now, I patrol the city and see lots of white faces, and things being put in order and running smoother and cleaner, too, maybe; although no one's got any money for fresh paint, but it's starting to clean up and look American in a way.

Food is still spotty and will be for a while, I guess, except we on the front lines are getting the best of it. We're starting our own boot camps to build up an army so when the NAR leave, we can hold all the territory they took.

The Mecks are spitting mad, of course. We hear (translations) of all the things they plan to do in the near future like recruit, rearm, attack; their sacred soil this and holy lands that, to their last dying breath, blah blah blah. Sure, maybe a million guys armed with spears would beat a few thousand with bows and arrows, but from what I've seen, war is mostly high tech now. Ground pounders have to be there running the stuff, but it's going to come down to who can build the best and most bots, drones, lasers, missile shields, and so on.

From what I've heard, the NAR have bots that build bots. Smaller and smaller, too. You want to beat the NAR, you're going to have to nuke 'em into oblivion.

I heard one guy say that maybe a nice plague of some sort might take care of them, knock them down to size, but it's not like they haven't thought of that, too. Maybe it's just a rumor or fantasy, but I know a smart man who said that it was possible to engineer disease or bacteria that would only kill you if you were a certain race, had certain genetic markers or lack of them, and so the NAR has let it be known on the down low that the Chinese, the Hindus, the Russians and Arabs, or any other trouble makers days as a race or people might be limited if they so much as cast the evil eye at the new Americans.

Mean, cold hearted bastards these people are; and you know what? I think I get it. If I don't like the way things are going in our new New Mexico, they said I have a home with them. Lots of great land grants available in California. Think of all that beautiful coastline, and all those great homes already there. And then there's the Baja. They claimed it for themselves. Told us that if we want some great coastal land, to take it from the Mecks. Just make babies, they say. Lots of babies. No legal birth control in New America, I'm told. Men marry young, women stay home, and they make babies and keep the women busy; and divorce isn't as easy as it used to be. The men are doing the screwing instead of being taken for a ride, they say. Fine by me.

I could retire at thirty-seven a multi-millionaire and lie on the beach all day if I want to. Or quit the army in a year or so and start working my farms or factories. What could be better? Or maybe I climb the ranks, retire and run my holdings while being senator or president or secretary of defense or something. Anything's possible, and I'm only seventeen years old! What a world this is now.

And it seems light years ago when I was a kid in Bellingham worried about acne, getting my first kiss, and maybe copping a feel somewhere on a sweet girl I wished would notice me.

My mom says things are topsy-turvy, but once I decided to fight back in the Dark Time, and learn the ways of using violence to defend or attack, I must have grown up a mile or two, because I'm a man now and ready to marry, work, fight, and learn how to run things. I had no idea before that the human will could change from being passive and accepting to become aggressive and defiant.

But hey! As far as I know, I could be dead tomorrow and all this stuff might be useless effort, but I'm not dead yet so I think I'll stick with the plan, and make life good for me and mine to come. Come what may.

29706897R00137

Made in the USA
Lexington, KY
10 February 2014